W9-AXI-017

GONE TOMORROW

Also by the author:

Horse Crazy
Scar Tissue and Other Stories
White Trash Boulevard

GONE TOMORROW

GARY INDIANA

PANTHEON BOOKS   NEW YORK

Library of Congress Cataloging-in-Publication Data
Indiana, Gary.
Gone tomorrow/Gary Indiana.
p.   cm.
ISBN 0-679-41888-1
I. Title.
PS3559.N335G66 1993
813'.54—dc20   92–50476

First Edition

For Dieter Schidor (1948–1987)

and for Bette Gordon, Wolf Wondratschek,
Vera Lehndorff, and Holger Trulzsch,
with gratitude

La vie c'est pas une question de coeur.

L. F. Céline, *Mort à crédit*

PART ONE

mala hierba
no muere

1

At the Chelsea, 1991

I once had cancer on my face and when it was excised a fine web of scars embedded itself in my right cheek like the soft crust of a soufflé. Over the years the skin smoothed itself, but if light caught it at the wrong angle the flesh appeared bloated, trapped between intersecting keloid fissures. I would never again get parts that depended on my good looks; I changed careers and started writing for the magazines. I sued for malpractice the doctor who sewed me up and won a bundle in court. As I walked into the Chelsea, I fingered the dented filigree beside my mouth as if to rub a bit more of it away.

It surprised me to instantly recognize Robert Sheib, who sat on a sofa under an abstract painting. We had met only two or three times—in Munich, with Paul Grosvenor—when, as best friends of the same friend, we had assumed a superficial familiarity. Robert was an object of near reverence for people I had known, at various times, in various places: because he was esteemed as a poet, because as a public figure he'd come down on the worthy side of certain political questions, signed petitions and open letters and lent himself to committees for the general welfare, in former West Germany, former Munich, because he seemed to need very little from other people, and finally because he made an agreeable drunk. Now that Paul Grosvenor was dead (mysteriously dead, from my point of view), Robert was the only source of facts and rumors I thought it important to find out.

His plaid shirt, puffy cotton pants, and beige ankle boots evoked the costume of an early aviator—an effect, I realized, of the painting above his head, which suggested a small airplane whirring through muddy skies. The art in the Chelsea lobby has never looked entirely real or valuable to me, in spite of its cool pedigree.

"Well, so." Robert grinned expectantly, a pale face coming into focus. I contrasted his relaxed English, unaccented enough to pass for American, with my memory of Paul's overprecise diction. "It's been years and years."

Robert rose to his feet and offered a freckled hand.

"Four years, I think."

"Where does the time go."

"After forty it just races past."

"The good times race," Robert sighed. "Suffering crawls."

"We should wish people a short life, I guess."

"A wish often granted, alas," said Robert, making my remark sound fatuous.

You have to climb up to the valley, I thought, and many lose their breath. My inner vision conjured a giant eye in the crater of a volcano, shuddering bloblike in time to a deafening heartbeat. Robert reminded me of Munich and Munich reminded me of a country house near Salzburg where, seven years earlier, I'd left a copy of *The Other Side of the Mountain* by Michel Bernanos, the one who died at forty. And those seven years were gone in the flutter of an eyelid.

That morning I had come across a postcard of a pensione I'd

once stayed in in Positano. In my mind I saw steep cement steps wending down to a rocky beach, hairy torsos broiling in the sun, and echoing walkways threaded between damp stucco walls. The memory came attached to another dead friend: we had climbed one afternoon to a cemetery full of sweet clover and rosemary and dessicated weeds perched on a mountainside above Amalfi Drive. *When this you see, remember me.*

Standing, Robert looked like photographs of Rimbaud, handsome and bleary and spoiled, with short curls (in Robert's case, red ones) and a subtle air of self-possession. He was the type of unaggressive male I had to remind myself wasn't gay—"sensitive," European, *muy simpatico.*

A blast of freon greeted us in El Quijote. There was something metallic about the restaurant's vaguely controlled chaos.

When we had a booth and a pitcher of margaritas, Robert repeated what he'd told me on the phone: that he was sharing a suite upstairs with a television director named Dina, and writing bits for her ZDF documentary on hotels. They had a few more days of shooting at the Chelsea, then they'd go to the Marmont in L.A. Robert normally wrote books. In Munich, he and Paul had drifted together in the loose mix of cinema and literary types who inhabited the Deutsche Eiche and Harry's New York Bar in the seventies and early eighties.

"I can't sleep lately," I said. "So a lot of times I try to drift off with the television on."

"Uh-huh."

"At four-thirty in the morning I hear this familiar voice. I open my eyes and look at the screen. And there's Paul, all blond on blond, in Nazi drag—"

"*The Guns of Koburg?*"

"No, the American one, *Cross of Glory,* where he's kind of an Ernst Junger type with a butterfly collection and hides a Jewish family in his wine cellar. I got up and took a pill."

"Rudolph always ragged him about how natural he looked in an SS uniform."

"Yeah. Well. Paul had the look, Rudolph had the behavior." The image of Rudolph Bauer rippled across the tangled circuits of memory. The Fat Man. Or, as Paul and I often joked, the *largest* German director of his day. Paul Grosvenor had produced one of Rudolph's films—the last one, as it turned out, a big homo wet dream called *Tarantella*. Paul also directed a documentary film about Rudolph, for which Robert Sheib wrote a memorably unflattering narration. Most of the Germans I knew had been somehow mixed up with Rudolph, if not totally controlled by him. Paul, for instance, had had great plans of producing all Rudolph's future movies, but then the great director overdosed on Mandrax in his Munich flat, dying with his head wedged into the toilet bowl. Since Rudolph had been a tyrannical, crazily vicious person (not consistently, that was the odd thing about Rudolph, he could also be the nicest person in the world, and there was never any logical reason for his viciousness, unless it was an irrational fear of abandonment) his passing wasn't an unmitigated tragedy for his stunned circle. "A cross," Paul once eulogized, "between the goose that laid the golden eggs and Dracula."

I had met Paul in Paris after Rudolph's death. Paul was still dining out on *Tarantella* then, and acted very grand, rather as if Rudolph were only temporarily dead and would soon launch a new project. Shortly after we became friends, Paul suffered a series of reversals, including lawsuits from Rudolph's family, and at some juncture he filed for bankruptcy. Paul found his producing ambitions completely blocked. He kept busy with acting. He also directed several low-budget movies. These were all short subjects except one, *The Laughter in the Next Room*, which he'd hired me to appear in and shot in South America.

I remembered Cartagena as I scanned my forearms, unable to

decide if particular tiny moles had been there for a long time. I remembered the bowl of the outer city, hills pockmarked with fortresses. In my memory the city had become a recumbent, scar-pestered body whose breath was the soughing of the tide.

"Do these little dots look normal to you?"

Robert examined my arm with pretended gravity.

"Yes," he said. "Everybody gets those."

I withdrew my arm. "I can't help it," I said. "When people drop all around you like flies. Not that you see so many dead flies. I'm always looking for tokens of the plague. I tell myself I should pitch a tent in the cemetery, since everyone will end up there eventually." I said this as a charm against calamity.

Robert sucked salt from the rim of his glass. He leaned back against the padded booth and squared his shoulders, puffing his cigarette with a luxurious air.

"These are rotten times," he said without elaboration.

"I've been trying to reconstruct my memories of Paul. And I run up against the fact that I used to get so goddam drunk with him, my memory's full of holes."

Robert swallowed. "I will always remember Paul and the times we had," he declared. "But I often wish we'd spoken more about inward things, not just to entertain ourselves." He looked at me over a tasseled menu the color of dried blood. "Maybe we'll have some little appetizers, sausages or what do you think?"

The waiter was stout and barrel-chested, and his oily black hair was going back. He bared his teeth in a rictus of grim cordiality. We ordered appetizers.

"Can you tell, Robert? Some of the help here really hates waiting on faggots." I said it lightly, chewing my thumbnail.

"Surely not," Robert scoffed. "I mean it's the Chelsea, isn't it."

"I'm not oversensitive about that sort of thing. So if I think so, it's probably true."

The tables near our booth had filled with middle-aged couples whose outfits suggested the high fashion of an alternative universe. Two women wore fringed dresses with jet beads and tight hats. With them were two men, differently bald, who had hair sprouting from their cuffs and shirt cleavage, everywhere except their heads. I felt the Cuervo rising from my stomach to my brain, making me expansive and theatrical.

"I don't want to make out that I'm *haunted,*" I said. "What actually makes everything hard to reconcile is that the whole . . . finale is so murky. Paul came here in May or June of that year, and then I never saw him again. You had more of a day-to-day relationship with him, maybe it makes more sense to you. I feel certain that it makes more sense to you than to me. I like to think Paul and I were as close as we always said we were—I mean, I'm sure we *were,* but so often, things would be cranked up to a high nervous pitch. Either he was in transit, or I was, or one of us was somehow always wired. Boats passing in the night. There were times he came to New York, and we'd have dinner, but he'd also have ten other people to see, and business meetings, everything rushed, and you'd end up very concerned about having a 'perfect moment.' Then down in Colombia, when we really did have some time, he had to shoot the film. You couldn't kick back and relax. Down there it was a lot of stress for me, too." I took one of Robert's cigarettes. I looked again at my moles. "I feel you get to know certain sides of people in the down time when there's nothing happening, and there's no pressure to put up a front. It just makes me wonder sometimes," I sighed angrily, "if I ever really fucking knew him."

There is no anger more pointless than that of people left behind. Robert topped off our drinks from the pitcher as a plate of sausages arrived. The waiter positioned it with a thoughtfulness that made me revise my opinion of him.

"Him and me . . ." Robert dipped his finger in the oily sauce, tasted it, nodded approval. "For years we saw each other every day. Played tennis, swam in the Isar, snorted fifty tons of coke together. But in the end . . . even when you're quite clear about how a person is put together, events throw everything in doubt. Especially when the person's not around to explain himself."

"I never saw Paul as somebody who'd go out like that," I said. "I don't know why I didn't. He was very Roman when all's said and done."

"Roman, yes. Yes, he was. But how can we ever predict such things?" Robert speared a sausage. He twirled his fork while his eyes probed the chandeliers philosophically. "Chekhov says, 'Suicide is an undesirable phenomenon.' It's certainly true for the survivors." He chewed a gob of meat and washed it down with his margarita. "Ever since I'm in New York, I drink like there's no tomorrow."

The chandeliers reminded me of a male brothel in Barcelona where I had paid a Tunisian mechanic per penetration, as if the boy had been a taxi with its meter running.

"Some days," Robert was saying, "I want to drink the whole day off and just let everybody go to hell. Life can be such *shit*, who says we have to *live* every day of it? You should have days you can pull the blankets over your head and listen to Schubert as if you were dead. This is my philosophy: I'm forty-five, I've successfully lived a whole life without ever doing an honest day's work, and if I want to drink, I'm entitled. If I want to smoke, I'll smoke. Eat like a pig, fuck like a Turk, fine."

"I'm too high strung," I said, "to embrace that as a *philosophy*."

Robert dabbed his lips. "Perhaps *philosophy* is a little grand," he laughed. "I still have moments when I stupidly believe I'm going to live forever, you see, if I play my cards right. It's then, as a rule, that I embark on some cosmic scheme of self-improvement."

"If you start too ambitiously, your efforts are doomed to failure."

"Set your sights low, in other words."

"Haven't we?"

A marimba band moved through the restaurant playing "La Paloma." Since "La Paloma" was the theme music of a film we both had sentimental associations with, we shook our heads in amazement at the changes wrought by passing time. The waiter, whose resemblance to Peter Lorre became more pronounced each time he materialized, unloaded our dinner from a metal trolley.

Robert explained the libel suit that Valentina Vogel—Rudolph Bauer's film editor, the woman who'd lived with Paul at the end—had recently brought against him. "In Germany, you need only one person to accuse you. That person says that you said such-and-such about them to a third person, who testifies. Probably it's something left over from Nazi times."

The third party was an actress I knew only from her movies. As Robert talked, the faces of both women sprayed across the video screen in my head: Valentina's sinister features, imperious as a Wagnerian demiurge. The actress named Carmen, a decade older, wraith-thin and spaced out, the way she'd looked as a morphine-addicted, Third Reich glamour queen in one of Rudolph's last movies.

"She's not unpleasant-looking," Robert said. "After all, she's a movie star. But she gives off that dissatisfaction, like a personal smell. She's like a ferret or a rat, sniffing in mucky corners, prancing on her hind legs for anyone placed a bit higher than herself.

"So I ran right into her at Bochum, outside a screening—there she is, snout poised for opportunity. She's one of those brittle people one always wants to win over and loosen up. I hate those kinds of people! It brings out my masochist complex. I become a little child begging for approval. Stupidly, I invite her for a brandy, since the theater has a bar. Carmen tells me she's working on a film that Valentina's editing, and I say something like, 'Oh, you better watch out for her, she's the Angel of Death'—"

"She can't sue you for *that*," I protested, thinking it ironic that none of Paul's friends, including me, had registered the extent of Valentina's weirdness until quite recently, when one person talking to another person and then another puzzled out that her version of Paul's death didn't really add up.

Robert, wielding a nutcracker, snapped a lobster claw in half.

"By law, yes, she can, defecation of character or whatever it's called," he sighed, dipping lobster meat in a cup of butter. "Even if she wins, though, her lawyers will cost her more than she can get from me. Funny, these days you can kill people with no problem. You just have to watch what you say about them."

"She always was a strange sort of person." I recalled her voice: a sharp alto given to sudden harsh intakes of breath as if the utterances of other people shocked her. "In Colombia, she kept herself a bit aloof, a little . . . *precious* is the word that comes to mind." But very much a player, I thought, remembering: something inside me resisted telling Robert about our games, our little intrigues, during the shooting of that film, but I knew I would spill them out eventually. "I should think bringing this kind of lawsuit would just focus more attention on, uh, the strange fact that she was around when all these people died. There was Rudolph, there was Ray, finally Paul . . ." I ticked them off on my fingers. "Even if she's not the Black Widow, she's certainly some kind of *death groupie* . . ."

Robert waved off the specter of Valentina Vogel.

"Later for her. Tell me about New York."

We finished dinner in the welcome afterglow of the departed musicians.

"Let's go to the roof," Robert said.

We fetched cigarettes from Robert's room on the fifth floor, and then knocked at a top floor apartment belonging to a social worker he had interviewed for his documentary. The social worker was a nervous woman of fifty with short salt-and-pepper hair. Her apartment was clean, beige, invested-in. She wanted us to look at videotapes of teen gangs in the South Bronx. Several of her friends, residents of the hotel, lounged on modular furniture, smoking grass, watching the tapes. An Eric Dolphy album was playing. Robert focused his charm on the task of boosting two large vodka drinks. Then we went up to the roof.

There was a redwood picnic table near an opaque skylight, surrounded by clay pots of ficus and cacti. Robert pointed out a wiry profusion of sensitive plant and ran his fingertip along a frond, causing the leaves to curl. The floodlit tips of the cityscape resembled a painted backdrop. Thin, black clouds bruised the indigo sky.

"In this trial," I said, "I bet I could testify for you, as a character witness or whatever."

Robert seemed to consider the effect of me on a witness stand and said he didn't think it would be necessary. Eric Dolphy riffs swelled pleasantly from below.

"It's complicated," he said. He straddled the redwood bench and stared at the Empire State Building. Over the roof's edge a faint nimbus of night traffic glowed. He lit a small cigar, forgetting not to inhale.

I said, somewhat more dramatically than I intended: "Well? What's true and what isn't?"

Robert, choking, waved the cigar like a spunk. His expression said that all truth was relative and the truth of what we were talking about was even more relative than most truth. A thin shell of light from the skylight backlit the picnic table and Robert's plaid shirt, his brushy hair.

"Valentina can't afford to lose this lawsuit," he said, "because Paul's family is suing her for his property. If I prove in court that she was somehow improperly involved in his death, the parents can use that to dispute this document she has—"

"He left a will?"

"It's a kind of will. Technically, legally, I don't know exactly what it's considered to be. Paul *was* a lawyer, though, so either it's valid, or else he was really clever, and it isn't."

Robert said that Valentina's suit against him, though important to her, was frivolous, and would be settled quickly. But the parents' suit against Valentina might drag on for years.

"Who has the movies," I asked. "I mean the ones he directed. Who has them right this minute?"

Robert went down for more liquor. He came back with a bottle, tonic, a tumbler of ice, a small dish of lime slices. I exclaimed at the sudden abundance and lit a joint.

"Let me tell you about Colombia," I offered, wheezing out a lungful of dope.

"Excellent," Robert said. "This will be the third or fourth version I've gotten. The novelist inside me rejoices."

"We had no idea what fate held in store for anybody," I said. "You have to picture all this by the way I tell it to you. I mean it was *his* movie, but it's kind of *my* movie too. Bearing us all to the bloody slaughterhouse."

"Fantasy island," Robert said, coughing up smoke, splashing vodka over ice.

"The way is slippery, you understand. No flares or impaled natives' heads to mark the route." I began to whisper. "Only this bottle of Smirnoff's and these blinking skyscrapers." They were starting to inhabit me, all of them: Paul, Irma, Ray, Valentina. And Michael. Yes, especially Michael. "Oh yes, amigo. There we were, playing a hand of Where He Shoves It . . ." Moved by a stoned, mournful, expansive impulse I burst into song: "South of the border, down Mexico way . . ."

"You are bombed, my dear."

"Just setting up the mood. We want that Orson Welles, Marlene Dietrich atmosphere . . ." I stalked around the picnic table, hunching my shoulder like Nosferatu. I had an exalting sense of the Chelsea roof as the recurring center of a cosmic, convoluted narrative. I really did feel myself a tenant in space and time, whisked back to the patio of the Caribe or the Capilla del Mar, flanked by sex-hungry soldiers waving their submachine guns. "You are getting the altitude sickness, señor. And now we are in the bruise-purple clouds that squat bestride the majestic Andes . . . it was a long time ago, amigo . . . Who would believe we would ever be this old this tired-out this hopeless . . . our sagging bellies dewlapped like bulls' throats, these hanging wallets of flesh . . . and as far as my memory goes, I had him buried as decently as the place would permit . . ."

I took a long hit off the joint and felt the empty air where I thought my head was.

2
Bogotá, 1984

*I*t was hideously muggy in the airport and no one on the ground spoke anything except Spanish. The air had the cloying dampness of doom-freighted dreams, and as I wandered under the vaulted ceiling of the upper deck, details of the previous night's dream came back to me. It had involved a restaurant kitchen and an exchange of automobiles and repeatedly thwarted escapes from a setting my brain had manufactured from bits of my hometown outside Rochester, the housing projects near the Fourteenth Street exit of FDR Drive, and the island of Santorini in Greece. The green bag slung over my shoulder had also been with me in the dream.

Unhelpful phrases drifted into my mind from some flight-numb Babel of movie lingo. *Las teclas de mando. El cristal opaco. Dispositivo de sincronization.* Chaotic crowds surged through the building, marching over the shiny ecru floors and strips of crimson carpeting, up and down stubby escalators. I pictured tropically costumed fire ants gnawing their way through the landscape, bearing off shreds of linoleum, wrought iron, plastic, and plush leatherette in their clacking mandibles. They would leave nothing behind but the building outline, a blueprint of filaments that would stand for a moment like something in a cartoon before it collapsed into smouldering dust.

Loudspeakers layered the confusion. Flights were boarding, flights were departing, flights were delayed. But which flights, at what gates, how soon, how long, it was impossible to tell. Through the massive windows a sky dotted with white pastry clouds. From the density of human traffic it looked as though the entire population had chosen to flee on the same afternoon. Yet there was something inertial and self-defeating in all the excited motion, a feeling that the swarm was really going nowhere, circling boarding lounges and duty-free shops and the incongruous neon cocktail bars like jaded shoppers picking over a depleted mall.

It was the kind of airport where inconvenient political types and luckless bystanders were sometimes mowed down in crossfire. Fear wafted off certain people, rolled through the air of departure gates, pooled around public telephones and ticket counters. Fear laced the ambient chill of souvenir shops and boutiques, and in the sultry open passages that caught the heat of the day, fear led the fearful traveler to anticipate the stench of something large and dead trapped under the glistening floor.

Sound and image peeled apart. In a men's room mirror I saw a short, narrow man, his face lined by incipient jowls, shaggy black hair turning glossy with sweat. "That's you," I told myself disgustedly. I had "retired" from acting and now acknowledged my reluctance to commit my postsurgical face to celluloid, tracing the lines of my scars with a finger. Blue sunglasses completed a punky abstraction. I removed the shades and examined my Levi's, ripped at the knees in advance of the fashion, my hand-stitched shirt wilting in the heat, my clown-white skin. I looked enough like a queer to cause trouble in South America. I hoped the trouble would come later on. At a row of urinals behind me, men pulled their cocks out wearily, as if handling unreliable appliances.

I leaned into my reflection and bared my teeth. My mouth is one of my better features. Somewhere along the gum behind the last of my upper molars, I felt the jagged outcrop of what I concluded was an emerging wisdom tooth. It felt like a tiny chicken bone or metal spoke. The tissue around it was raw, since my finger came out red.

It was easy to lose my identity in a place that was more or less nowhere. If someone had asked my business, I might have pulled Paul's film script from my bag and pointed out my lines, run through with yellow marker. On the other hand, my link to any film set or indeed to any narrative felt extremely tenuous.

The agent at the Avianca counter had the wary face of a scavenging owl, puce fingernails honed into lethal weapons. With insistent gestures, irritatingly overdrawn for the amusement of people behind me on line, she indicated that connecting flights to Barranquilla Santa Marta Cartagena departed from a different airport. I had missed the 2:30 shuttle. I could get another one. Yes, I could use the same ticket. The bus was outside.

As she enumerated these facts in a brutal parody of American-ese, the agent's face conveyed disgust at my presence in the airport, and in the country generally. She threw in "have a nice day" as a parting malediction.

I stumbled through automatic doors into the glare of day. A fluttering, fiery wind smelling of gasoline and putrefaction rolled across my face and clattered through the diseased palms along the road divider. On the bus, I pretended not to understand that the driver wanted money for the trip. I waved my ticket, gestured at the receding airport. I emitted a variety of frustrated noises to convey my belief that the ticket included the price of the bus ride.

Through the oblong windows, a landscape of agricultural monotony refuted the myth of El Dorado. The driver did not insist.

He was a round man with a pencil moustache and mousy brown eyes who could not use any trouble. I considered this a good omen. It would have been difficult to surrender the five-dollar fare, since I had boarded the plane in New York with eight dollars and some change.

At a smaller version of the main airport, I booked a seat on the coastbound shuttle. I discovered that I'd left the sunglasses on the bus—a bad sign, I thought, that canceled out the free ride. On the upper deck I found an empty cafeteria with a view of the airfield. The diffuse sunlight falling into the gray-carpeted gallery gave it a spectral chill, like a black-and-white crime scene photo. I drank a beer and ate a pork sandwich at a littered formica table. I lit cigarettes and smoked them and crushed them out on a gold cardboard ashtray and watched planes touch down and lift off. Through the soundproof windows they looked like fragile silver toys.

From the table I could view the departure gate. A spectacularly ugly soldier with a stringy moustache rocked on his boot heels beside a phallus-shaped trash cylinder. Accidentally catching his eye, I found myself engaging his vulpine gaze with something like defiance, working a gradual, ambiguous smile onto my perspiring face.

The soldier spat thoughtfully through his fingers. He wiped the snot on his snot-green trousers. I swallowed a mouthful of beer suds. I put down the cup. I willed a foggy look into my eyes and fisted all but my middle finger, which I tapped "absently" against my lips. His scowl expanded. He stroked his submachine gun with unconscious lubricity. The possibility of senseless homicide flickered briefly in humid eyes, followed by a glaze of tropical lassitude.

I had only one book in my bag, *The Portable Prescott*. I dug it out and began reading about the trial of Atahuallpa, the last of the Incas, who had been condemned for breaking the laws of a church he did not belong to. The arrival of white men and their microbes into the Americas coincided with apocalyptic prophecies, astral portents, comets, shooting stars, the superstitious tokens of an ancient, flawed science.

The flight was delayed. The boarding area filled with flashy Colombians exuding a Halloween esprit. I purchased another waxed paper cup of beer with a U.S. dollar. I now had six dollars. I pictured my late arrival in Cartagena, and related complications. I was not clear about my destination, having written "Plaza de Bolivar" on the back of an envelope while Paul gabbed my ear off on the phone. "Write it down," he'd said, "if we're not at the airport go there and look for us." Paul had told me a lot of things I hadn't really paid attention to. "You're going to love how stupid everything is," he had assured me with asperity. Perhaps Plaza de Bolivar was not a hotel but a general location, there could be many hotels there. A pleasant feeling of alcoholic decrepitude warred inside me with a mildly alarmist trend. I wondered how things would play out if I blew my remaining dollars on drink. Not so wonderfully, perhaps.

Across the airfield, the sun sank behind a perimeter of plane trees and umbrella pines. Orange and purple wrinkles fissured the lower sky, furrowed clouds like watered silk catching in a cosmic drain. I hauled my bag to the boarding gate. Very Mardi Gras. Several swarthy Medellín-cartel types, their open shirts baring medallions and chains nestled in rampant chest hair, were traveling with large, effervescent women with dramatically piled hair and livid eye makeup who resembled professional transvestites. It was some sort of ghoul party of Bogotá high rollers, nerved up for a weekend of fancy fucking. A cocktail wagon had been rolled out. A stewardess ladled punch from a plastic punchbowl, handing it out with sacramental fervor.

I felt that these large, awful people were using the air I needed to breathe. Olfactory surprises mined the area—patchouli oil,

Paco Rabanne, Opium, sweat. A cloud of tobacco smoke swirled at waist level, roiling under metallic ceiling lights. The airfield darkened against the glowing necklaces of runway lights.

Time lumbered along. A sour, overdrawn feeling spread among the crowd. Finally a rope barring the boarding corridor was unhooked. The revelers nearest the drinks wagon scrambled onto the DC-10 first, shrieking, tripping over luggage carts, their laughter swallowed by the roar of idling jet engines.

When the plane reached altitude the seatbelt sign blinked off. A number of people interpreted this as a signal to amble through the cabin. I was strapped in beside an ample woman wearing a cowrie necklace and the maquillage of a Times Square B-girl. Pumpkin faces inflamed with liquor and dread floated through the cabin on waves of rancid cologne. I heard singing. Hearty, off-key choruses about fiesta time in Cali. The plane entered a lightning storm that knocked it violently through the clouds.

Screams rose as the plane dipped sickeningly down, slashing through strata of atmospheric muck. It quickly fell to an altitude where the quiltwork land became visible through the double plastic windows. Moisture was condensing between the thicknesses of Plexiglas. The aubergine veins of river tributaries suggested ideal crash sites. The evening light was dissolving in darkness. Suddenly the plane lurched back up into the clouds, obeying some fixed, suicidal instrumentation. I felt my bowels turn to pudding.

In scattered moments of equilibrium the more determined passengers resumed singing and stumbling down the aisles, as if to fill the stale recycled air with proof of their calypso élan.

The storm broke a few moments before landing. Then the plane went in so smoothly it surprised everybody, provoking a big ovation for the pilots.

The aircraft emptied in a curious hush. Rainwater stippled the oily tarmac. Amber floodlights marked the route into the terminal.

The desuetude of a jungle backwater greeted me. Two military cops stood near a closed customs table beside the arrival gate, yawning as they waved the debarking passengers through. The rain-slaked air muffled footsteps, absorbed voices like thicknesses of cotton. I walked down an empty corridor parallel to the building entrance. Behind me the clamor of footsteps was matched, outside the building, with car engines coughing into life. The corridor led nowhere. Shuttered kiosks and darkened ticket counters lined the way to a metal gate drawn across a black thruway linking separate wings of the building. Through the rust-smeared gate I watched a mound of rags squirming inside a wet cardboard tent. A black foot livid with scabs poked from the rags, its yellow heel planted in a long, shallow puddle.

I hurried back toward the echoes of departing passengers. After the flight crew left the building, the whole airport would shut down like an unplugged refrigerator. In the main hall, the police were now sapping derelicts in the shadowy boarding lounges. Tacky rows of modular seating ranged beneath framed tourist posters. SEE PICO COLON read one, reminding me that intestinal parasites were a common hazard of the tropics.

A policeman whose moist pink lips and shiny teeth looked terrifying from seven feet away smashed his club against a prostrate, emaciated beggar's medulla oblongata. He pounded the man's skull methodically, each blow crisply audible and followed by howls of brain-obliterating pain. The last passengers of the Bogotá flight hurried past the cop and his victim, eyes fixed on the cream paneling and aluminum trim of the arrivals corridor, the backlit Duratrans ads for American Express, Bacardi, and Avianca. The lunging club and its supine target were met by the determined, discreet march of expensive heels toward the exit doors. The prone body, dressed in a gray shirt and red shorts, thrashed from side to side avoiding the club, which nevertheless sank into shoulders, biceps, and hips. When the body stopped moving the cop tucked the club into his thick belt with a snort of flustered satisfaction. He mopped sweat from his face with a soiled white handkerchief and then began kicking the moaning body at his feet. His thick boots struck ribs, making sharp sounds like the snapping of tree branches. The squirming derelict coiled in a fetal position, guarding his belly and groin with knees and elbows, hawking and spitting for breath.

The cop retracted a fastidiously pressed pantleg and slammed his boot into the man's face, mashing the nose, shattering the teeth, muttering amused curses in a language I didn't recognize. To my complete horror, he glanced up at me standing there and broke into a wide, idiotic grin, his pink tongue slavering behind his teeth like some giant, malefic infant.

"You go along now." The rubbery black face spoke with maniacal benevolence, grinning as his boot continued kicking the pulped, dusky face on the floor. I saw a meat-red wound where the skin around the sallow eyes had been kicked open. Blood dappled the floor under his head, spidery filaments of blood had sprayed far from the body, like the trail of an insect brood emerging from hibernation underground.

The air in the carport was fresher than on the tarmac. Men wearing shorts and straw hats lounged against vintage sedans. A taxi caravan rumbled away from the building, exhaust trailing across slick pavement. Across the road, billboards for hotels hovered above a stone wall, overhanging vines casting intricate shadows over pastel swimming pools and deluxe cabanas.

A shirtless driver with coal-black skin and angular features waved from a fender. I nodded and went over. He mumbled something in Spanish.

"Plaza de Bolivar?" I asked in a hopeful way.

"Plaza de Bolivar," he said thoughtfully, to himself, eyes fixed on the curb. He wore white shorts stained with what looked like pomegranate juice and plastic flipflops on wide feet. The nails on his big toes were raised and rocklike as if they had grown back deformed after an accident. His nappy hair was shorn in artistic tiers close to the scalp of a delicate oval head. He hawked up a bright green oyster of phlegm and studied its configuration on the asphalt for a moment, then said, "Okay, okay."

I climbed into the rusted sedan. The car was a color redolent of the 1950s, a dusky avocado. Matted excelsior and sharp springs poked through tears in the seat cover. A tangled scapular swayed from the rearview mirror. The radio was picking up a crackly offshore station.

Where the road went into the rain forest it crumbled into cracks, lumps, and flooded trenches, like the cursed path in a Gothic opera. Lagoons of shallow mud slithered through pitch black villages of wattled shacks. The headlights swept overgrown savannahs of rubbish and spectral wooden longhouses. Brackish roadside ponds brimmed with hacked-up industrial tires, smashed wooden debris, and copious fecal matter. The road and the passing villages were solemn as graves, the only movement that of wandering livestock, blocky mammalian shapes lumbering through vegetal blackness. The passing landscape stank of rotting compost, mixed with gusting odors of polluted seawater.

The driver's fierce, narrow face shifted with jolts of the road. A silver crucifix glinted on his sweat-dappled chest. I stared at him in the gleam of dashboard instruments, wondering what sort of living he made and what he spent his money on. Paul had touted Cartagena as a "fun town," but Paul's ideas of fun encompassed many places where half the people were starving to death.

"Antonio," the driver said abruptly, pointing at his own chest.

"Antonio," I repeated, and gave my own name. My pulse was still racing from the scene in the terminal. "A clear case where one can do nothing," I thought, uncomfortably aware that an earlier generation of travelers, the kind you find in Graham Greene novels, would certainly have tried to intervene, even if it involved a lot of unpleasantness for themselves. I have often been forced to see that I belong to the race that sings under torture. Like most people.

I lit a cigarette and passed it to Antonio. He grunted and slowed the car. I let my fingertips rest on his hand a few seconds too long. He did not move his hand away. I had been a passive sack of water trapped in the machinery of travel for many hours, and almost instinctively wanted to make something happen. He gave me a look of frank inquiry. I nodded and made a gesture with my fingers.

He left the engine running while we coupled against the rear fender. Drizzle coated us like an aerosol spray. His long, skinny penis thrusting inside my rectum felt like a toothache dulled with Novocaine. I thought, "just like dogs," and the animal spontaneity of this jungle fuck suggested a rich, secret world older than money, family, and private property. The radio throbbed eerily in the hushed forest. I would not have been surprised if, after the act, Antonio had thrown me in the ditch like a used condom.

Woody odors spread through the forest on the soft rain. On the far threshold of the forest floor, a rime of ghostly phosphorescence, a red-violet tracery skimmed the ground like a furry band of moving hieroglyphics.

The slippery flesh of the Colombian's hips and stomach slapped against my buttocks. He came with a grunt and we got back in the car, heading for the sea. The moon lit up greenish mists between the trees. The crumbling road ultimately segued into a smooth coastal highway.

We arrived in Cartagena. The sea filled one side of a lunar landscape, penciled waves like corrugated iron fibrillating on a slithery column of moonlight. A blue moon hung over the bay, brushed by dark clouds. The walled city rose on the left, a giant pastry crust with cannons poking from its crenellations. Floodlights spiking across the grass moat lit the massive stones as if for a Hollywood premiere.

The curving road revealed the outer city. Fishing boats clustered in a marina that flowed to a T-shaped esplanade and continued on the other side as a narrow, unnavigable canal. At the head of the esplanade stood a gelid bronze figure of Bolivar. At its far end, set back from the street, a gaudy nest of gingerbread baroque buildings with arched windows and sagging balconies crowded above a long, rotting arcade. Palms lined the sidewalks, fronds half-brown from dessication. A glass-and-steel cakebox palace, its flag-lined plaza adrool with fountains, floated on the black water of the marina.

Human figures crowded the esplanade, which had the look of a perpetual carnival. There were wagons selling boiled peanuts and ices, wheeled steam tables, people in straw hats and sandwich boards hawking lottery tickets, balloons, grotesquely fat women working the crowd with trays of smashed coconuts and sliced papaya balanced on their heads, refugees from a Botero painting.

The cab slipped through an opening in the walls. The inner city was a maze of Spanish houses crowded on cobbled streets. Dank gardens flashed behind wrought iron gates. Balconies overhung the wet streets. We passed several squares built around statues of saints and conquistadors. Odd patches of sidewalk and street were floodlit and occupied by slight soldiers who ambled, guns drawn, in the blue-white glare of mobile klieg lights. Antonio pointed out the soldiers, snorting contemptuously: "Cheeldren," he explained.

A curtain of warm rain obscured the Plaza de Bolivar. There was a long arcade, anchored at one end by the Banco Nacionale de la Republica. At another corner of the park, the Palace of the Inquisition with thick wooden pillars. The desultory square itself, flower beds bristling with jasmine and birds of paradise, coconut palms soaring to the rooftops.

Antonio stopped the taxi in front of the hotel. I handed him the rest of my cash.

"I see you again," he said. He rubbed his crotch and grinned. "Some night, here in the Plaza."

I smiled awkwardly and lurched from the taxi into the rain, stepping into the protection of the arcade. The cab farted off down the jigsaw streets. I wondered what I would do if I had come to the wrong place, who would rescue an American without money in the asshole of the world.

3

Hotel Bolivar

I stepped out of the rain into the arcade. A line of wrought iron lanterns running down the middle of the vaulted ceiling threw gray light into recesses along the slick tiles. At the distant end of the walkway, in front of the national bank, a uniformed figure smoked a cigarette in the shadow of an arch, shoulders and a raised foot resting against the pillar, hustler-style.

Lightning branched in the livid air above the palms, solarizing the dull plaster columns and baroque façades. Feeling tense and excited, I rushed into the Hotel Bolivar. In the lobby I had to stop dead and take my bearings.

It was all strangely familiar. Drab walls, flaking portraits of third-rate conquistadors, aquiline dukes and swan-necked duchesses in lace collars and velvet greatcoats. Ceiling fans knifed the motionless air. Lights hung in fluted bowls of frosted glass. Like a proscenium dressed for a play on the theme of miscegenation or incest.

Green and black floor tiles. A scarred oak staircase. An elevator cage. In the paneled office enclosure, a vulpine Ricardo Montalban type counted receipts on a baize desk blotter.

With a sleepwalker's certainty, I knew the corridor behind the desk would lead into the patio, and that I would find Paul out there in the vegetation. The desk clerk's fishy gaze swept over me, indifferently tagging my place in the food chain. I heard the same scratchy music that had played in the taxi, its island staccato lending mechanical gaiety to the dank garden behind the hotel.

Leaving my bag in the hall, I stood in the patio doorway. Numerous square tables were scattered around. The movie people sat in the open getting soaked, ignoring the drizzle, fussing over storyboards and script notes amid dirty plates and overflowing ashtrays. The familiar evidence of compulsive orality was almost heartwarming. Paul was flanked by his technical crew, nondescript young people sucking cigarettes, hands poking and flailing to illustrate their jumpy thoughts. Their voices were loud, contentious, workaholic. Paul had removed his spattered glasses and was oblivious to my arrival.

He was an intense-looking man of thirty-five with a steeply angled nose, disdainful lips, and an expression of incipient hilarity . . . and something dark, sardonic and secretive, in the unexpected grins, the caustic asides, the casual, vast erudition . . . Delicate fingers rummaged through wet papers as his eyes skipped myopically from face to face, as if pondering the special absurdity of each interlocutor. He wore what I called his Jean-Paul Sartre look, froglike and skeptical. He heard everyone out impassively, then replied with exact, jaded intelligence, meanwhile squeezing water from his matted hair.

He was speaking German, English, and Spanish without any transitional pauses, translating from one language to another. The table, actually several tables pushed together, was bowered by a vast rubber tree, its foliage shunting the rain into erratic streams.

Water gushed from a drainpipe near my head, splattering a trail of jagged flagstones. Rain galloped on a tin awning over the doorway, pattered through the tree's endless canopy.

"Nicht arbeit, der Kamera ist hier. Und hier."

"Aber die Elemente des Bildes in bestimmter—"

"Es ist möglich?"

As I moved out of a violet light under the awning—a light equipped with some crackling device for electrocuting small insects—I noticed Irma Irma's platinum hair among a gaggle of heads, in the shelter of a bar shack under the hotel wall. The shack had a thatch roof and some tall stools, and was strewn with red chili pepper lights, as if for a voodoo Christmas. One group was loudly abandoning the place, staging a drunken dash for the lobby. As they fled past, I recognized passengers from the Bogotá flight.

Approaching the truncated Last Supper scene where Paul held forth, I became uneasily conscious of a young man sitting beside him in the swaying shadows of a low-hanging bough. While this stranger was still a peripheral object I found myself standing behind him and then became paralyzed by his beauty, which hit me with the force of a blunt instrument when I looked him full in the face. I ignored his presence so emphatically that I might as well have groveled at his feet. However, no one noticed a thing.

White T-shirt, tanned arms, sculpted biceps in rolled sleeves . . . I thought of some rare, pornographically detailed jungle orchid. I couldn't look at him: such faces are not for me. He was overpoweringly phallic, male, inhuman . . . sitting rather primly beside *him,* whose crisp efficiency was such a devious mask . . .

"You could at least have sent someone to the airport." I announced my presence with the swagger of somebody in jodhpurs with a riding crop. I felt that this . . . person was a surprise Paul had saved in order to devastate my sensibilities. He had not mentioned any great beauty hired for the film. Very few people could still make me crazy with sexual desire, but this boy . . . young man, I should say . . . had something ecstatic about him, like the aura of a saint. I caught myself "acting" for him, not saying what I meant to say but striking a certain unconvincing pose, cravenly dissembling my rising excitement.

Paul betrayed nothing. He assumed a familiar joviality full of cunning and secrecy.

"I have," he said, snapping a lighter flame to the tip of a cigarette, "perfect faith in your ability to find a taxi." His voice plunked a note of warning to save my acting for later. "We knew you'd find your way here. Everyone was busy shooting. We've just finished up for the day." They had also finished dinner, I noticed: the soggy remains of a broiled white fish, fried potatoes, and slimy green beans occupied a plate at his elbow. Despite the humidity, Paul wore a light jacket over his shirt. He fanned his face with a sheaf of damp papers.

I began to describe what I had seen at the airport. "You see, Paul, I'd just gotten off the plane . . ." The boy's eyes roamed over my face. The harder he stared, the less I could follow my own narrative. I began losing track of my words, my voice rising in panic. What I had just witnessed started to lose its reality . . . to the degree that I actually felt I was lying, or at least embroidering a tall tale out of something small and insignificant. The words coming out of my mouth, the phrases I picked, were "for" the boy, meant to impress him with my worldliness, my wit, the danger I had been in, wanting to excite his . . . protective instincts? So the whole episode became a piece of fiction. Even before I let my account trail off into nothingness I sensed that the gorgeous stranger must have understood how his presence derailed me, making me stupid with desire.

"Somehow deliberately choosing this climate makes it slightly more tolerable," Paul said, pointedly changing the subject. "At any rate, once we finish this little meeting, I'll check you in here. You must be wanting a shower."

"I thought I was—"

"Staying at the villa, yes, we had it all arranged, and then this morning our hostess descended from her hotel and announced a change in the arrangements. She has limited the villa to five. It's infuriating, but what can I do? We have five in there already, as they all arrived before you."

This was a drastic shift.

"You can't make her make room for one more person?"

"Can't *make* her do anything. Even Alex can't make his old mama do anything, can he?" This was directed at a square-headed man with bad skin who was puffing a cigar and squinting through clouds of malodorous smoke. He emitted a coughing chuckle. "Poor Michael here," Paul continued, indicating the youth, whose candid look gave me an immediate, unwanted boner, "also must stay at the Bolivar." He let that sink in. He waved at his companions like a bishop flicking holy water, reciting their names. They nodded and grunted indifferent welcome. Deflecting further protest, Paul pointed out that they, too, resided at the hotel. Obviously, I couldn't reply that they were "only" crew, though Paul read the thought on my face, and so did they.

So there was a name attached to that terrifying beauty: Michael Simard.

Sulking at the head of the table, Alex Gavro was already familiar from numerous Lionel Stander–type roles he'd played in German New Wave movies. Like many persons associated with Rudolph Bauer, Alex Gavro had a potted minor legend, endlessly repeated in reviews and press releases: rejecting his bourgeois background, he'd joined a criminal gang in his twenties, in nebulous solidarity with the Red Army Fraktion. He spent three years in prison, where he wrote two "hard-boiled" novels.

These brought him cult fame, as a kind of discount-house Genet. Now he wrote, produced, and acted in movies. In Paul's movie he would incarnate a Nazi fugitive who had designed concentration camps for the local government (supposedly Paraguay) and trained its security forces. He was also producing the movie. The fabled villa Paul had promised belonged to Alex's mother, Carlotta.

He was a big white man in his late thirties whose stiffness made him seem to preside over all activity, a wooden ringmaster around whom others swirled. This impression was misleading. His charisma was only the heavy charge of fear and mistrust he inspired, like that of a sour patriarch whom relatives placate in hopes of inheriting money. I disliked Alex Gavro immediately. I had disliked him in most of his films: he played brutal characters in a way that convinced you he was that way in life. What disturbed me even more was something willfully unreal about him. Something incredible about his "casual" outfit of jeans and pinstripe shirt. Something forced and unbelievable in the stony expressions rolling across his face as he listened to the table talk, his square jaw falling open and clamping shut like a steam shovel, while his pale gray eyes bored holes in the sodden tablecloth. Here was someone who needed to believe he was as much an icon as Jack Palance or Eddie Constantine, and if you reminded him that he wasn't, he would hate you forever. He was . . . like Rudolph, I suddenly realized, Rudolph without the fame and adulation. Rudolph as a bit player.

"If you don't mind," Paul said, "I want to just finish up here . . ." If I had imagined they'd gathered on the patio to await my arrival, he squashed this illusion. "Why not get yourself a drink? Look, your friend Irma Irma is waving to you."

Irma Irma was miming a samba in front of the bar, rattling air marimbas, tits and hips jiggling in an absurd parody of local exuberance. She was projecting the impression of idiocy she had gleaned from her new surroundings. Irma's chunky hourglass figure had been tortured into a white dress resembling a mutant Ace bandage. As she shook to the sounds of the bar radio, she kept up a breathless monologue aimed at a black-haired girl whose tight yellow skirt barely covered her crotch.

"You never call to *Berlin* anymore," she shouted to me in mock reproach. How mock it was I couldn't tell. "Weiland always says, 'What's happened to him, why doesn't he call me, he doesn't care about us any more. He's forgotten us. Off in his glamour world of famous people.' " Her choppy diction put a rising lilt in the middle of sentences, as if she'd learned English strictly for rhythm rather than sense. Aside from the lilt her voice was incredibly flat.

"Weiland," I said, "should send me a ticket and give me parts in his movies. Calling Berlin on the phone from New York isn't cheap."

"This is what I tell him." Irma shrugged. Her voice trailed away into a chanting monotone, a medium channeling bored spirits from the other side. "But don't expect anything from Weiland. If you were there, yes, he'd put you in a movie. To fly from New York? That is hundreds of marks he can use to pay his apartment, or for Turks to come and massage him. What do you think Weiland pays me all these years? For ten, eleven films? When I need money he tells me, 'Thanks to me, you are underground superstar, you will make money from other directors because of me.' So well he pays me, I need public welfare for my children. Ja, *eine superstar* . . ." In a fading voice she repeated, "*Ja, eine superstar* . . ."

"I'd like to know what kind of glamour world he thinks I live in," I said.

She smirked and waved her hand across the vista of the gloomy patio.

"Well," she said, "for example . . ."

I had once been a close friend of Weiland, her usual director, for about two years. My marginal life dropped me in one city after another without many preconceived plans or coherent purpose (in those days, I would uproot myself on the strength of the haziest promise of money or work) and so my friendships tended to bloom and wither in occult patterns, often fading out for years. I . . . lacked continuity. Weiland, Irma, Berlin . . . until that moment, they had belonged to a different period, one not so removed in time as in its general code of sentiments. We had shared a feeling of deprivation, of being more . . . authentic, up-to-date, than the no-longer-bohemian, well-off Rudolph Bauer crowd . . . and, let's face it, those social melodramas Rudolph churned out, full of operatic self-pity, in his smug little "Hollywood on the Isar"—a bit pathetic, really . . . Well, and then Weiland had moved on to bigger budgets, bigger films . . . he now made his own versions of Rudolph Bauer movies, showing how cruel and cold life really is . . . I'd heard he still paid Irma practically nothing . . . I had gone back to Paris, plunging into fresh difficulties . . . then New York . . .

(With Paul, things had developed almost subliminally, in little stray motes of time, after Rudolph's death . . . in Paris, Munich, and New York . . . developed more strangely . . . that is, without seeming to develop at all . . . based on a certain . . . shared pathology, I suppose . . .)

"And now Dr. Grosvenor will make us real superstars," Irma said sarcastically. She clutched a whiskey and soda in a fierce proprietary grip.

I shrugged. "We are already immortal, Irma. This is only a postscript of additional glory."

I associated Irma with a sexual flamboyance for which her high-cheeked face with its slightly crossed eyes and dramatic angles predestined her. It was hard to decide if Irma was beautiful or not, but Weiland had so often cast her as a platinum "sex bomb" that her neurotic tics, even her disinterest in most erotic situations enhanced a silvery illusion of perverse insatiability. Her screen persona had come to overshadow her deeper, real personality. The celluloid Irma was easily amused, thick-skinned, wacky, amorous . . . while the real Irma was complicated, insecure, earnest, easily hurt, and boringly malcontented. Yet she could be coaxed, manipulated into behaving like the frivolous slut Weiland had invented, merging with her fictional self.

I shared this weak-willed desire to gratify other people's wishes. It now crossed my mind that Paul had selected this current menagerie precisely for its malleability. The beautiful boy, for example . . . a model? Anxious to please in his first movie role? Willing to . . . perform beyond the call of duty? With Irma, possibly?

Slouching under the imperfect thatch of the bar ceiling, I perceived an eerie link between Irma's flawed, smartly made-up eyes and his hooded "bedroom" eyes in the swaying shadows of the rubber tree . . . her agile, gesturing fingers and his fingers, which absently rubbed the brown flesh of his bottom lip or supported his boyish, round chin . . . her mouth and his mouth, meshing together somehow . . .

Behind the bar, a colossal white woman swayed to the sputtering radio, her vaguely defiant motions emphatically meant to give only herself any pleasure. At odd moments this woman tossed a scathing Spanish phrase to Irma's companion, who had been following our conversation with uncomprehending interest. The girl's masculine face reminded me of Chimu pottery.

"Here, meet Maria," Irma said. "While the others decide how to ruin tomorrow's shooting. Maria *comes* from Colombia." And under her breath she repeated, "Maria *comes* from Colombia."

Maria giggled. It was a disturbing sound. She was holding a cigarette between sharpened crimson fingernails, and occasionally bringing it to her lips to suck without inhaling. Her English was practically Californian compared to Irma's.

"Ah," she said, "you're Jo-Jo." This was a reference to my character in Paul's script. The girl seemed in high spirits. Drug-induced, it seemed to me.

"Not if I can help it," I assured her with irritation. At the very least, I planned to get the character's name changed to something less stupid.

Maria cocked her head and grinned as if I were a lovable curmudgeon she had known for years. It was just the kind of presumption that put my back up.

"Don't tell me you don't like your part," she scolded, wagging a finger. "Because it's a wonderful part."

I hoped to like this attractive girl but sensed that I wasn't going to. She had "come aboard," evidently, in all dewy innocence, being only twenty-two, a native of Cali, whom somebody—Alex? Carlotta?—had hired to be the art director and interpreter for the company. No doubt she'd also appear in the film, having a decid-edly filmic if underdeveloped look, something like a juvenile vampire in a horror comedy. Her naively patronizing manner wasn't the most winning quality she could have brought to the production, but her energy and evident willingness to do menial jobs would definitely endear her to the undoubtedly torpid cast and crew—she was already offering to take my passport to the desk and check me into my room, "where your bag'll be safe, anyway," and later, she proposed, we might go through my clothes together, "to see what can be used in the film."

I ordered a Cuba libre. The barwoman, instantly hostile, stomped through her enclosure, chanting a litany of disgust that concluded with the words "Cuba libre" spat out with incredulity. This startling performance repelled me. I hate fools. Then it occurred to me that the woman might be insane. She had been dancing and mumbling to herself in her bottle-lined cage like a bomb waiting to go off. In Spanish, Maria explained that I was an important movie star who did not give a shit about Cuba. I had to admire this improvisation, since none of it was true.

"Rum cola," the barmaid chanted correctively, her big limbs hacking the air, porky hands seizing lime, knife, and Coke spigot in exasperation. The purple-blue lighting over the bar's work counters had a soothing underwater effect. The woman's fat, busy feet shuffled on grooved wooden planks designed to drain spills into the earthen floor. "Rum cola."

The group at Paul's table appeared to be breaking up. A song crowded with laid-back Jamaican voices, a song that had played three times in a half hour, came on the radio.

"Shit," said Irma.

"You'll hear this one everywhere," said Maria. She mouthed a line of the song, making a brainless face. "It means, 'Mama, my sister's gone off with a Negro.' Pretty racist," she added.

"What is the race situation down here?"

"Oh, you'll see. It doesn't take long to figure out."

"Well, there's what? Spanish, black, and Indian."

"And Germans," Irma put in. To Maria: "Germans came here as well as to Paraguay and Argentina? Some friends of Martin Bormann's, I'm sure."

"There are German farmers in the interior," Maria said, not recognizing the name. "German businesses in the cities. In terms of races, though, it's the Spanish who own everything, and below them are blacks, all by degrees of color, see? And at the bottom are the Indians."

"In other words the people who were here originally."

"Exactly. Tragic, isn't it?" Maria spoke of tragedy in precisely the vexed tone one speaks about the weather.

The rain had dithered to a residue dripping off the rubber tree and the wattled bar roof. Maria again offered to arrange the room. I surrendered my passport with vague misgivings. What was keeping me glued to the patio was Michael Simard, who smoked quietly five yards away while Paul and the others yapped about locations and camera angles and budget constraints. The interminable discussion had concluded several times, each conclusion trailing a wake of postscriptive chatter. I stood with my back against the bar facing the table, savoring the discreet view of the comely actor, a view repeatedly broken by hunching backs and gesticulating arms. I searched out his legs among other legs under the table. I mentally removed his white shirt clingy with sweat, his khaki shorts, the bright yellow socks ribbed around his ankles, the canvas espadrilles on his long feet. Now and then he tilted back his chair; in the shifting light I saw his shorts bunched in the middle by his jock strap and what was in it. Irma, oblivious, continued a wry lament about the local climate, the twice-daily rainstorms I should expect, the unfavorable terms of the housing arrangements. Tenants of the villa, she said, were obliged to pay over a major chunk of their salaries for rent and maintenance, the servants' pay, and daily meals. Even the gin in your cocktails was itemized and billed to you at week's end.

"I don't say you're lucky staying here," she said. "But that house isn't so special, neither."

I wondered if Paul had coached her in resigning me to the squalid Bolivar, not fully appreciating that the hotel's strongest selling point was sitting beside him, restlessly crossing and uncrossing his shins and stretching his sleek arms, fingers locked over his head, cracking his knuckles. The fleshy mouth opened in a luxurious animal yawn. Nonsense. Paul had measured the allure of every inch of Michael Simard's flesh, calibrated the spell of those heavy-lidded eyes, the (conscious?) invitation of his spread-limbed body language. It only remained to discover whether Michael was as big a narcissist as most people would be if they looked like him.

4

Room Tone

"*M*onstrous woman," Paul said, with curious light-heartedness, half an hour later in my room. He was referring to Carlotta Gavro. "Of course these silly conditions are really from Alex, not from her. She's letting him cast her as the dragon lady, what does she care? Not that she couldn't be. But in this case . . . I'm sure Alex thinks if he doesn't splinter up the group, we'll all get too close and form a cabal against him."

Alex and Carlotta were staying at the opulent Caribe in Boca Grande, he said, "outside the inner circle." In Paul's mind, the inner circle consisted of himself, his lover Ray, Irma, the editor Valentina Vogel—and, he implied, me. And then there were Maria and Michael, sort of the outer inner circle. Paul claimed that Alex had already entered a conspiracy with the cameraman and the line producer to sabotage his, Paul's, authority.

"Or else it's just a petty way of showing that he's in control. We can't get dailies, for example," Paul said. "Mainly because he says to have dailies flown from Miami is too expensive. My suspicion is that that cameraman changes my shots when my back is turned, especially when I'm acting in the scene, according to things Alex tells him. He doesn't want me to see what they've been doing," he concluded. Realizing that this sounded paranoid, he added in a less certain voice, "It's possible, isn't it?"

I shrugged. Anything was possible.

"I don't understand the script." I pulled off my sneakers and wriggled out of my Levi's. I stood at the window naked except for athletic socks and underpants. I smelt foully of travel.

"That's all right. I don't really understand it either." Paul was now wearing a Panama hat as well as his pale striped jacket and looked, I thought, a little louche. He had uncapped a small amber bottle. A tiny spoon dangled from the cap, on a tiny chain. With scientific patience, he scraped the bottle's insides with the spoon. He lifted the spoon to his nostril and inhaled brusquely.

"Yes, but you wrote it."

"What don't you understand?"

"Okay," I said, staring at my hairy chest. My body looked like something bloated from long immersion, white as lard. It repulsed me. "You secretly run the country. Alex is the official torturer and drug kingpin, the Kurtz character. Irma is his mistress. Then Michael and I show up as two investigative reporters—"

"Yes, yes, he's writing a story on the Nazi underground railroad. You're the photographer."

"I would think I'd be the writer and he'd be the photographer, but anyway. Alex tells Irma to find out what we're after . . . but this other plot, the revenge story, the guns . . . it's a little opaque, isn't it."

Paul rose from the bedside and extended the amber bottle. I shook my head.

"I hate that shit."

"You must have some. It's the national product."

"Oh, all right."

As I sniffed the white powder I took in more of the room, to avoid looking at my legs. It was mint green. The window shutters, folded open for the night breezes, were darker green. My green luggage was sitting open on a brown chair. A fan with white wooden blades whirred overhead, a useless decoration. The heat got into everything. The room contained a dresser and a shuttered closet and a Spanish copy of *The Watchtower* in the night table drawer.

"The plot is expendable," Paul said. I thought of white stones soaking up solar heat, of animals driven mad in high temperatures. "The script was thrown together as soon as the chance to do a film came up. Alex gathered all these state grants on the basis of a one-page treatment. The only condition, as far as he was concerned, was that it had to be shot in Cartagena."

"Why Cartagena, particularly?"

"Because Carlotta owns that house. People do this all the time. The company rents the villa as housing and rents it again as a location. So you also have insurance clauses and so on and so forth. Maybe certain pricey things get broken. Say Carlotta has a little cash flow problem. A sixteenth-century crucifix she picked up in a flea market, valued at ten thousand marks, is smashed by a careless gaffer. The rental monies filter through Carlotta back into Alex's pocket. That's another reason for putting some people in this place. He works out a deal with the management, they give him padded receipts, he takes half the declared price of the rooms."

"Charming."

"Well, he's a crook, what do you expect? I mean, he did go to jail for robbing a bank."

"He looks more like a petty holdup type. Convenience stores and gas stations."

"In any event, the script isn't engraved in concrete. I'm definitely changing it."

"Wonderful. If you make my part any smaller I can just phone the performance in."

"It won't affect you. Calm down."

"I assure you, it doesn't make any difference to *me*. I'm just pleased to get a vacation." That sounded too generous; I added, "Even here."

Paul fussed with his drug and contemplated the ceiling. He had a way of seeming entirely at peace with the larger movement of reality while remaining overwrought about all its particulars. Now he became avid. His voice turned urgent:

"You do see the *possibilities*, don't you? With *him*? Even from where I was sitting downstairs, I saw you staring at him—"

"That obvious, huh?"

"Only to me, my dear. Because you and I think just alike." He let that sit there while I peeled off my socks and stomped to the bathroom. I paused uncertainly in the doorway. I knew he had already set into motion whatever convoluted scenario was infecting his imagination. I remembered a party we had both attended in Paris three years earlier; this moment and that one seemed fused, spliced together in the same waking dream. The image of the two mouths returned, now strangely linked in my mind with the partial wisdom tooth I'd felt in my mouth earlier in the day.

"Her and him, you mean."

Paul chortled. "Of course her and him. You weren't thinking him and you, by any chance? Or me and him? We don't want something so obvious or vulgar—you *can* see it, can't you?"

A long silence.

"This isn't a bad room," I said. It came out sounding like a question. I felt nausea stir in my stomach, at the same moment the drug began spreading out in euphoric waves. I removed my glasses. I folded them and placed them on the night table. "I mean I've been in worse rooms. That phone doesn't work, though."

Paul plucked off his hat and idly ran the brim between his fingers. He placed the hat on his knee. Then he lifted the old-fashioned Bakelite receiver and pressed it to his ear. After a moment he muttered something in Spanish and hung up.

"It works. You have to go through the switchboard."

He rearranged his floppy body on the bed. Paul had a bit more bulk to him than I did. Pressing one nostril shut with his middle finger, he ingested a smudge of cocaine.

"I can try, maybe by next week, to put you in the villa," he sniffled. "Don't forget, though, you might not really want to stay there."

The coke had spread a sour taste through my throat. I tugged off my underpants.

"He looks sort of Russian," I said.

"Russian?" Paul chased the coke down with bemused drags of a Marlboro. With his glasses on he seemed to take in every detail of the room, adding it to a vast inner catalogue of geographic oddities. "You think so? To me he's a French schoolboy, or a French sailor. He has a perfect ass, by the way. Two solid cantalopes."

I went into the bathroom and closed the door. I thought about men wanting things from other men and the odd, contradictory forms those things could take. The shower hissed out full strength and quickly shrank to a lukewarm trickle. Michael's mouth came into my mind as I soaped my testicles, Michael's mouth overshadowed by Irma's mouth, the two mouths lining up somehow like graph lines on a three-dimensional grid. I could not reach the jagged bit of tooth with my tongue but imagined it inside my mouth. The flimsy shower stall with its plastic curtain felt like a clammy nesting spot for spiders or scorpions. I put my finger inside my mouth and felt in back for the tooth.

He was on the phone when I came out: ". . . tell her there's nowhere to buy it. Not after seven. Unless she wants to go into Boca Grande. There's a pharmacy near the Hilton. You go up past the Caribe, around that little peninsula. The shops, everything up there stays open for some reason. Not everything, but the pharmacy does. She won't tell you it's her pussy? *Make* her admit it. And tell her we're looking for a big, big Negro to bang her pussy for her." He listened for a moment, then started laughing. "All right. In a few minutes. I kiss your big prick, darling. All right."

I walked around the bed to look in my suitcase, adjusting the towel around my waist.

"Ray says hello."

"How is Ray?"

"You know how I rely on him. He's honestly my favorite person in the world. He hates it here. Says it reminds him of shitholes he saw in the merchant marine. Rangoon, and so forth."

"Good old Ray." It crossed my mind that I did not really know Ray very well.

"He's quite a special person, isn't he? It's a pity, perhaps, that we don't share everything. It's too bad there are areas where he doesn't—well, certainly parts of *me* he doesn't appreciate. Aspects of my psyche or whatever. But maybe it's a good thing really. Otherwise I would make his life too complicated."

"I don't believe Maria has gone through my luggage. Look at this."

"Now you're angry."

"Not at all. There's nothing very private in here."

"She was just checking out your wardrobe."

"*What* parts of you doesn't Ray appreciate?"

Paul sat up straight with his legs in a semilotus position.

"Various parts," he said.

"Anyway," I said, "I do appreciate the fact that we're here. Some people seem to think that travel's bad for you, but I've never found that."

"Why, because it corrupts people? How would we learn how

terrible where we come from is, without some vacations in real nightmares like this place. It's sexy here. The constant threat of violence and the sultry weather driving everybody out of their skin. And you know, down here you can get anything you want. Really anything."

"You sound positively depraved when you say that. Don't put your feet on the bed."

"Except good coffee. Isn't it incredible?" Paul sank back against the pillows, stretching out his legs so his shoes hovered over the side. "They export it all."

"Paul."

"All we can get is instant."

I leaned out the window. The window faced a high, dark, stucco wall. If I strained my neck I could make out part of the street where some teenage boys were playing stickball, and a portion of the spired cathedral roof. The air was hot, but ruffled by cool gusts. The breeze carried the young people's voices, a motorcycle exhaust, the brief rattle of a tambourine and a man singing over it, a rumbling truck.

"Strange town," Paul said. I glanced at him across the night table light, which gave his head the nimbus of a corpse in a funeral parlor. He squeezed his eyes shut as if the noises played over his nerves like the padded hammers of a piano.

"It looks it."

"But you haven't seen anything yet." He sat up a bit. I blew a cloud of white smoke into the blue darkness and watched it scatter in the breeze. I liked Paul more than almost anyone. "If you want a boy, you can always have Alex fix you up with someone."

I tossed my cigarette out. I pictured it landing in somebody's hair. The idea pleased me. I decided to put on the Levi's I'd taken off earlier. I slipped into them without underpants. Paul retrieved the drug from his pocket. His single-breasted jacket was made from a soft, thin material that had wrinkled in the moist heat, like parboiled flesh.

"I don't want boys that Alex gets. I don't want Alex knowing my business."

Paul snorted. A mosquito with horrible long appendages dangled around the bedside lamp.

"Life certainly is full of ridiculous lessons." The mosquito bobbed closer to Paul's face. "You can't imagine what it was like going from the high of producing Rudolph's films, then after his death having the whole bankruptcy thing come down, and now, in my stupid little optimistic way, making a movie with *Alex*— Rudolph despised him, you know—but I keep thinking, it would turn things around if we did something that would pick up a few prizes. Maybe I delude myself. You're right, the script isn't very good."

His eyes were huge behind his eyeglasses. I considered for the thousandth time that Paul and I could pass for brothers. He was a little more solid, maybe a little handsomer, too. And blond. But the resemblance was striking.

"Who knows. Things may never be good again, but . . . it's too bad I have to take Alex for the main actor."

"He's a good actor," I said, though I didn't really think so.

"His skin is like cottage cheese."

"So? That could be interesting. I don't know why we always want to look at beauty. Beauty is boring," I said, putting up what I knew was a doomed, elliptical defense against the strange power of Michael Simard and whatever real-life script Paul was conjuring. "It's redundant. That's what Breton should've written, 'Beauty will be REDUNDANT or it won't be at all.' Anyway, Irma's fabulous, you have a big part; it ought to be very antic and glamorous and smart, even if it doesn't quite make sense."

46

"And you, don't leave out."

"Yes, with my face all wrecked. Well, that proves my point."

"I wish you'd realize that most people can't even see those little scars. They've become less and less noticeable in the years I've known you." Paul smashed the mosquito by clapping his hands. He bounded off the bed and got a bathroom tissue to wipe off the bug guts.

"The camera sees them."

"In a certain light." He tossed the scrunched tissue on the night table and resumed his recumbent pose. "But you're the one who zooms right in on them, no one else does."

The drug bottle came out again and he sniffed several hits, quickly, to close the subject.

"Take more," he said.

I folded back the shutters of the other window in the room, which offered basically the same view. There was a lighted window low on the opposite wall, in which I saw the corner of a wooden table and a hairy arm resting on it. A big cigar was planted in the fingers at the end of the arm. The cigar and the arm bobbed up and out of view, fell back in gray trails of smoke, at regular intervals.

"Be discreet," said Paul. He said the town was full of police spies. Ignoring him, I snuffled up some powder.

"Tell me the truth," he went on. "You don't think the script makes sense? I'm not a script magician the way he was."

I burst into explosive laughter and tossed him the bottle. I thought I detected a startled movement of the faraway arm holding the cigar. The hand and the arm vanished. A moment later the window was slammed shut.

"My god, you still say 'him' as if you were talking about Jesus Christ," I said with more derision than I intended. "I've got my scars, and you've got Rudolph. I mean, no offense, Paul, but who cares at this late date, what a genius he was? At least you're not under his thumb for the next twenty years. Let's face it, he wasn't any picnic."

Paul flushed. He bounced up and strode around the room, shaking out his pantlegs and arms as if centipedes were trapped in his clothing.

"It's no picnic since he died, either."

"Instead of feeling like you had the rug pulled out from under you," I said, "you should consider how likely it is that he would've fired you in the middle of the next picture. On some whim. And then it would've been even worse, no one would've worked with you out of fear of offending him."

"I don't believe Rudolph would have done that. We had a good relationship."

"Yeah, but he did things like that to plenty of people he had a good relationship with. Don't get me wrong, I'm not saying it's a good thing he croaked or anything." Basically, of course, that was exactly what I was saying. "I just think we've got to move on with what we have."

"Oh, no question."

"So," I said, in a summarizing spirit. "Let's see what adventures we can have. This town must be full of horny studs with big fat cocks and dirty girls and drugs until the cows come home. Why not run with it? The local *ambiente?*" We had both moved beyond such pedestrian pleasures, but for a moment I felt a kind of desire as I spoke.

"Yes, why not? I should tell you, they only do it for money down here."

"Then I need an advance on my pay. I have something like eighty-five cents, I think." I began putting on my sneakers, without socks. As I laced them I studied Paul's face: he had something slightly maniacal going on there. We had agreed to join Irma and Alex and the others at a gay bar outside the city walls, along the canal—the only gay bar, actually. I was noticing that the room was full of small insects, moths and so forth, besides lacking all amenities. A soft knock sounded on the door. I opened it a crack. Michael Simard stood in the hall, dressed now in long pants and a black-and-gray crepe shirt.

"I'm ready," he said, with a timid, almost supplicating look. "Let's go out."

5

El Dorado

*N*ext day began with more knocking at the door, this time pounding, the noise invading an apocalyptic dream I woke from with a hangover as big as the Ritz. Thrashing free of some tangled sheets I sprang out of bed, a big mistake as it turned out, and threw open the door. Paul's boyfriend Ray looked at me with the nervous self-effacing air of an importunate bellhop.

"Eughuugh," I said, looking down at his shoes. Only then did I recognize my surroundings. My mouth tasted like a reptile hatchery. I was wearing the clothes I'd passed out in.

Ray giggled nervously, as though he had serious business to discuss and any levity was an awkward distraction from his real mood—whatever that might be. Other people's lovers, like other people's husbands and other people's wives, have often been inscrutable and menacing presences in my life. I had often been told that Ray "liked" me, but our relations seemed arrested at the stage of circumspect politeness. I thought it entirely possible that Ray could stop liking me at any time.

The fifth-floor hallway was flooded with horrible, brilliant sunlight. The arches at both ends of the hall were open to the elements. One faced the palms in the square, the other framed the grimy dome of the cathedral. Between them the green-and-black floor gleamed like polished glass.

I held up a finger and gently closed the door. I vomited quietly into the toilet, then went back to the door. Ray hadn't moved.

"Paul thought you'd like to visit the set," he offered. His shrewd eyes examined me for residual inebriation. He was a small, compact Australian with a long patrician nose and an Adolphe Menjou moustache. That morning he wore faded denims and a darker blue sport shirt with a little alligator on the breast. "Didn't you want to come?"

I agreed to meet him on the second-floor terrace and then searched desperately for aspirin, finding instead a box of amphetamine pills that Irma had handed me sometime the previous evening. I found that I could recall only the movement of her hand inside her purse and the passage of the box from her hand to my pocket, like a tight iris shot without any explanatory footage before or after: I could not remember where we'd been or anything beyond our initial movements through dark, narrow streets to a cramped discotheque. Faces appeared to me in the shower, strange faces with bits of nameless feeling attached.

I probed the outcrop of tooth lodged in my upper gum. Today it felt queerly like a chip of quartz or mica. Pressing the soft tissue around it with my fingernail, I could not feel any larger incipient mass. The bleeding had stopped, at least temporarily.

I stood under the shower long enough for the first waves of speed to rill through my headache.

"Looking a bit more human," Ray hailed cheerfully. He sat alone on the long empty balcony, flicking cigarette ash into the greasy remains of his breakfast. The spaces between the tables contained palms in cement tubs. Window boxes of begonias balanced on the balcony railing. The tables themselves featured checkered oilcloths, paper napkins, and Woolworth's cutlery and dishware. I resented these cheap touches through my first two cups of coffee, until the amphetamine fully kicked in.

In the plaza directly below, a small army of boys with shoe-shine kits and old men selling *tinto* and lottery tickets swarmed over the tar pavement and lounged in the cool shadows of the fountains. The curb beside the Palace of the Inquisition was lined with taxis. I wondered with vague alarm if one of them contained the driver I'd made it with the previous evening.

"Quite a night, quite a night." Roy's avuncular tone sounded ominous.

"Oh God," I said. "What happened?"

He displayed his easy smile button grin. Ray normally had a guileless, friendly, mildly subservient attitude. Yet he was a brittle person, inhibited, touchy, and terrified of rudeness.

"Well, *you* were in top form," he said. He ruffled his hair, almost singeing it with his cigarette.

"Wait a minute, though, I don't remember seeing *you*." A mirrored ball refracting blue and orange constellations on peach walls, a stuffed marlin, fishnets, nautical decorations, young dudes with leather vests over bare chests, earsplitting ye-ye music, Irma and Michael and Maria shaking on the dance floor: some things came to me like slides flashing through a projector. Paul drank Midori sours and described his correspondence with Leni Riefenstahl. Alex introduced a bald man who ran the local film festival. But Ray was in none of my pictures.

"Do you remember what you said to Alex?"

"Oh God. Oh God."

As I drank my coffee and tried to chew some toast slices smeared with guava jelly I noticed that Ray was trying very hard to seem relaxed but was lighting one cigarette from another. The hair on my neck bristled. Had I committed some atrocity that had seriously changed the state of things? The combination of alcohol and cocaine was completely lethal, I reminded myself. Whatever pent frustrations or tamped rages I held inside me were bound to come splattering out if I indulged my usual recklessness vis-à-vis "substances."

Ray told me what I had told Alex, described a conversation we had both had with Carlotta Gavro, and said I had offered a blowjob to the Arsenal Bar bartender: nothing especially horrific. Other things were bothering Ray, it seemed.

"I don't remember any of this," I said. "How embarrassing."

"The bartender sort of went for the idea. But then you were really too drunk. It couldn't go on like that so we brought you back."

"You mean to say I went down on him?"

"You honestly don't remember?"

I could not summon any picture of the bartender, or of Carlotta.

"It's hard to believe Alex actually has a mother. What's she look like?"

"Really blonde, and really old. Full of spunk, though. In every sense of the word, from what I hear. Good figure for an old broad. She was wearing a brocade thing with sequins sprinkled through it. Hair up like this. Almost Irma's color."

"Uh."

"Next to each other she looks like Irma's mother, actually. Or grandmother."

Ray had parked the production pickup truck on a side street. It was an old white thing all filthy in back, with dents in both doors and the side panels. He looked small to be driving it.

"How's that room?"

"Hardly been there, have I."

"Seems like a decent establishment."

"Pisshole full of bugs."

"Rudolph stayed there once."

"Must've been slumming," I said.

We were rolling through streets with cars parked on both sides leaving a single negotiable lane. People swarmed out of shops in shawls and campy headgear. Mule-drawn wagons clopped along the wider avenues. Indians bowed under bales of straw and sacks of fertilizer lumbered through sidewalk markets where produce and clothing and all sorts of junk were sold out of wooden bins, kiosks, and car trunks. Alongside these antiquarian figures strode young urban people in smart European clothes, shop assistants and office workers and petty capitalists. The stucco architecture all dated from the same period, at least two hundred years ago. Storefronts had been gouged out of ancient façades, tricked out with corrugated metal aprons, security systems, and plate glass.

"Rudolph came here two or three times. Alex brought the head of the film festival to dinner a few nights ago, this Luis Vasquez— you met him last night, no? I think he's an old smuggling buddy of Alex or something, he was telling us. Rudolph went to the Bolivar because he got himself barred from the Hilton. He was bringing his twelve-year-old tricks up to the room and so forth. Not just one, five or six of them. Must've looked like Menudo up there."

"Lovely."

"Six a night at twenty a pop. Marks, not dollars. Sounds like Rudolph, don't it."

"Sounds like everything else down here, actually."

"It's possible to miss him." Ray looked around, steering with his wrists resting on the wheel, studying the profusion of life in Cartagena. We were, quite suddenly, two guys from another town, in the middle of our lives in a foreign city, experiencing a sort of peace, an inconsequential curiosity, a moment of something very close to nothing.

"Don't hold it against Paul about the villa. He's really pissed about it himself."

"Well, I do blame him for letting this happen. For the past four months he talked and talked to me about the villa every time he called, what a fabulous place it was. Look, Ray, you people have a pool and privacy and a staff. The dump I'm in hasn't even got room service. That isn't right."

Ray chewed the middle of his moustache. "It *is* an unfortunate, uh, problem," he said. "No argument there. The situation really sucks. Paul was ready to throw in the towel over it, don't tell him I told you. If there's anything I can do to make things easier, don't hesitate to ask. And you know, you can always come over and use the pool."

"Be that as it may," I said. The concept of Paul canceling the film over a minor difficulty, even one that inconvenienced me, was disturbing. Of course it probably wasn't true.

A dog ran through the crowd in front of the truck. Ray jammed the brakes on, tossing us both at the windshield.

"Fucking man's-best-friend. They'll probably be stuffing him into empanadas by dinnertime." He braced himself and watched the animal streak past a corner supermarket, disappearing into an extensive galleria. The truck inched forward.

"Plenty of shops," Ray said neutrally. "Paul tell you about Colombia paying off the national debt with cash from the big drug dealers? *He* claims García Marquez organized some big conference, here in Cartagena. And they paid off billions, in cash. To frustrate the North Americans."

"It's probably the North Americans who came up with the idea," I said. "Everybody likes cash. Paul says you're not enjoying yourself." I wasn't really curious about it; it was just something to say.

Ray's slightly mousy face took on a guarded look. He seemed flustered at becoming a subject instead of an observer. The idea that he was secretive had never occurred to me until that moment. I realized that in the years I'd known him I had hardly given him two consecutive thoughts.

"I wouldn't say that," he said, downshifting the stick and tapping the brake to let a bus cross an intersection. The Cartagena buses were festooned with decals, Day-Glo emblems, and shimmering lenticular panels, like wheeled acid flashbacks. "I will say, I have trouble tolerating the people down here," he let out after a brooding silence. "I mean, look at this bottleneck here. They're like monkeys. I mean they really carry on like pigs."

The vista in front of the windshield, an avenue constricted by traffic and variegated humanity, looked completely normal. The only difference from a street in Munich or Sydney, as far as I could tell, was that the people were darker and had more life.

"I know it sounds racist," he went on, "but you get to the point of thinking they really are dirty and smelly and lazy. Some of them are all right of course but the majority, you can have them."

I pretended to think distant thoughts. I didn't see what good it would do to argue. I didn't think Ray believed what he was saying, anyway. Something else was bothering him about the situation, about being down there, that he wouldn't express. It had to be about Paul, and maybe, I thought, it also concerned me, my friendship with Paul. The idea formed that possibly Ray had insisted on having me stay at the Bolivar, to keep us separate. In that case, Paul, in order not to alienate me from Ray, had persuaded Alex to pretend that it had been Carlotta's idea. Ray probably believed it was my bad influence that made Paul go over the top, but it was really the other way around.

I tried to "push the thought out of my mind," as a smoke-quitting class I'd attended in New York had urged, on the grounds that "the mind can only have one idea at a time." I concentrated hard on the idea of Michael Simard's genitalia.

Ray piloted the truck through a maze of bright streets. Dank vegetable smells hung in the air, wafting off the filth packed into odd corners and heaped around trash bins. The trash of Cartagena had a particularly blunt, naked appearance, composed as it was of matter too rotten and useless for any trash picker.

Some of the streets ran flat out to a horizon line where a vast blue sky obliterated the sense of boundaries. Others switched back on themselves, snakes claustrophobically coiled in a basket. Eventually we passed outside the city walls and took a tar road that hugged the meadowy grass moat, through a sparse zone of trees and greenery and a valley overlook, passing a willow grove beside an ancient cloisters converted into tourist shops.

". . . like this Hector, this little spic that works at the villa," Ray was saying, now gripping the steering wheel with both hands. "He must be all of sixteen, I suppose what he really does is sodomize Carlotta for a living, but he's supposed to be a servant—you know, make the beds, set the table, and I promise you, you have never seen such a *grudging* performance in your life. It's not that I like the idea of people waiting on me, as a matter of fact it repulses me. There's so much abuse and sadomasochism built into the whole fucking concept. In this case, though, the more human you try to act with this Hector, the more vicious he becomes. He hates all of us, I'm sure of that. I don't blame him, either. But if he's paid to do x, y, z, he fucking ought to do x, y, and z—period. End of fucking message."

We entered a thickly settled area where one-story white houses were grouped beside the road, and other white houses filled an entire small valley riven with alley-size streets. The grass moat under the city walls ran along the opposite side of the road, a wide marshy belt with muddy paths scuffed through it. A twenty-year-old Buick and a black van were parked on the shoulder. Paul sat on the Buick's fender, balancing a clipboard on his knee. His hair blazed red and gold in the bright sun. On the moat, equipment was being assembled, and actors primped in the shade of a wall buttress.

"Here we go," said Ray, pulling up behind the van. He shut

the engine off but made no move to get out. We sat in the truck cab finishing our cigarettes and watched the technicians and actors stroll back and forth on the bare grassy plain, each in his own world, the cameraman, the sound man, an actress in a black slip, Maria with a makeup box, the camera assistant, Michael in olive twill pants and a white cardigan, a scrawny local boy wearing a Bundeswehr tank top. It was that interminable interlude when everything is being set up and no sense of organization has yet settled in, the sun climbing to its zenith, scattered fibrous clouds dissolving in the azure sky.

I flipped through my copy of the bound script. "What's he called in the movie?"

"I can tell this script grabbed you as much as it did me. This," Ray said, shoving his door open with his shoulder as he indicated the surrounding vista, "is on page twenty-seven."

I found the scene as we trudged along opposite sides of the black van and converged at the Buick's trunk. The pebbly ground crunched underfoot. Michael, known in the film as "Max," would buy a gun from the prostitute Imelda. "She pulls a newspaper package from under the chintzy bed. The room has a grease-coated fan, scarves tacked to the plaster, and posters of Delores del Rio and Maria Felix." First he would pick her up near the wall, then they would cross the moat into the warren of slum housing, camera tracking in long shot.

"There you are," said Paul. His face looked absurdly determined, weary, and absent, all at the same time. He was one of those people depleted by any prolonged effort to take things seriously, and his current situation obliged him to pretend more forcefully than usual. In the distance, the cameraman was planting a tripod on a dry patch of earth. Paul put aside his clipboard and slid off the fender to his feet. "A man's having anal sex," he said, stepping over to reach into the car's side window.

"This one's bloody sick," Ray chuckled, then walked away in the direction of the wall, Maria, the actors, shaking his head.

Paul pulled out an opaque plastic bag containing numerous small objects. He fished out a pack of cigarettes and after lighting one tossed the pack back in, then took out a large brown rubber dildo.

"And he finishes," Paul continued, "and he says to the girl, 'That was great! How was it for you?' "

Across the white road, electric blue graffiti was sprayed across a house wall. Spidery letters partly obscured by a candy green Toyota: ESTA *something* YANKI *something* NICARAGUA.

" 'Humiliating,' the girl tells him. Then he says, 'That's a pretty big word for a nine-year-old.' "

Maria met Ray in the middle of the grass, a few feet from where the camera was being mounted. They studied the mise-en-scène together, then Maria came running up, Louise Brooks hair slapping her cheeks. She panted extravagantly.

"Any makeup is going to melt right off them," she told Paul, who wagged the dildo at her, holding it by the perfunctory testicles at its base.

"This," he said, "should go into Imelda's room so it's in the first shot."

"Quite a catzo."

"If mine were this big I would rule the world by this time," Paul said.

Ray returned from conferring with the cameraman. I detected a brittle edge in his banter with Paul, as if a long-running argument were being held in abeyance until they could get each other alone.

The next hour was full of desultory exchanges, snippets of gossip, disputes about camera angles, light readings, rehearsals of Michael walking from the sidewalk to the wall, of Michael and Imelda walking from the wall to the sidewalk . . .

"It's too mechanical," Paul said, agitated, pacing the ground behind the camera while the cameraman, a Dutch hippie with a moon face and wispy little moustache, turned the apparatus to track Michael. In broad daylight, Michael looked even more a miracle of genetics, nearly six feet tall, with perfect muscle tone evident under the clothes, a face out of Caravaggio, broad forehead squared by a mop of fluffy ink-black hair. And the dazzling teeth, the dimpled smile of pure seduction . . . there was, I decided, something horribly repulsive about him.

"What about this?" Paul solicited Ray with a curious urgency, as if he did not really want his opinion but wished instead to reassure himself that Ray took an interest in the project. "Michael doesn't speak Spanish, so Chino, the little pimp kid, figures Alex wants a prostitute . . . and when he introduces Imelda, she takes him off to her room, she lies down on the bed, she pulls her dress up, that's when Michael sees there's been a mistake, so he comes back and talks to the kid again, this time the kid understands, and takes him somewhere else. *Then* he gets the gun."

"It could work." Ray squinted into the middle distance. He seemed to seriously consider the problem. Maria sauntered back from repainting Michael's face. They had been crouched in the shade directly under the wall, Michael impassive as Maria's long fingers cradled his jaw, dabbed his fleshy nose with foundation, good-natured laughter infecting the two bored local actors nearby. The massive ocher wall seemed red in the sun. "Ask Maria."

Maria thought it could be done. She would knock on some houses and find a backyard they could use. Most houses in this many-balconied warren were split into tiny apartments, often single rooms, crammed with huge, melancholy families.

This was the slum quarter called San Diego, where the nearest road through the town walls empties out at a vast weekend marketplace, much of it domiciled in a giant tent. Just within the city walls is the huge sienna thumbprint of the abandoned bull ring, its plywood whorls blanched in the relentless sun. A few hundred yards in the opposite direction is the modern business district, a patch of printed circuit board with low-rise offices of Olivetti, IBM, Mitsubishi, like a steel oasis in a desert of dust and sleep. There is a new bull ring on the road to Santa Marta, under the fortressed hills, mainly used for religious revivals and the annual music festival.

Irma arrived in a sky blue Cadillac convertible driven by Alex, who refused to stay, claiming urgent business in Boca Grande. He was plainly not interested in any scene he was not in. Irma wore huge white-framed sunglasses and no makeup, which made her look old and rather battered. They were still setting up the shots. Like every film set, this one was all about waiting and waiting and doing a shot and then doing the shot again and doing it again and waiting some more. Irma said she had thought to watch the shooting but saw that it was unbelievably dull. We walked to the dip in the road where the market tent was collapsed and roped up like a deflated, grimy dirigible. There was light foot traffic through the arched openings in the walls, an occasional bus, sporadic cars. The idea of people doing business, going to jobs, and living conventional lives in that demoralizing heat made me infinitely weary of the human swarm. A massive anthill built from the debris of possibilities.

Irma was in a bleak mood. She had gone for a walk in the Parque del Centenario, a man had followed her, she took a taxi into Boca Grande and walked down Carrera 2, another man followed her, she went into an emerald shop and the salesman hit on her. She had days like that, she said, when every man in the world was a walking boner with a big mouth. She had gone to the coffee shop in the Capilla del Mar, drunk a pot of tea, and listened to women talking at the other tables, women who were traveling with absent men; two particular women, she said, seemed to have met because these men worked for the same company, and left alone with time on their hands, they'd made a date to go shopping. Now they were finished shopping. The only things worth buying in Cartagena were emeralds, so they had obviously bought a lot of junk. They were sitting in the Capilla del Mar coffee shop surrounded by bags and packages, telling each other every single intimate thing about the men they were traveling with. The younger of the two was not married to her man, and the older one was urging her to get a ring on her finger. They get everything from you and when they're through with you they throw you away and leave you with nothing, the older one said, unless you've got that ring on your finger. Palimony, forget it, the case drags on forever and you lose a fortune in legal fees.

They talked about everything, Irma said, they had never seen each other before and in ten minutes flat every detail of their sexual lives, every physical oddity and flaw of the people they lived with had been gone into in incredible detail.

"Imagine," Irma said, shaking her head in disbelief. "Loving someone so much you give all their secrets away to a stranger over coffee."

"But it's kind of nice, too," I argued. "Two women that don't know each other, in a strange town. It has a nice existentialist thing to it. Like a Marguerite Duras novel."

Irma shook her head. "They were not even a Jackie Collins novel, really not. She's telling the other one about the boyfriend's shit stains in his underpants and how his armpits smell. The other one tells her how to get more money from him. 'And I make sure he does this for me, and does that,' and so on. Very banal, in fact."

I wondered if Irma was now sleeping with Alex. We walked back up the dusty road. Gray-bellied clouds moved over the city from inland hills. The crew was packing equipment, the two tracking shots having gone off surprisingly fast once they'd started shooting, Paul assured us, though Ray rolled his eyes and rubbed his moustache with his teeth as if he, veteran assistant to Rudolph Bauer on twenty pictures, doubted very much that Paul would be thrilled when he saw the rushes. This silent skepticism was burning a hole in the air between the two men, who stood obstructing the equipment van as the crew deposited a half a ton of lenses, slates, earphones, and boom microphones inside. Maria, desperately cheerful, flirted with Michael on the hood of the Buick, where she was swabbing his handsome face with Kleenex. She seemed eager to offset the tension between Paul and Ray with the force of her banal chatter, and her voice was getting louder and shriller by the minute.

Paul had his own plans for relieving the tension. They would not shoot the follow-up scenes in the prostitute's room until after lunch, and maybe not until the next day. He proposed an outdoor restaurant on the inland road to Barranquilla, and after much palaver the whole production got under way, crew in the van, Ray, Michael, Imelda, and Chino in the truck, Paul and me and Irma and Maria in the Buick. Why that configuration and not another? And what was Paul talking about? There was always a great fracas of people piling into vehicles to go from one place to another; the exact disposition of bodies seeming to define the shifting magnetic affinities and polarities . . .

Paul was feuding with Alex, Alex opposed some idea of Paul's that involved borrowing costumes from the Historic Institute in Bogotá, Alex was jealous of Michael and wanted the script rewritten to make Michael's part smaller or his own part bigger, it sounded like a typical male thing, somebody's part had to be bigger than somebody else's . . . Irma wisecracking, ridiculing Alex . . . I gathered they weren't having an affair, after all, though you could never tell . . . And Maria, suddenly gone quiet, seemed to be rolling something soft and delicious through her mind, an erotic hankering, no doubt . . .

The countryside was overshadowed by the moving clouds. The

road was entirely empty, a strip of black licorice between sepulchral fields and spectral patches of "development," a closed bauxite mine sporting hills of decaying slag, and then a rich green forest pressing close to the road on both sides.

The restaurant was a hacienda set back from the road on a sloping drive ringed by jacaranda trees, with long beds of pink hydrangeas flanking the gravel horseshoe entrance. As luck had it, Alex's Cadillac was in the parking lot. We went into the rear garden, a maze of hedges and clematis and little gurgling fountains. Alex sat a table of attractive food, under a Cinzano umbrella, with an indestructible-looking old lady who was certainly his mother. Across from him was Luis Vasquez, the festival president, who had a long oval infant's face and a glabrous bald head fringed with wooly hair. Luis Vasquez looked like a clown, and he was laughing like a clown at something that had just been said by a horsey, big-boned woman in a ruffled crepe blouse, a string of gold beads resting on her ship's prow of a bosom: Valentina Vogel.

After a due amount of verbal seething and boiling, the froth subsided, the agitation melted away, and we found ourselves dispersed over neighboring tables. Paul was not thrilled to see Alex. He disguised this with his usual fastidious manners, but his expression was engulfed in a kind of woe.

I was fascinated by Carlotta Gavro and the tall, severe woman beside her. They did not look at all alike, as Ray had said: Carlotta looked much more like Irma than like Valentina, but Carlotta and Valentina both looked like Germany, specifically Germany on the march through the Sudetenland. Carlotta was a grotesque, someone through whom the vital forces continued to pump at an exalted rate, despite her advanced age. She was more animated, heartier, lustier than anyone around her, a wrinkled ingenue. She gabbed continually, making fearsome, energetic gestures, half-rising out of her chair to emphasize her points, barking out saucy observations about the whole company. Carlotta was hardly as intelligent or as witty as she thought she was, but she was far from stupid, even if her frame of reference had been more or less sealed off two decades earlier. Her humor pleased us, her *gemutlekeit* jokes, her barbed remarks about people's appearances . . . even at a distance, we felt the atmosphere enlivened by her élan . . . Let's face it, a very old person full of animation reminds you that it's possible to live a long life . . .

On the other hand, though, everything amused her, everything sent her into gales of laughter; all this . . . *life,* in a person so obviously nearing the completion of life's journey, to put it diplomatically, made a bizarre impression. After twenty minutes or so, Carlotta's well-bred raucousness, her apparent compulsion to make the occasion a high-spirited romp, began to seem a bit gauche—after all, this woman had voted for Adolph Hitler fifty years earlier . . . Inexorably, as the afternoon wore on, the residue of the Third Reich settled on Carlotta like a toxic powder . . . A feeling of revulsion overtook my earlier fascination . . .

And Valentina, that imperious waxworks figure less than half Carlotta's age, with her high forehead, her pencil eyebrows, suspicious eyes, her rueful, twisted, mean-looking mouth . . . She resembled a handsome but overweight, spoiled scion of some profoundly middle-class fiefdom, a dynasty of toilet manufacturers or slumlords . . .

From my vantage point several feet away I could see them glancing at us between bites of steak—practically everyone had ordered steak, since this was one of two restaurants in Cartagena that could be relied upon not to serve horsemeat—almost pityingly, as though their table were the only one worth sitting at. In fact, Maria defected to their camp, along with the local actress and the boy. Our table had gained Ray, Michael, and the cameraman. Luis Vasquez wandered over, ensorcelled by Michael, no doubt, or by Irma (whose films he knew and complimented rather nicely), but the flame of Carlotta drew him back, mothlike, to her side.

"Well?" Paul whispered in my ear. "Is he a big queer or what?"

"Who? Herr Vasquez?"

"Yes, but never mind. Let's play Most Insignificant Person."

"All right. Who is the most insignificant person in this room?"

His gaze swept in one direction, mine in another, searching, considering, sifting: Luis Carlotta Maria Imelda Chino Ciro Alex Vale Hannah Willie Ray me Michael Irma Paul Valentina Michael Hannah Chino Ciro . . .

And then something strange occurred, something that I find rather difficult to describe even now, years after the fact, even after telling it to Robert Scheib: because, in effect, it was something only Paul and I paid attention to, on that bright backyard terrace, with bees humming nearby in the clematis and waiters trampling in and out of the fragrant kitchen. Paul had finished eating and was smoking a cigarette, tamping the ashes into a round ashtray covered with a fine sort of steel mesh. Michael's hand was on the table, blunt and inert, but when you looked more closely you perceived some tiny tremors, for example, of the skin at the bottom of his fourth finger, and sometimes his third and fourth fingers touched; sometimes such embryonic movements developed into real ones, as when he touched the tablecloth with his forefinger or cradled the stem of his wine glass.

These things seemed so remote from Michael himself that he might have been a great country full of internal movements that were impossible to apprehend. One of these movements consisted of a slow closing of the hand and folding of the fingers, a chaste, fugitive movement. It was curious that it generally coincided with a lowering of his eyes (which I hardly ever saw); he never raised his eyes when he did it.

Irma's hand, a remarkable object that was charged with eroticism "through" its proximity to Michael's hand, lay beside her plate, a long, elegant, restive sort of hand. Her hand seemed busy with its own choreography, the bunching of certain fingers that rubbed and broke apart, the worrying of one nail with another nail, pressing her thumb-tip between her second and third fingers . . . and the gnawed, fatty remains of her steak sat congealing on a blue plate.

"I've got to go to the bathroom," she announced, glancing around to locate its likeliest spot. She was seated at the head of the table, with Ray on her left and Michael on her right, and next to Michael, Paul, and across from Paul, the cameraman, and beside Paul, me. As Irma left the table, I noticed again the peculiar affinity between her strong, broad mouth and Michael's Italianate, big-lipped mouth, and I imagined, for no reason at all, those two mouths coming together through the wire mesh of Paul's ashtray, I imagined the mesh caked with tar and ash inserted between the two sets of lips . . . His hand with its virile fingers, interlocked with her delicate fingers . . . And then on the mosaic tiles that paved the dining area, quite near our table, something came out from under a hedge, a tawny oval about two inches in length, its movements slow and cautious. It was a cockroach, one of those monstrous southern roaches that are, I am told, often caged as pets in Madagascar . . . Its whiplike feelers trembled in the searing, humid air. . .

There was a space of perhaps five feet between the end of our table and a fieldstone wall wrapped around some kalanchoe bushes beside the building. The floor was an odd Mediterranean surface of sea shells and smashed, varicolored ceramic tiles embedded in a cement grout, an intricate obstacle course for the roach, which seemed headed toward Alex's table in the distance. After noticing the bug I continued talking with Paul, who was describing, in a defiantly loud voice, his idea for a long "historical flashback" in the very middle of the picture, an idea Alex had apparently vetoed earlier in the day, and meanwhile Ray took one finger of his left hand in two of his right and carefully examined it while a dreamy smile spread over his face. Michael, languidly and inexpertly puffing on a French cigarette he'd gotten from the cameraman, was telling us that he played the saxophone, just in case Paul felt like giving him a saxophone solo in the film. I pictured this Greek divinity sitting in his underpants, beefy legs spread, blowing into a saxophone. His eyes looked over to register the flicker of sexual attraction in my eyes. Paul's eyes picked up the telegraphy of our eyes. Meanwhile Ray and the cameraman saw everything without really seeing anything. They carried on smoking, telling dirty jokes, and each would go blank for a moment and stare at me, or Michael, or Paul, and then decide to move a piece of cutlery or push an ashtray across the table a few inches. Ray crossed his legs, uncrossed them, cleared his throat, coughed, and so forth. In the slithering language of glances I followed Paul's gaze to the crawling roach on the mosaic tiles, and saw that Michael, too, kept returning to the labored movement of the insect.

Suddenly there was a sharp crack, as if a strip of sealing tape had been ripped from a package. It wasn't a loud noise, but it was strange enough to stand out from the other noises. A kind of "now it's coming" feeling flashed through my head. Irma resumed her seat at the end of the table, Valentina swooped over from her table to gossip with Paul about Alex, Paul introduced me and Michael to Valentina, Ray began a salty anecdote about a friend of his who smuggled heroin, a cacophony rose in the surrounding air, and then I saw that Irma had crushed the cockroach en route to the table, it lay there flattened against the whorled crown of a conch shell protruding from the cement . . . worse, the thing was trying to crawl on its two or three remaining legs, wobbling crookedly a few millimeters and then collapsing onto its crushed side . . . I looked away, my eyes immediately locking on Paul's, for he had noticed the feeble efforts of the roach . . . an inferno of pain had opened up a few inches from our feet. From out of the clear sky an indifferent god had transformed this writhing organism into a lump of apocalyptic agony . . . By this time Irma's glance had also fastened on the cockroach. Her elbows rested on the table, her left hand cradled the wrist of her right hand. The cigarette in her right-hand fingers dissembled the trajectory of her gaze. She caught Michael's eyes with her eyes, directing them to the death throes of the insect, which was pushing itself forward with repulsive determination, a shiny trail of olive viscera oozing over its path of broken shells and crockery . . .

Irma smiled, lightly, almost imperceptibly . . . and her smile coaxed a wicked, corrupt smile onto Michael's genial face, a smile of casual complicity . . . Paul and I watched them watch the crawling, dying thing on the ground while Valentina laughed at one of Ray's jokes, and then Michael stood up, stretched conspicuously with a forced yawn, his eyes twinkling, and moved around the table in an elaborately casual manner, unhurriedly heading for the toilet . . . all this so he could stand facing the table rather than the restaurant when, with a theatrical deliberation all the more impressive because he was also making himself inconspicuous to everyone except myself, Paul, and Irma, he brought his foot down on the scaly back of the struggling creature, cracking its spine, crushing the rest of its legs, smashing all its internal organs . . . so that a flattened carapace remained glued by its own guts to a smooth rhomboid of pink ceramic when his shoe moved off toward the WC. He paused once on his way to turn and smile at Irma, the wide, lascivious smile of a man confident of having given total pleasure.

6

Laughter in the Next Room

*D*iseased palms formed a visual fence between the wattled huts and a sandy beach where sewage from Boca Grande, borne on a trick current, washed up in stringy clumps. The village smelled of brackish water, pig feces, charred lumber. It had the rudiments of a community but it was in no way clear where people living in the huts made their money or bought food, the only business in the area being a clapboard shack with a rusted Coca-Cola sign nailed to its side. The shack sold cold drinks out of a rusted metal cooler and small bags of potato chips. There were other foodlike things for sale but nothing you would want to eat. Long structures set back among the trees had black glassless openings full of staring, huddled faces. The blacks living there did not appreciate being told to move out of camera range and ambled into shots to display their resentment. When Paul gave the most aggressive ones money to vanish, others materialized. It didn't help that the cameraman and his assistant shouted and waved at the natives like Nordic conquerors clearing a Munich sidewalk. Maria had attempted diplomacy in the local dialect. Since she was a woman, the villagers smiled and nodded and pretended to agree and then resumed their interference.

Paul's obsession with Michael Simard had begun to determine the alterations of the script, which Paul took with him at night in a canvas shoulder bag, along with a Polaroid camera and other paraphernalia to be used during dinner to record a promising location or a comely potential extra. He would amend the next day's shooting pages over strong rum drinks in the Arsenal Disco (where a number of local transvestites battled for his attention, hoping to secure parts in the film), scribble more dialogue in the taxis shuttling us between the old city and the resort peninsula of Boca Grande, and improvise scenes as we sat in the basement casino of the Don Blas Hotel, feverishly losing thousands of Alex's pesos at roulette. Paul believed that Irma and Michael were "coming together" in some occult way, and kept adding scenes between the two of them to urge things along.

That morning, for example, a love scene between Irma and Alex had been postponed on Paul's insistence, and something entirely different was arranged, a scene at the market just below San Diego. The cameraman was permitted to shoot inside the block-long tent, using a crucifix of battery-powered floodlamps and a hand camera. He followed Michael and Irma through the loamy fragrances of the bazaar, into crowds thronging around vast piles of vegetables, sweating Mayan pyramids of cheese, and butcher stalls where the fetor of dried blood swaddled impaled goats and rabbits. An endless profusion of straw baskets and balsa crates overflowed with tomatoes, carrots, peppers, guavas, and mangoes. Filtered cathedral light sprinkled down on makeshift shrines to the Virgin, cardboard altars festooned with garlic necklaces and clumps of squash. The sound technician contentedly trailed the camera, headphones clamped to his ears, his omnidirectional mike recording an unbelievable cacophony of voices, breathy flutes, cackling hens, butchers' saws and cleavers chopping dead flesh, the cries of ragged children, the shrill electronic gurgle of hand-held video games.

Outside the tent, among sellers of pistachios and Brazil nuts, Paul filmed Irma and Michael strolling away from the market into a field where the grass was chewed up by truck tires and utility trailers. In a secluded spot near the edge of a woods, she was directed to stand looking up at the uneasy sky with an expectant expression, to point her arm up at the clouds, to hold this pose for several seconds until Michael, likewise, reached toward the sky, his hand angling until it brushed against hers; at the moment they touched, they threw themselves on the ground side by side. Paul rehearsed the actors several times, giving elaborate instructions about the configuration he wanted them in. Next, he had them each remove one shoe, and told Michael to take his sock off and roll up his pant leg. Lying on their backs, the couple stared into space. Her knees pulled up, Irma crossed her bare left foot over her right knee, while Michael's naked right foot came up and crossed his left knee, until their feet touched in midair . . . then they dropped their feet to the dirt.

"What's he doing?" Ray wanted to know. We were standing behind some parked cars several yards away from the filming, watching the cryptic choreography of arms and legs. We could hear the sibilant nattering of Paul's breathless directions, unintelligible from that distance but audibly rapt and exacting.

"It looks like some sort of ritual," I said, wondering how Irma would choose to interpret Paul's fetishism. Ray acted puzzled and dismayed.

"Alex is just livid," he commented drily. "Paul's been cutting his scenes down. What's worse, he's making Michael's longer. Those shots back and forth the other day. What for? Look at this! It's unnecessary! And I mean, what are they doing? What is that? It's . . . it's *obscene*."

It was true. The stilted, artificial movements of Michael's hand

and Irma's hand, Michael's foot and Irma's foot, the unnatural way these parts of their bodies met and flew away from each other, exhibited a powerful, bewildering eroticism, a studied carnality—it was indecent, in a way that an actual sexual act wouldn't have been. From a distance, the actors might have been signaling a passing aircraft, such was the initial impression of innocence, yet the longer you looked, the more perplexing and naked these symmetrical movements became, charged with a pornographic bluntness . . .

An hour later, Paul observed, "Between the two of them is developing the possibility of murder," as he scanned the baleful Boca Chica sky, its ragged clouds raking low over the palms, pointing his Coke bottle at the long avenue of mud ribboning into the rain forest. We were sitting on the tailgate of the white truck, as Maria resumed her negotiations with the locals. We might have been in Central Africa, Cameroons, Mozambique: the poverty of the surroundings verged on the conditions associated with life in the wild.

"Between their characters," I said, encouraging clarification.

"Well . . . yes, naturally. The possibility exists that they'll conspire to murder Alex."

Paul craned his head around and smiled at Michael, who stood with his back against the bulkhead of the truck, technicians at his feet unpacking reflectors and magazines of film stock. Michael grinned back disarmingly. I realize that I have described him as Russian-looking, Italiante, Greek, a French schoolboy, etc., etc.: the fact is that Michael's beauty was, like all extreme beauty, indescribable. Certainly he was "dark" rather than Nordic, Mediterranean rather than Celt, let's say, closer to Slav or Arabic than to WASP; he was probably an inch or so short of six feet, his body type somewhere between a "swimmer's build" and "body-builder." His face had smooth, regular features, thick black eyebrows, piercing gray eyes with green-brown aureoles, a fleshy, longish nose, wide lips, a wide, squared chin . . . but it's futile to itemize his attractions. Michael Simard was the shepherd you hope will stumble over you in the forest. As far as what he was actually like is concerned, this was still, improbably, mysterious. For one thing, the boy was so laconic that we had learned almost nothing about him. His résumé was simple: a friend of Paul's had discovered Michael modeling nude at the Art Students League in New York. ("That doesn't mean he's a prostitute," Paul assured me. "It just means he's comfortable without his clothes on.") He also worked as a chauffeur for a limousine company.

He had a ready smile and an apparent willingness to do anything Paul asked of him. But he seemed utterly incurious about the film—except when he became interested in things the technical crew was doing—and he spent a great deal of time staring off into the clouds. Michael drifted in and out of our thoughts, an object of intense preoccupation and at the same time a complete irrelevance, like some childhood fetish bedeviling your responsible, adult self . . .

Meanwhile, Alex Gavro, alarmed at Paul's script changes, afraid not merely of being upstaged by Michael but also of losing money (since every departure from the established shooting schedule risked prolonging our stay), had driven into Boca Chica to supervise, with the line producer (a dour woman named Hannah) and Valentina Vogel, who sat in the front seat of the Cadillac preening her long auburn hair with a plastic brush. For several days, Valentina had stayed in the villa on the pretext of some obscure indisposition; Irma reported that the haughty editor (like Ray, a longtime veteran of Rudolph Bauer's celebrated films) emitted a subtly disparaging view of Paul's project. She had only agreed to edit the movie out of friendship, and to have a paid vacation in South America. Today she had condescended to "take a look" at the shooting, to groan good-naturedly over Paul's amateurishness, maybe to interject a wise if obvious suggestion.

I was supposed to walk beside Michael along the mud road, past a corral full of pigs and a large pink building on stilts, the local schoolhouse. We carried suitcases, the premise being that a transportation strike obliged us to walk into the city from the airport, through the fetid marshland between the forest and the harbor. We had agreed to play the scene for comedy, my impish character struggling in the heat with a luggage that was loaded down with bricks while regaling Michael aka Max with risqué gossip about Ava Gardner and Lana Turner. Michael remained silent, impassive, preoccupied with his own thoughts. The first shots took us past the pig corral and into the deserted outskirts of the village. From there the camera, mounted on the truck, would track us front-on.

We had already shot a few takes, none of them to Paul's liking, when a cloudburst supervened. My sneakers were caked with mud; Michael was cleaning grime from his shoes with a rag. Paul had just reiterated his desire to use this timeless, primitive colony in his "historical flashback." Alex had once again proclaimed his aversion to this proposed sequence, claiming the movie would grind to a halt as soon as it came on. The first sheets of rain fell without preamble. Alex stopped haranguing Paul to hop back into the Cadillac and put the roof up, while Ray and the crew men spread greasy tarps over the equipment in the pickup.

I jumped into the Cadillac with Paul and Valentina. The others huddled in the rear of the black van. Through the splattered windshield we saw them framed between the open doors, figures in parentheses, sitting with knees up along the van floor, passing joints around.

"I haven't been up this way in years," Alex said, lighting a joint of his own and extending it to Paul like a peace offering. Valentina and I politely ignored each other's body in the backseat, like strangers on a subway car. The smell of rain mingled with a stale dusty scent of the upholstery, a smell redolent of old powder puffs and closets choking with mothballs, ruched gowns and faded taffeta in forgotten cedar chests. With the raindrops rattling on the soft vinyl roof, this smell transported me to some long-ago moment of childhood, exploring the attic of our family house. Some desultory talk among the three of them followed, starting in English but lapsing into German, effectively locking me out of the conversation. Every so often Valentina looked at me and smiled a bit helplessly, her severe face softening, as if in apology for the language barrier. "Would you like some more of this?" she asked in English, holding out the joint.

Since I only understood one in six or seven German words, I couldn't really follow Alex's ruminations. The most I caught was his reminiscent tone, as he waved the dwindling cigarette at the rain, recounting past escapades in wonder at his former daring. Alex had unsuspected narrative gifts—when he got going, he loved spinning out a tale, replete with strangely nuanced observations. The wooden self-importance he carried around on his face was only one, daunting side of an off-putting personality. You can turn a rock over with your foot and find a whole world crawling around.

Alex had every reason to turn on the charm: the rest of us didn't trust him. His part was being whittled down, not in any systematic way that he could fight with his powers as producer, but in supple, deft, logical-sounding strokes. Alex seemed incapable of ordinary social pleasure, so I assumed that this plangent interlude had an ulterior motive—but perhaps it was simply what it was. Paul, with whom he'd been bickering only minutes before, sat spellbound, and soon was translating Alex's spiel for my benefit.

In the less organized early days of drug smuggling, Alex had operated a small air service between the islands, one single-engine Dakota that flew between Boca Chica, the Caymans, and the Everglades, and numerous unmarked islands and sandspits along the way. It was in the sixties, before Alex's stretch in prison, and the drugs were mainly marijuana and peyote plants instead of coke. "And of course," he added wickedly, "heroin." Valentina clucked and guffawed throughout the recitation, exactly like a goose, I thought, nervous and silly: what was the Edith Sitwell poem Paul was forever quoting? "Daisy and Lily, lazy and silly, walk by the shore of the wan grassy sea—"

Those had been days of manly adventure. And if anyone subscribed to Paul's ponderous credo that fucking and killing were the only actual events in life, it was Alex. He spoke of dodging DEA agents and drug pirates, sinking competitors' boats on the high seas, jettisoning a half a ton of weed in advance of a bust. He hinted, darkly, that in the kill-or-be-killed circles he had traveled in, murder was all in the day's work, though he himself had never done a hit—but he had witnessed a few. Yes, the whole area was saturated in lore.

"He says that behind the mountain near Santa Marta there's a tribe of Indians," Paul said. "The men can only have sex with their wives once every three months, according to the lunar calendar or something . . . and if you go on the beach over there and spread out your towel, the men will come out of the forest and fuck you, one at a time, until the whole tribe has had you."

"It's true," Alex asseverated, hunching around behind the steering wheel.

"Fuck you and then eat you, probably," Valentina suggested. "I suppose this is only for boys?"

"Stupid," Paul said savagely, "the whole point is not to have to enter that horrible vagina."

The moment froze, since Paul's anger almost never surfaced, and when it did its meaning was never clear. Alex coasted over the brittle patch in German while Paul told me in English, "Alex has a friend he thinks we should meet. He lives in the hills over there."

Up ahead, the three-man crew, abetted by Michael, Ray, and

Hannah, were pretending to dance inside the van, squatting in the doorway, pumping their arms up and down, and chanting something unintelligible. Maria climbed out of the front of the van and ran over to us. She climbed in next to Paul, black hair dripping:

"They want food," she said. "Like always."

Paul glanced at his watch. It meant going all the way into the city, and several lost hours, since each time the equipment was boxed up and moved it took forever to unpack it again.

"Alex, what do you think?"

Alex looked at his own watch. He answered Paul in German. Valentina had some objection. Alex nodded, considering it, then made an "it's all the same" gesture with his hand. Paul twisted his face ambivalently. Maria and I looked at each other with goofy, clueless expressions. Something was decided, at any rate, since Valentina started gathering her things up.

"We're going?" I said.

Paul thought about it.

"You can either go," he said, "or . . . maybe come with us to meet this person."

I shrugged. Valentina was nudging Paul's half of the front seat forward, obliging Maria to scrunch against him. Valentina was obviously smarting from Paul's insult, though when he spoke to her in an imploring tone, to smooth it over, she laughed and waved him away. "I need food," she said flatly, stepping out of the car and skipping toward the pickup. Maria poised herself for a dash back to the van.

"I've taken enough speed that I'm not going to eat anything, anyway," I said. "So who is this person?"

I noticed that Alex's grim face wore a dreamy, idiotic smile. As soon as Maria had bolted for the van, Ray jumped out of it and came up to Paul's window, knocking on it furiously. The keys to the pickup were clenched in his fingers. Through the steam and driblets on the plastic rear window, I got a weirdly distorted glimpse of Valentina climbing into the pickup, her large purse impeding her progress. Paul rolled down the window.

"How about meeting us at Paco's?" Ray said. The rain dripped off his petite face, collecting at the fringe of his moustache. His eyes were sore and red in the corners. I wondered again if my influence on Paul, Paul's influence on me, terrified this bland, excitable man.

"Well, of course, maybe—"

"You have other plans?"

"I have to discuss things with Alex," Paul protested.

Ray cast a significant look at me in the backseat.

"Concerning the next scenes," Paul added. "Look, you're soaked, go on ahead and we'll meet you there."

"Paco's," Ray reminded him.

"Yes, yes, Paco's," Paul said with exasperation after Ray had walked off to the pickup. "Why on earth he wants a ginger-bread cottage in the forest of Hansel and Gretel, after all this time . . ."

"He only wants you to love him," I said, with feeling. As I said it I felt excluded from all love, but flooded with altruism.

"It isn't so simple to love what you love," Paul said.

Soon we were driving into the woods, under the dense forest canopy, the shrinking road developing an acne of sinkholes and boulders.

"It's necessary to *hate*," Paul shouted as the car dipped into a gully of spraying stones then lurched up through mud.

"Hate what?"

"All affectional ties are predicated on hate," he said. "Hatred of the others. I'm sure it's a perversion of Kant's universal ethics. We want all to be as we would wish in order to be right, and if we think it's right, then all should do as we do, and they don't."

The car bounced through a pothole.

"Therefore," Paul concluded, "we must hate them."

Alex adjusted his Tonton Macoute sunglasses as though he had long ago accepted the practical necessity of hatred.

Behind the flatlands of Boca Chica there were hills that rose into a vertiginous zone of emerald verdure. The road became straighter, less onerous, wending across meadows and groves of cultivated fruit trees before plunging back into the jungle. The rain stopped abruptly, as it always did, and Alex put the top down. Sunlight poured through the treetops.

The house was set back several yards from the road in the shade of monstrously tall trees: a plain, well-appointed little house whose main area was a terraced living room with no front wall, the open space overlooking hundreds of miles of forest spread out in the direction of Venezuela. A dog started barking as soon as the car pulled into the dirt drive, and then came galloping around the house, a skinny Airedale-looking mutt tethered to a clothesline wire by a retractable leash.

Skirting the perimeter of the dog's terrain we approached the veranda, which had a flagstone subterrace as a repository for potted ferns and metal flower boxes full of jasmine and gardenias. On the upper level a large, powerful-looking man was seated in a motorized wheelchair, gazing out across the million treetops through which a wide, sluggish, gray river snaked, streaked like the treetops by thick bands of sunlight. Behind the strong fragrance of the flowers lay a stronger odor of mulch or compost lifting from the forest floor, a smell that summoned thoughts of boa constrictors and other slithering things.

"Who coming there?" The man lifted his shaggy head and fixed an intense, level gaze on Alex.

"It's me, Jaybill. Alex Gavro."

"Who be talking to Jaybill?"

"What, you are blind and deaf now as well as crippled?"

"Shee-it, Alex, you come on up here now. Let me look at you. How's yoah mutha? These your friends?"

"No, my enemies. I always travel round with my enemies, don't you?"

Jaybill Hanratty, as he was called, had a harsh sensuous mouth framed by a rakish beard and moustache. His face had a saturnine cast, the skin light brown, like a North African Arab's. He wore an orange, short-sleeved Villanova sweatshirt and denim cutoffs. Almost the first thing you noticed about him was that his arms ended in stumps just below the sweatshirt sleeves and his thighs tapered into smooth rounded tips where his knees should have been.

Behind his wheelchair was a long elegant sofa covered in dark green silk with a pattern of white daffodils. Piled on the sofa cushions were numerous prosthetic limbs, plastic arms and legs with sectioned steel and flesh-colored surgical straps lying askew like the overcoats of party guests heaped on a bed.

"*Simone—!*" Jaybill yelled, tilting his head back, aiming his voice at the hidden depths of the house. High-heeled footsteps clattered on bare floors and the dog resumed barking, without much conviction.

Alex introduced us to Jaybill, who told us we should take a look around God's country. In fact, the area around the house had a monumental quality, like the Ecuadorian panoramas painted by Frederick Church: endless woods borne down by a whole democracy of climbing plants, an infinite entanglement of sylvan loveliness.

"Someday this will all be a desert of soil erosion," Jaybill said with satisfaction. "Much of what you see has already been sold to cattle ranchers."

"And you still have to go to Paco's for a decent hamburger," Alex said. He sounded nostalgic. "What is it, Jaybill, that dooms the Orinoco valley to this kind of third-class, third-world style of shitty half-done development?" He waved his arm at the panorama, becoming vehement: "This, this here, it was El Dorado!"

Jaybill Hanratty nodded his head, looking like a fifties jazz musician on goofballs.

"That is true," he said finally. "We are looking straight at what the Spanish thought was El Dorado. Pizarro thought it was and Ferdinand and Isabella thought it was, Sepulveda and Herrera and De Soto and Alvarado thought it was, quoth the raven, El Fuckin' Do-ra-do." He paused, stuck out his lower lip, hawked and spat across the lower terrace into the yard. "I do believe they were correct, too. It *was* El Dorado. Trouble is, Alex, it ain't El Dorado anymore."

Paul and I stood on the lower terrace taking in the view, while Alex crouched beside the wheelchair, conferring with Jaybill in an unfamiliar patois. In the depths of the house the sharp footsteps of Simone clacked back and forth, as if she, whoever she was, could not make up her mind to come out.

"Let me tell you what I'd like to happen with your character," Paul said ostentatiously, leading me off to the far corner of the terrace. I could hear the dog's leash scuttling along the wire on the other side of the house. "Alex's friend was a big drug dealer," Paul murmured. "He used to control this whole part of Colombia, not Cartagena but the countryside and all the inlets along the coast. He still takes a lot of drugs and he's really out there, you know?"

I looked back over Paul's shoulder to the rather strange tableau of Jaybill Hanratty in his wheelchair, staring Nietzsche-like at the teeming jungle, Alex off to the side in a wicker chair, bursting now and then into hacking laughter. It was odd that Jaybill, judging from the way his clothes hung, had an athletically proportioned body despite his missing limbs.

A woman came into the living room, a scrawny woman in a strawberry sundress, a blonde Marilyn wig, and red spike heels. She spoke to Jaybill in a sharp voice, then turned to Alex, ignoring us. As she talked she gripped the handles of the wheelchair and began pushing it gently back and forth.

"How did he . . . ?"

"That's the best part," Paul whispered. "He burnt some people in the Cali cartel, for something like a million dollars. That's what Alex says anyway. And they did this to him—they didn't want to kill him. They knocked him out with chloroform in the parking lot of El Laguita. Then they kept him in a cabin in the mountains, on morphine, chopping off one limb every four or five days. There was a doctor who sewed him up each time so he wouldn't bleed to death."

The information gave Jaybill a sudden freakish glamour, like a movie star disfigured in a car crash. I tried to imagine his exposed stumps as objects of a keen, adventurous eroticism. Simone was running her fingers through his thick black hair, brightly painted nails flashing.

"Y'all wanna whiskey or somethin'?" Her American voice with its strong southern accent was distinctly male. I now noticed the muscular calves under the sundress hem, the bulky shoulders. Now she came clacking over to the edge of the veranda. "Yew prob'ly think we're peculiar or just demoralized to start so early in the afternoon, but this is the tropics, gentlemen. And besides," she winked, "things bein' as they are, they ain't very much else to do."

Paul lit up with appreciation: Simone's gender delighted him.

"I wouldn't mind a little breath of whiskey," he called. "Unless of course you've got gin. And my friend here would like whiskey also unless you have gin."

"No," I told him.

"Your friend there can say for hisself, cancha darlin'." Simone laughed. "I have gin, I have vodka. I have tequila. I can make you a gin and tonic, a gin and lime, or a gin and orange squash. I can give you gin and vodka, as far as that goes. I can even," she said with a leer, "make you a gin and piss, if you give me a minute or two."

"Maybe some ice water," I said. "If that's okay?"

"Might not be okay down at the Bolivar," Simone said, letting us know she knew a little bit about our arrangements already. She moved off toward the kitchen. "But I make my ice with spring watta 'stedda tap watta. Keeps that *malaria* at bay, keeps the *piss* outta the ice cubes."

"I have to act this afternoon," I reminded Paul, though it sounded like an apology for not drinking.

The sun was evaporating the last of the rainfall. A luxurious wet heat rose from the forest floor, with the twitter of a million insects and small animals making a muggy symphony.

"I want to change that scene in the village," Paul said, keeping his voice low. He paced the edge of the lower terrace, pulling me along with his arm around my neck. "The way it is, it's just a comedy scene floating in the void, where what we really want is something much darker . . ."

Alex and Jaybill, deep in conversation, looked like astral opposites, one white as chalk, the other dusky, romantically disfigured. Alex's chair was in the shade of the interior wall, Jaybill in a blade of sunlight. There was a haze in the air, a fine mist that put a white sheen on the spaces between things.

We stood at the base of the terrace, watching Simone move in and out of an outdoor pantry off the kitchen. Paul jumped down into the undergrowth. He strolled beside the house, picking tall weeds out of the wild grass, while I followed just above him. The architectural distinction between inside and outside obtained nowhere in Cartagena: parts of the inside extruded out, and vice versa.

"Instead of just playing it for laughs, I thought we could foreshadow this possible act of violence with the gun—let's say that you and Michael, walking along, get into an argument, he loses his temper and hits you, knocks you to the ground, he shouts abuse at you . . . ?"

"It's up to you." I shrugged. Certainly this inspiration had nothing to do with Paul's script. The question was, what part did it play in his private movie, the one unfolding in his head?

Simone brought the drinks. We perched on the edge of the upper terrace, near Jaybill's wheelchair. Simone pushed the prostheses to one end of the couch, clearing a space to stretch out. She lay on her side with her elbow on the rail-thin couch arm, a transvestite Cleopatra. It occurred to me that the elegant fabrics and conservative decor of the house were completely at odds with its inhabitants, whose own tastes would undoubtedly run to the arriviste. Their money had come from pimping and whoring and dope. They carried that atmosphere around with them. There was nothing wrong with that as far as I was concerned, but it didn't go with the furniture.

"How *is* your mutha, Alex," "she" asked languidly, craning her neck and clinking her ice cubes. "She still doin' fine?"

Alex interrupted himself to answer her. "Oh, you know Carlotta, she's a rock of life."

"A rock of life. That would be a way of putting it. What's her opinion on these bodies they found in the canal?" Simone turned to us. "Old Reen Wilson that owns that Sandwichy Cubanos over next to the Hotel Medellín, drove all the way up here the otha day just to describe the horror. He went on in such gross detail I practically fainted. Just imagine, two separate bodies, all cut up, with the heads sliced off, and from what Reen Wilson says, some stuff inside all missing too . . ." Simone made a pained face. "Seems like you neva get any normal kind of killin' around this area."

"That is the Bible-thumpin' truth," intoned Jaybill in a James Earl Jones voice. "It's the army that sets the example. It's not enough to make one person disappear; the wife has to be tortured, the daughter raped, the father decapitated, the mother burnt alive, the sister's children gang-banged by twenty soldiers and so on. Why, they even kill your pets in terrible ways."

"Killed Reen Wilson's toucan, and his dawg. Course that they say was a accident. There's always them American advisers out at the Caribe," Simone said. "Always see their cars parked out at the yacht club too."

"The bodies are incredibly mutilated, they say," Paul told me. "They found them quite near the Arsenal."

"I guess you want Jaybill to act in your movie," Simone told Alex. She looked at us. "Seems like everybody wants to see him perform. Don't they, Jaybill."

"Damn if that ain't true," Jaybill muttered. He smiled to himself. Some white spittle appeared on his dark lips. Alex shifted in his chair. He looked at Paul. A little conference in German ensued. As they talked across Simone and Jaybill, the latter both looked at me with sly, knowing faces. I could see that under its vivid makeup Simone's face was bland and even slightly ugly, the nose wide and flat and the eyes a queer round shape, the face of an unloved boy-child grown to quotidian monsterhood.

"She" spun herself into a sitting posture on the sofa and crouched forward, lightly gripping a handle of the wheelchair, attempting a sleek, imperious, Diana Ross album cover stance. Alex and Paul continued to chatter and Jaybill's big brown eyes continued staring into space. Simone's little movements were accelerating—"she" gave the impression of someone pacing rapidly inside her own skull. In some indefinite way she had fixed on our arrival as a golden opportunity that Jaybill remained insensible to. She also looked completely stoned on freebase, beyond the stage of verbal diarrhea, at the level where words, if they come at all, eject in a mad gabble and hang in the air as a sort of spoor.

Amid the many noises in the air—Alex and Paul jabbering in German, chirping insects, forest sounds—I now heard a sucking and surging noise, as regular and unobtrusive as the purr of a refrigerator. I realized it was Jaybill's breathing. His upper torso rocked gently against the beige leather backrest of his wheelchair.

Simone was talking. "She" had been talking for some time, her mouth against Jaybill's ear. "Gotta be paid, paid plenty," she was chanting, slurring her words, between great belts of whiskey that sometimes poured down her chin. "Jaybill here been in plenty of motion pictures. He's what you might call a specialty act—for a special type of audience. Go 'head, show him the merchandise, ask him what he thinks."

"Alex ain't making that typa movie, Simone," Jaybill rasped. But Simone was implacable, down on her knees beside the wheelchair, tearing at his shorts.

"Take it out, go 'head, don't be shy, *show* that thang! This boy'd like to see it, I am *sure*, Jaybill . . ."

Now Paul and Alex were paying attention, and I felt that an invisible wall keeping one thing apart from another was suddenly being torn down, one thing becoming mixed up with another. Jaybill's penis sprang out of his open fly, even in its flaccid state a true curiosity of nature: its length and width easily rivaled that of a donkey's love pole, which it also resembled in color.

"Ain't that something?" Simone wanted to know. Jaybill, of course, was unable to replace the organ in his shorts, and after some useless grumbling let himself be handled with an air of philosophical resignation. His meat rested in Simone's firm grip like an engorged python. He was looking down at it as if he had never seen it before and had no idea how it got there. For some reason I thought of those funnels of ragged flesh that revolve on spits in Greek restaurants. "Feel this thing, it all muscle."

"Magnificent," Paul crooned. I looked at him. His face was

"ironic." Something was taking its course, an image developing in the red light of his brain's darkroom. He did not take up Simone's invitation.

"Anyhow, now you know," "she" babbled, "what a South American movie star looks like." A moment later, Jaybill released a long, thunderous, wet-sounding fart, which spread a thick cloud of stink across the veranda.

A second later the whole episode was over, Jaybill's business was tucked safely back into his shorts, Alex conferred once again with Paul, then the two of them with Jaybill, while Simone straightened up the pile of prosthetic limbs at the foot of the couch, talking to herself the whole time. The veranda resembled a proscenium stage on which some quirky minimalist drama had just been acted out.

"Don't you think he's *perfect?*" Alex asked Paul as we drove back to Boca Chica. Since he phrased the question in English, it was clear that he wanted me to understand him. He was signaling his own complicity with Paul's unstated schemes, the scenarios hatching in Paul's unconscious. Exactly what these schemes were, however, remained opaque. And I was confident that Alex was more a pawn than a conspirator.

I slouched against the rear seat of the Cadillac, probing the back of my teeth with a fingernail. The scaly, rocklike protrusion in my gum moved slightly when I pressed it. In my mind, it was connected to the convergence of Irma's mouth with Michael's mouth, of both mouths with the wire mesh top of the restaurant ashtray, and now with the arm and leg prostheses lying askew on Jaybill Hanratty's couch. Tooth, mouth, mesh, mouth, leg, arm, tooth.

7

Insignificance

*T*ime was moving in a deep, black river. Cartagena felt like a hot loaf of bread. Days passed hazily in thick, pounding heat, and at night we were all bone tired from the day or else artificially wired from cocaine. And that could mean a frantic, brittle evening in Boca Grande at the casino or the discotheque, sloppy, wine-dilated meals in the beach restaurants, winding up at the Arsenal Bar after midnight.

Typically, though, the residents of the villa kept to their pool and watered drinks and late dinners in. Miles away, Alex ate with his mother at the Caribe and tried to pick up vacationing American girls. Those of us marooned in the Hotel Bolivar went our odd, independent ways, sometimes meeting in the patio bar or crossing paths in the plaza. Since Michael's room was directly across the hall from my own, his movements acquired a certain interest. I listened for him in the evenings, and sometimes timed my own exits so that we would meet.

He was a curiously changeable young man. Sometimes he came out of his room wearing a look of luxurious contentment. He wrapped me in a muscular embrace that was either tinged with lust or a put-on, insisting on buying us beers, there in the Bolivar or around the corner at Paco's. There was a spring in his walk and a strutting self-assurance that made him even more desirable, if that were possible. At other times he seemed startled or annoyed to see me, his eyes hooded, and skulked evasively to the stairwell or fled back into his room.

Even when Michael was obviously high on coke and unable to suppress a torrent of speech, I found it difficult to recall later on any single thing he had spoken about. Except his body. Michael could speak inexhaustibly about his physical envelope and its discrete parts: his fingers, hands, elbows, chest, abdomen, hair, knees, abdomen, moles, feet, teeth, penis, testicles, ears, eyelashes, and internal organs provided him with endless conversational material. He spoke of the various events these pieces of himself had undergone, the myriad sensations they had experienced, injuries they'd sustained, always with a kind of enthralled detachment, as though his possession of such superb corporeal merchandise never ceased to amaze him. He was especially loquacious when describing his various brushes with discomfort and pain. He tended to get backache. He once described his aching back in such explicit detail that I began having the same aches and twinges. It crossed my mind that this may have been an invitation to offer him a massage, but I felt inhibited by his beauty.

At Paul's insistence our characters had fought in the middle of the dirt road in Boca Chica, "Max" supposedly provoked by my failure to reserve a rental car at the airport, also by the heat and the dust. I understood that our rehearsal of various stage combat feints was a ruse: behind Paul's directions there were other directions, behind the narrative another narrative, real violence behind the fake violence. This would be partly for him and partly for me, we would both have some of it, and with any luck it would taste good, like the blood in a rare steak.

Paul expected me, at the crucial moment, to bring my arms up too slowly to deflect Michael's fists. Two rapid, strong blows struck the sides of my head. I blacked out for a few seconds. I blinked awake in Michael's arms. His face was a rictus of guilt and concern. Hovering behind him, Paul beamed ecstatically.

"You see? He's really a . . . a brawler," Paul marveled later in the Arsenal. We had wrapped early and gone by ourselves to the bar, stopping beside the brackish canal to look at the warm sunlight, the mottled stones and weedy moss of the embankment, and the indistinct clouds scudding in the blue-white sky. The Arsenal had just opened, the sound system was mercifully silent, and only two other people were in there, both part owners of the place who were sweeping and prepping the bar.

"That's ridiculous," I said. "Michael's docile as a kitten. You just rigged it so he had to hit me. You know he'll do whatever you tell him. I mean he *has* to."

"He didn't say no," Paul said, licking his lips with satisfaction. "Besides, that wasn't some love tap he gave you."

I shook my head. "I'd like to know what this is leading up to," I said. "I mean if you want . . . well, him and Irma . . ."

Paul's blue eyes glistened. At times he resembled an ancient tortoise peering from its shell. His partly tanned neck was loose in his shirt collar. "You'd like that as well, wouldn't you?"

"To see them . . . yes, sure." I shrugged. "Although I'm sure he'll be sleeping with Maria before long." Despite her frequent references to a dashing banker-lover in Cali, Maria had been more or less throwing herself at Michael for days. In his quiet way, he appeared to return her interest, or at least acquiesce in it, though his public demonstrations of affection were always perfunctory and strangely impersonal, as if to emphasize his equal availability to everyone.

Other liaisons were also forming. Valentina had begun "dating" Luis Vasquez, and the line producer, Hannah, had started sleeping with the Dutch cameraman. Irma had a chaste friendship going with the sound technician, a fat leather queen from Berlin named Ciro, with whom she went swimming in Boca Grande on our days off.

"Imagine," she told me. "He goes off into those outdoor toilets with soldiers . . ." While remaining hazy about her own erotic life, Irma always savored the exact details of these encounters, reporting that Ciro loved it when a man in uniform "made pee into his beard" or squirted come on his large, hairy belly.

Paul and Ray . . . argued. Paul replayed their arguments in all their particulars, rolling details around until every possible meaning had been considered. I can reconstruct these arguments as though I'd been present, having them from both parties, see them today in my mind's eye: the two men in the northwest second-floor bedroom of Villa Gavro; Ray, whose crumpled-handsome face (the face of a runty but dashing corsair, its fleshy proboscis firm as marble above his sculpted mustache) looks oily in the candlelight, has donned his white linen jacket and a pink St. Laurent shirt, stiff at the collar and cuffs. He wears nothing below but a tight pair of red silk underpants. Ray's scrotum is conspicuously large. Paul, athletic and baby pink after a lukewarm shower, has dressed in a gray Armani suit too thick for the heat. He sits on a soft bundle of mosquito netting folded at the foot of a frilly canopied bed, holding one of his shoes.

The ghosts of Effi Briest and Major Crampas, of Warren Beatty and Elizabeth Taylor hover in the enormous room. The electricity has sputtered out, as it does three or four times every evening. The terra-cotta sconces in the ancient stucco, their stout yellow candles exuding a faint gardenia scent, have been pirated from a cathedral in Lima, along with a voluptuous marble Christ impaled on a sectioned two-by-four of worm-eaten teakwood. All the villa's furniture is massive, incredibly old, and seems to have migrated from a looted monastery or museum.

Paul claims that Carlotta Gavro has been the lucky beneficiary of myriad pillagings. That after the war she was an essential link in the vast network that spirited the likes of Mengele and Barbie out of Germany into the depths of Bolivia and Paraguay. These grateful fascists have funneled objects of virtu to her over the years, until her villa has become a virtual museum. Paul thinks about the Elgin Marbles, about the weird, bloody circulation of money through the universe. About exploited peasants and the piquant depravity of dictators. When Paul pictures himself rectifying life's injustices—relief worker in the Congo, signer of petitions and indignant newspaper letters, member of the RAF—he gets a mental cramp. He would like to plant bombs at Springer Verlag, smuggle plastique aboard transatlantic flights, shoot an I. G. Farben CEO. But he can't, and much of his imagination expends itself in stepping over the rubble of ruined dreams.

Instead he imagines "pictures." As work on the film proceeds, each day requires the fresh invention of images, positioning of bodies in space, numerous hours in an unreal world.

Ray stands at an inlaid African dresser, contemplating his diminutive but manly features and the room behind him in a tall, oval mirror. The silver nitrate behind the glass has cracked and peeled in several spots. The mottled reflection breaks Ray's body and the room into jigsaw pieces. Ray resists suggesting that Paul use the mirror in his film. Ray thought the cock-shaped turrets of the city walls were made for the movie, too, and Paul instantly rejected them: they'd remind people, he insisted, of the fantasy city of Rudolph's film *Tarantella*. "People will think I've got no ideas of my own."

The mellow room cools after a day of soggy, listless heat. Under the balcony overlooking the courtyard the monkeys scream in their cages.

"I don't see what you're driving at," Paul tells Ray, jimmying a white-stockinged foot into his shoe. "We shot eleven pages today and we're three days ahead of schedule. We don't have dailies but I'm almost certain what we've got looks great."

"I just wonder," snorts Ray, amiably, admiring the fractured image of himself thrown back by the scaling glass, "whether what you've got makes any sense. That boy is supposed to be a *reporter*. I mean I know he fucks her, but we never said the audience was supposed to drool over his body every time he's on screen."

"Why not? He looks better than Alex." Paul ties his shoelace, walks to the dresser with an air of decision, and embraces Ray from behind. They contemplate themselves in the leprous glass.

Ray has been wallowing in the weaker regions of his will. He did not think coming to Cartagena a good idea. He resisted it for many weeks and then changed his mind, whimsically. Paul slides his crotch against Ray's taut buttocks, his hands caressing the well-toned abdomen through the pink shirt. Moisture oozes from Ray's skin.

Ray detaches himself from Paul's body, faintly irritated. "I just think it distracts from the story line," he offers weakly. He spins on his heel. "But look here. Here I'm telling you what to do and really it's *none* of my business—no, really, Paul, it isn't. We're lovers, not artistic collaborators. What *I* think is that I should go back to Sydney and get out of your hair."

Since shortly after Rudolph's death they have lived more apart than together, Ray in Australia managing a film distribution company, Paul in Munich filing bankruptcy and hatching plans. There is some unstated intention to resume connubial life in the middle future, somewhere.

In the wardrobe with Renaissance carvings where their things hang intermixed, Ray locates his cream-colored trousers. There's a streak of dried, dark mustard on the fly, from Paul wearing them.

"But you have a part to play," Paul protests. He joins Ray at the wardrobe. He nibbles Ray's earlobe. He squeezes Ray's penis. "You have to play the piano."

Ray tousles Paul's sun-whitened hair and makes a sour face, looking like a sober, steadfast, whiskered rodent.

"Get Maria to play the piano. *I wonder who's kissing her now,*" Ray sings in a pleasant, tuneful voice.

"Maria is my wife, you're my biographer. I need you both. Also, she doesn't play."

Paul slips his hand inside Ray's underpants. He has given himself the role of the "secret genius" running the government through proxies like Alex and Luis Vasquez, who plays the chief of police. It is a good role for Paul: witness to the crimes of others, a puller of strings, Svengali. He cups Ray's damp balls in his palm. The stringy hairs feel grainy. Ray's penis stirs a fraction. Paul slides his hand out, smells it.

"Your crotch still has the sweetest odor," Paul rasps.

"What about this," Ray offers, stepping away to the bed. "I'll go to Sydney and work for a few weeks . . . then meet you in Sosua. We'll have a vacation. Jacmel, if you prefer."

"Jacmel." Paul sifts through a tangle of neckties. He picks out two and stalks to the dresser. "World capital of AIDS. Lovely."

"Carriacou. The Grenadines. Look, Paul, I *know* what you're getting into with this. And if it . . . proceeds, I'm just afraid we're going to scrap—and I don't *want* to scrap. We should just have done with all the bloody fussing. I want us to get along."

Paul considers this, along with a blue tie, which he knots under his collar, then undoes and tosses aside. Ray farts a cheesy raspberry.

"Sorry."

"We could have a week or two holiday but we can't afford you flying over there and back again. It's just too much. Look, we've both got to go to Sydney afterwards anyway. Jesus, what did you eat today?"

"What we can't afford," Ray says, waving a coiled belt at the walls, "is *this*, Carlotta's bloody pisshole Kempinski. Everybody's whole salary's going into the damn—" He slips on his white trousers. He sighs as if tired of his own anger. "And a bunch of jibbering nignogs shaking us down for every ice cube. You know, you could call Alex on that. We never said we were doing a film just to launder money for Alex Gavro. This is your *art*, for the love of God."

"Well," Paul says with irony, "not for the love of *God*, certainly, but I see what you mean . . ."

Ray zips his trousers. His gaze lingers on the stain. He darts barefoot across the stone floor to a table, digs a Marlboro from a crumpled pack. The possibilities of argument are endless, he thinks, picking up a lighter: rightly to be great is not to stir without great argument, blah blah blah. Near the ashtray, a many-legged and -armed Hindu deity in jade. It, like the stain, annoys him.

"This house," Ray says. "This house is so pretentious. I know you like these fancy digs but, I mean, really." He flops onto his back on the springy bed. He stretches out his legs and rubs his groin with his fist.

"I'll tell you what's pretentious," Paul says. "This tie. Do you know the origin of the tie?"

"Yes, I do."

"In the middle ages," says Paul, ignoring him, "noblemen had to wear them like a garotte to show the king that he had the right to strangle them at his pleasure. You can hardly call this a pisshole," he adds, standing before the peeling mirror. "Besides, we aren't paying for it. It's all Alex's money, in a sense." He puckers his lips. The spirit of Marilyn Monroe flutters at his elbow.

"I'm not sorry Alex parked himself at the Caribe," Ray says.

"And I do appreciate your putting *him* at the Bolivar, I'm sure you two would be giving live shows over here by this time."

"Well, there you are. I've done everything you wanted, you can't leave now."

"All that stuff with Michael and Irma. His feet with her feet and lying about in the grass, Paul, what's all that supposed to mean? It's not natural, it's . . . bizarre."

There are wicker baskets in the room, Greek Orthodox icons, the screaming Christ with tears of blood dripping from its crown of thorns.

"Oh, we won't even use it, probably. I was simply trying a little experiment. Kind of a carryover from the stage. Those mechanical gestures and so forth, a little like Oskar Schlemmer automata, if you see what I mean."

Paul idly wraps a tie around his fingers. "You realize," he continues, "you don't have to come to the set every day if you don't want to. No one asked you to help the crew, that isn't your job, lugging and fetching—I only want you to play your scenes. The rest of the time you can stay here lounging by the pool! Or go out and fuck a nice boy. Why not? I don't mind, you know. A nice Colombian youth, or one of these child prostitutes they have. Haven't you ever felt like . . . sticking that big cock of yours into a nine-year-old?"

Ray has put out his cigarette in the ashtray planted on his chest and lit another. Paul turns from the dresser. His face looks goofy. Ray feels, for the moment, pleasantly defeated. He sucks in smoke and wrinkles his eyes shut.

"I . . . *did,*" he confesses in a whisper.

Paul's eyebrow arches in a circumflex. "How interesting."

"In Bangkok. I mean, it was twenty years ago."

"You were twenty. It doesn't count. Anyway, I bet it was a girl . . ."

"Well . . . once it was a girl, that's true, but it wasn't only that time. You realize, Paul, you're free to have a party, too, if you want."

"No desire." Paul shakes his head. "I mean I *do* have a party in mind, but not one where—well, let's say I've got a special sort of thing in mind. By the way, darling, Hector Luis and Juan Carlos aren't Negroes. They're Indian and Spanish, mixed. *All* Spanish, if you ask them."

"Hector Luis is a weasly little thief."

Paul sighs. "It's part of his charm. These servants are paid shit, you realize. If they rob us we should be glad for them." He brings his face close to the mirror. It looks no older than when he last paid attention to it. "Glamorous screen star," he asks his scattered reflection, "or aging pederast? Mirror, mirror, *you* be the judge."

He follows the mirrored candle-lit nimbus of Ray's form as the latter stands up, strides to the foot of the bed, and sits down on the mosquito netting. Paul slips on his tortoiseshell glasses, assuming a look of blond efficiency and control. Ray's pale bare feet perch on the bedframe.

"I *do* need you here," he insists once again. "I need to stay alert and strong and also *fucked* from time to time, and not by some piece of local trade. Don't forget I have to deal with these exasperating people."

Ray coughs on his cigarette. He finds this hilarious.

"You thought it all up yourself, fuckhead."

Paul nods, with energy. "I did, didn't I. What was I *thinking* about? You'd have to be . . . *unbelievably* stoned to dump all these people together in the same place. And this place is a perfect horror."

I imagine this little exchange taking place about three weeks into the project, on one of those sultry evenings when the vaunted inner circle was expected to join Carlotta Gavro at her regular poolside table, out on the peninsula. The Caribe was part of "modern," i.e., tourist, Cartagena, like everything out on that fat hook of landfill. It made a change from the Bolivar.

As Ray and Paul argued, Irma put the finishing touches on herself by candlelight. Irma hated her face, all severe angles and Max Beckmann lines. She hated her hair, clipped and dyed ash blonde, her Bride of Frankenstein crossed eyes. "She isn't beautiful," ran one line in Paul's movie, "but she has something. Men go crazy for her."

This happened to be true, but of no particular use to her most of the time. The ground-floor room was full of stagnant air. She moved the candelabrum closer to the bathroom sink. She hated her big tits that no one bothered noticing, the big fanny she'd put on, which everyone did notice. But she was starting to like herself a little, she thought. She liked her dress, which she wore in the film and got to keep—a see-through clingy silk thing, half myrtle green, half clown pink, the colors divided vertically.

She unhooked a small crescent bag from the bathroom doorknob. She blew out the candles and walked out of the room, but stood for a while in the darkness between the rear staircase and the tiled arcade enclosing the patio, listening to the monkeys screech. Across the thickets of the garden, in the blackness above the balustrade where the dining room would be, an indistinct bolt of white hung suspended. As her eyes adjusted, she realized it had to be Hector Luis's shirt. He had noticed her coming out of her room and was staring, watching to see what she'd do.

The villa bristled with freaky noises and abrupt silences. There was sometimes a riot of cicadas, sometimes birds, sometimes shouting from the street. And gunfire, she thought. The surflike soughing of wind in the palms. Before, she'd been able to hear Ray and Paul's voices carried faintly from the top of the house, and then a door had squealed shut and the voices stopped. She now heard a faint, dry slithering from the sitting room across the patio, fabric rubbing fabric.

The fuzzy specter of Hector Luis vanished. For a moment the house went still, and then a raking noise came from the monkey cages. A parrot leashed to a flame tree gurgled briefly in response. She remembered that the servants were supposed to bring the parrot down. The moon slipped free of a cloud bank, lighting the flagstones and vegetation and the vines crawling up the balconies. Irma thought, Everything in the world is connected.

As she started for the living room the power flicked back on, focusing the big picture a little more sharply than she would have liked. Her thoughts had been running on a downward spiral. She reminded herself not to drink too much.

Valentina Vogel sat near the join of an L-shaped couch. Her ample posterior sank into frothy lilac-patterned cushions. Her plump elbow rested on an onyx table where a lamp threw an oval of light across an Isfahan carpet. She had laid aside *Vogue* during the blackout and now picked it up again. She looked prepared to retreat bodily into its pages if anything further disrupted her composure.

Irma thought the brown cocktail dress Valentina had on, by some name designer no doubt, had cost at least three thousand marks. As the editor and ambiguous consort of Rudolph Bauer, Valentina's skills were much in demand, and expensive. Strap heels, tourmaline bracelet, a heavy gold necklace studded with dull amber stones. Straight auburn hair yanked back with pins to show off big gold earrings. "She looks like an Aztec pyramid," Irma thought.

Their eyes met in a flicker of suspicion. Since arriving in Cartagena, Irma had experienced a medley of emotions about Valentina Vogel. Mistrust figured prominently among them, the mistrust of Irma's working-class background toward a solid bourgeoise. She also felt a streak of defiance, against her fear of

Valentina's disapproval. And she also recognized in Valentina the strange obdurate authority her own older sister, who had recently died of cancer, had exerted over her throughout her lifetime. "If she ever asks me to do something," Irma thought, "I know I'll do it. Even if I don't want to."

"Well." Valentina's smile was masklike, automatic. She wasn't pretty, but she had a monumental sort of plainness. Irma's incipient masculinity came forward around women like Valentina, in spite of the latter's severity. "She's just a cunt," Irma told herself.

"What a nice dress." Irma stepped right over and felt it. "Very chic," she purred, forcing Valentina into a different sort of smile, an anxious Kilroy of a smile. Irma snatched up a gold bell and gave it a shake. She selected a five-year-old travel magazine from a wicker hamper and started fanning her face with it. She sat down on the far end of the couch: she and Valentina and the lamp now formed an isosceles triangle.

"Hector's crushed we're not having dinner here." Valentina giggled girlishly, thrusting her prominent round chin toward the villa's north end. From the sofa they both saw straight down across the dining room, to a crack of light where Hector Luis or Juan Carlos, differently irascible boy servants, would emerge from the kitchen. Uncharacteristically, one of them did come out almost instantly.

They watched the mote of red and white move slowly along the mortuary slabs of chair backs pressed against the dining table. From a distance, the servants looked identical. Hector Luis was distinguished by a refined profile and elegant extremities. He had the miniature quality achieved in certain dog breeds, wiry-haired, perfectly formed, but scaled for confinement indoors.

The dining room table was three hundred years old. It seated thirty. Irma did not believe there were thirty people worth having dinner with in Cartagena, from what she had seen so far. She halted Hector Luis in the archway with a look. His mischievous yet oddly worn-out face creased in idiotic amusement. A sarcastic smile bubbled to his thin lips. Valentina smiled. Irma smiled. The smiling mouths seemed to float in front of their owners, drift through the air, and stick to parts of their clothing or nearby furniture.

Valentina asks for a whiskey, in careful Spanish. Clutching *Vogue* by its spine and flapping it on her lap, she crosses her legs to angle it up for reading. Hector Luis shakes his curls adorably. He starts for the kitchen. *Dos whiskies,* Irma barks, *dos, dos*—the boy freezes. *Hector Luis,* she says in a rectifying voice, *unos rum cola instead.* It doesn't bother her not speaking a word of Spanish besides *mierda,* but she knows his trick of pretending not to hear. Hector Luis enjoys working people's nerves in small, irreproachable ways. Irma knows she would do the same in his shoes.

"I wonder if they would have books in German anywhere." Valentina is digging hard for a subject. Irma nudges off her canvas espadrilles and puts her feet on the cushions. Her toenails are shiny pink. The pink-and-green silk ripples along her thigh. She starts to say she's brought some novels, then almost guiltily closes her mouth and appears to think about it.

"Maybe at the Hilton," she finally says. "In Boca Grande."

A knock at the door. The sharp yawning noise produced when the servants open the front door. Footsteps crunch on the patio gravel. Michael and I have arrived together, and he, Mr. Perfect Perfection, has been having an allergy attack on our walk from the Bolivar, sneezing continuously, his face pale, eyes watering freely. Moments after our arrival, Luis Vasquez of the film festival shows up, in an elegantly sleazy suit: Irma notes his clothes, and the fact that he's bonded to Valentina.

Hector Luis returns with drinks. Irma grabs her glass and salutes Michael with it, brazening a wide, crazy-looking smile. Michael's mouth moves nervously.

"We're going?" Luis Vasquez asks Valentina.

"Well, I want to wait for Paul."

Michael sneezes twice, then a third time after some suspense, followed by a fourth and fifth sneeze. Luis Vasquez trails Hector Luis out of the room, into the kitchen. He has an easy proprietary air about the place that I can see bothers Irma.

"I wonder . . ." Valentina tosses her magazine aside. Michael plants himself in one of several leather sling chairs. I pace. Valentina leans back on the cushions as she stares at the ceiling. "I'd just as soon not go up there."

This appears to mean that she thinks Ray and Paul are having a fight. Or something else is up. Or nothing's up, and Valentina is giving a pointless inflection to the usual dead patch of time before dinner.

"Well, why should you?" asks Irma. She doesn't know if she is closing off a subject or challenging Valentina to bring it up. "This is a slow country. Things move slowly here. Relax."

Ray and Paul have been fighting but it has nothing to do with her. Ray wants to leave. Irma doesn't blame him. They've shot a good deal of Ray's part, so that will be bad, if he leaves they'll have to reshoot with somebody else or just cut him out or shorten the part. Well, if he wants to leave he should. Whenever you think a film will be fun there is always some little detail to ruin it, usually the mad hours and weeks of hardly any sleep and down here, she thinks, it is probably going to be cocaine that ruins it. Cocaine makes everybody eager to push things too far. To "get real" with each other. And in the last few days, Paul has been getting really real—which is to say, unreal.

Valentina stretches out her legs and looks at them admiringly.

"It's only that Carlotta will be put out if we're all late."

"Fuck Carlotta," Irma can't resist saying.

"Everyone hates Carlotta," Valentina says, deprecatingly. "I really wonder why." Her voice implies that she knows the answer and is eager to dispute it.

"I don't think 'hate' is exactly the word."

Valentina looks at me in challenge, then at Michael. We are speechless. Michael sneezes.

" 'Makes fun of her,' then. I honestly don't understand it. She's just an old woman."

Michael sneezes. Irma stares at Valentina, whose gaze shifts away. Her pointy nose, in Irma's mind, symbolizes some subtle difference in sensibility or genetics, she can't pin it down quite. Irma feels reproached by that nose, for her campy glamour compared to Valentina's sedate Lutheran dignity. She feels her style clashing against the style of Valentina and her nose.

We hear Paul's voice, crashing down from the second-floor balcony. A door slams, whether with intended violence or not, none of us can tell. Sharp steps on the balcony. Irma finds a magenta lighter in her bag. She lights a cigarette. She slides her feet back into her shoes. She feels suddenly weightless, silly, and closes her eyes and pictures Valentina's nose growing to the size of an alp. She opens her eyes. Paul comes across the veranda and down the steps into the room. As he glances at us, his prominent nose inhabits his face like a prosthesis stuck on with putty.

He nods and does his usual little dance around the furniture, debating where to alight, radiating commotion, with his nose sticking out.

"Well. So." He sits down in a scissor chair and deflates like a tire with a slow leak.

Luis Vasquez walks in ceremoniously with a tray of drinks. Glasses full of ice and fizzy something, an odd touch. The servants are fiercely protective of the booze: only they can handle it, so to speak. A volley of caustic looks passes. Luis Vasquez commences handing out drinks. A gliding motion of Michael's mouth, a sudden squawk from the parrot in the garden.

"Where's Maria?" Paul rotates his finger in his glass.

"She went to Paco's for a hamburger." Valentina jiggles the ice in her glass. "She hasn't eaten today. She couldn't hold out another minute. She said she'll meet us at the Caribe."

Irma swallows a lot of her rum cola. It tastes like vodka, not rum. It probably is. She watches Paul. Out of the corner of her eye she notices Luis Vasquez staring at her. He is squatting beside Paul's chair like a faithful dog, his bald head looking more and more like a circus clown's pate. He never looks at the person talking. His eyes crawl all over you when you aren't watching. The moment seems pregnant, but pregnant with nothing.

"She's out in the dark walking around by herself?" Paul's eyes bore into Valentina. The note of concern in his voice is meant to allude, no doubt, to the so-called Vampire of Cartagena, whose gruesome escapades have thrown sudden terror into the city. "Vampire" is a bit of a misnomer for what sounds like a serial killer with cannibalistic tendencies, but the Colombia press has firmly affixed the moniker.

"Well, actually, Luis, maybe we should join her at Paco's and take her with us to Boca Grande," says Valentina.

Luis grows restive. His knuckles fidget against his glass. His nose clings stubbornly to his face.

Valentina's nose is calm and decisive.

"Yes, we must go to Paco's." She throws her arms out to convey the naturalness of wanting to go to Paco's if you are all dressed up.

Irma settles her drink on the glass table and watches condensation puddle at its base. She believes that the villa's architecture, its grandiose excrescences, the monumental furniture, the expressionist lighting casting monstrous shadows, all conspire to suck people up and make them invisible.

Upstairs a door creaks open. Without even mentioning the Vampire of Cartagena we have managed to summon the idea of him, forgetting about Ray, who now hollers down something unintelligible.

Snail tracks of moisture dribble down Irma's glass. The underside of Valentina's shoe comes up and settles against the edge of the table. In silence, tensions gather at a vortex I imagine hovering above a square crystal vase in the center of the table. In the vase is a perfect cymbidium orchid. Michael sneezes.

"Jungle fever," someone whispers in a goosey voice: myself, I later realize. Then it all breaks up and melts into insignificance. Paul complains about something he ate the day before, Michael stares at his loafers, Valentina fondles her necklace and massages the muscles in her throat, Ray ambles into the room muttering about a handkerchief. The copy of *Vogue* on the sofa cushions. Paul's fingers rubbing his glass. Michael's fingers scrabbling at his hairline. Ray's palms smoothing his jacket lapels, the blue lamp, the lush potted palm, the orchid, the vase, the bit of tooth burgeoning inside my mouth, the shadows of the palm splashed across the upper wall, Luis Vasquez's gleaming baldness, the black iron ceiling fixture, the fan, footsteps in the dining room, Hector Luis's red jacket, insects croaking in the garden, Paul's glasses, Ray's mouth, Michael's mouth, Irma's mouth, Valentina's mouth, Hector Luis's mouth. Hector Luis smiles.

8

Looking Backward

As I said before, or maybe forgot to, telling this in retrospect has its pitfalls. The idea that I am anything like a reliable witness is a bit ridiculous. I know perfectly well that this is all an approximation, an attempt to make something with the texture of quicksand cohere into narrative . . .

That I had so little will of my own surprises me, looking backward. Paul, for that matter, though often grimly determined to "make things happen," was never terribly consistent in his wishes. He yearned to be a tyrant in the style of Rudolph Bauer, but he could never quite manage it. Paul really preferred the valet role, to be the inconspicuous witness of other people's excesses. But without a leader, a catalyst of some kind, people tend to dither and carry on meaninglessly, their secret desires never splashing to the surface . . . and therefore, by default, almost, Paul's actions spurred things along, against an opposing tide of entropy . . .

I used to spy on Paul. I seized any chance to observe him when he thought he was alone, hoping his private behavior would betray the "secret" that motivated his obscure fantasies. It had to be some sublime idea of degradation, I thought, a black vision that canceled all moral feeling. This did not consistently apply to Paul's actions, or even to Paul's opinions, but I could sometimes account for him in no other way. His casual, automatic betrayal of any confidence was only partly a gossipy compulsion; it was also his proof that your deepest secrets didn't matter at all in the larger scheme of things. In a life where the destiny of everything is to end up dead, the least interesting thing to do with a secret is to keep it. Paul, typically, would tell it to the person with whom it was likely to cause the most egregious trouble, just to see how both parties would deal with the resulting estrangement. It was useless to be angry with Paul—he never accepted your anger as real, and could wait forever until it blew over.

On the way to meet him in a café or a hotel lobby I picked him out of the crowd and then moved in on him surreptitiously, avoiding his sightlines, until I found myself lurking behind a damask curtain or a Chinese screen, or gazing out the slightly ajar door of a men's room. His white fingers curled around the beaded glass skin of a beer mug, the constant cigarette held a few millimeters from his lips, the mica blue eyes staring at other things in the room, sometimes as though these other things—the movements of waitresses, the dippy whizz and gurgle of a pinball machine, a palmetto rustling in a sudden breeze, scuffling teenage boys—confirmed some melancholy conclusion he had drawn about reality long ago. He smiled to himself, often. But I never found in his agitated, busy gestures, the bleary longueurs of cleaning his glasses with the corner of a tablecloth, any sign of that childish, regressive helplessness that often conquers people in solitude. Nor was anything in Paul's expressions or movements "for" other people, designed to make himself interesting to the passing crowd. I would think, "He is in himself for himself," and trembling with a thwarted sort of excitement I would enter his ken.

But who knows? Perhaps he saw me every time I crept up on him, and staged his "naturalness" to confound my curiosity.

Perhaps Paul could only be "natural," could only exist, if he was being observed.

The perfect place for him was Paris, that city where sensuous Germans come alive less bluntly and desperately than they do in Germany. Munich was his rut, and his life there always seemed to me impoverished. Even the "masculine" furniture in his apartment bespoke an inferior, bachelor life one insignificant step up from the proletariat. There were mementoes, for example hundreds of photos, all tacked to cork panels in the kitchen, and in the living room two big wicker baskets full of matchbooks from everywhere in the world, and various *objets*, paintings by a Cologne artist, a Warhol silkscreen of Liz Taylor, and little sculptures, little figurines, tiny African and Indian bric-a-brac, bought to commemorate or celebrate his marriage with Ray, but the apartment really felt like a dormitory, a slightly cruddy place where the carpets got damp from the two of them trailing bathwater into the hall, a place held together by the weekly ministrations of a housekeeper—it was an installment-plan environment, hastily furnished, indifferently laid out. Sometimes people who believe they are destined for quite different places will remain in such a transient location for years. Renovation is anathema because it implies permanence.

I knew Paul only after Rudolph died, but enough of Rudolph's scene persisted in his favorite hangouts to get the flavor of it: provincial, rough, and completely Bavarian, a milieu of starches and carbohydrates . . . rife with petty snobberies, feverish with peasant ambitions to "find one's place in the sun." A cosmos of pork loin and noodle soup and beer gardens and smelly underwear. And the siren song of fascism, the possibility of becoming haunted or possessed by the spirit of that raving lunatic from Linz, suffused everything like lingering funeral incense. In Munich, Paul always had too much insufferable time on his hands, too much bad company to waste it with . . . Robert, I think, was one of his few friends who actually forced himself out of bed in the morning. Strange to say, in those early days of the plague, as the horrific implications of the epidemic revealed themselves, the reckless behavior of the Munich crowd actually accelerated.

Cartagena—it wasn't his ideal setting, either. Paul struggled the whole time against his dissolute impulses, which were not as grandiose as Rudolph's, but trained in the same school, so to speak . . . And, at the same time, he plunged headlong into his more cerebral obsessions . . . with Michael, whose lap he insisted I sit on in the taxi that night, though I had nearly maneuvered Irma into that position, and so while he pretended to chatter on about the passing scenery, over the barrier of the front seat, Paul studied the effect of my own body snugly jammed against Michael's in an anal-receptive position, Irma beside us in her giant movie star sunglasses humming the latest hit by The Smiths, while Ray chewed his mustache and glared tersely out the side window at the silver spoor that the black waves deposited on the beach.

Paul's obsession with Michael, with Irma, and now with Jaybill, if I was not mistaken . . . and maybe with Jaybill's transvestite mistress, Simone, I couldn't really tell . . . the mouths merging in darkness, the insect trailing its guts on the broken tiles, those artificial legs . . . his foot rubbing her foot . . . and something else I'd noticed lately, a thin worm of indented skin in the spur between Valentina's nose and upper lip, the trail of a poorly basted harelip . . .

There were no roadblocks going into Boca Grande. This in itself was highly unusual. Since the second of the three recent homicides, night traffic between the old city and the peninsula was carefully monitored. When the cab whipped through the moonlit square in front of Paco's, a truck full of soldiers had just pulled up beside the fountain. Little khaki figures spilled out, yawning, scratching their balls. I came to believe it was always the same troop of fourteen-year-olds patrolling the city's odd corners and intersections, frisking people and rifling through their belongings. In normal times they searched for weapons rather than drugs, but if they found drugs they shook you down for all the money you had and would often snort the drugs right in front of you. (On one occasion, I purchased from a young soldier the coke he'd confiscated from me the night before.) Now, of course, they were searching for the Vampire of Cartagena. The local chamber of commerce, Alex had informed us, was frantically suppressing news items that referred to the Cartagena Vampire as "the tourist murderer." Two of the three victims had been North Americans, reportedly two gay boys from San Francisco. The third had been identified as a middle-aged Frenchwoman.

In the oval drive of the Caribe, a hansom carriage loaded with Americans clopped off into Carrera 2. "That's it, that's it," Irma hissed after them. "Show the whole city your big fat assholes." To us she smirked, "Maybe the vampire will get *them*."

We marched under the columned portico into the lobby, which was blindingly overlit and smelled of sawdust. Painters' scaffolds ran all the way up the center of the lobby into the rotunda. Drop cloths were scattered across the polished floor. Guests were using various "conversation areas," clumps of red modular seating arranged around square mirrored tables. The heavy smell of paint and the renovation clutter gave the lobby an obtuse backstage feeling. Officious brown-skinned men in cheap suits promenaded through the lobby with walkie-talkies, reporting their own useless movements to invisible colleagues with an air of avid importance.

The back of the Caribe was an intricate landscaped jungle mazed with flagstone trails to the restaurant and swimming pool. I felt myself locking into step with the gaudy march of the white race over all the world. No one questioned our absolute right to be there. Anyone with a tan line darker than angel cake would have been stopped by security.

Irma grabbed my sleeve.

"Now for the horror mother," she whispered.

Carlotta Gavro sat at a banquet table so close to the pool edge that I imagined I could look down and see her wrinkled smile floating on the water. A fat girl in a black and yellow bathing suit propelled herself through the water, kicking mightily.

Carlotta emanated an imperishable blondeness. She wore a patterned white suit and a substantial diamond choker. Her wrists were trapped in scads of turquoise Indian jewelry.

Alex sat beside her, grasping her hand and squeezing it. His sandy hair looked particularly wiglike in the garish "mood lighting" around the pool. He wore a black shirt, a blue-and-white houndstooth sports coat, and a fluffy cravat. The three crew men and Hannah, the sour-faced line producer, had arrived earlier and crowded around Carlotta. They were all overdressed in their idea of formal clothes, like country cousins at a city wedding. Paul moved quickly to take the chair beside Alex, leaving the rest of us to flounder. The vegetation had reignited Michael's allergies; walking just behind me he sneezed repeatedly, and I felt a spray of snot against my neck.

Ray decisively took a chair at the very end of the long table. Just as the maître d' approached, Maria and Valentina and Luis Vasquez appeared, in high spirits, voices amplified by cocaine.

The table had glass bowls with green-yellow orchids floating in them, and bottles of Korbel in buckets of ice. The corks began popping at close intervals. Luis Vasquez and Alex Gavro competed for "master of ceremonies," for each would rise and disappear into the enclosed part of the restaurant, conferring with the manager, or else duck into the dense shadows of the garden with one or another of the guests in turn, to snuffle epic quantities of white powder next to cages of slumbering parrots.

It was a peculiar, mad hatter's dinner. Carlotta dominated her end of the table, officiating like a high priestess. At our end, Irma pretended to translate Carlotta's chatter, whispering, "and then I put the Jews in the shower room and locked the door, then I turned on the gas, next I went back to the office and listened to Mozart . . ." Valentina was enraptured by the old horror, and Irma had her saying, "*Ach, ja,* if only I was born in the good days!"

Ray was knocking drinks back, his face becoming rubbery and savage-looking. It seemed that everyone was doing something strange with their hands. Tugging their hair or pinching their noses or scratching the tablecloth, and that seemed connected to the salsa music booming from inside the restaurant, and to a funny cocaine buzz that was making everything ridiculous. The chlorine ripple of the pool water, blobs of light bouncing against the wet pool tiles, the soaring palms clacking in the wind, the moon, the stars . . .

And then Alex, in an offhand way, said, "The manager is worried that the killings will scare people away from Carnaval."

The general conversation shifted to English at that point, for some reason.

"That's ridiculous," said Carlotta, dipping her wrinkled chin closer to her diamond necklace, which threw off sharp beams of brilliance.

Luis Vasquez had stood up to get a better grip on a champagne cork. He pouted his bottom lip and his face darkened as though he were burdened with terrible knowledge. Alex lit a cigar and blew out a fat plume of smoke.

"Even so," he said, "it's true there are cancellations at all the hotels. The tourists are leaving Cartagena."

"I heard," Maria said confidentially, "that they found more body parts in the canal, wrapped in plastic bags . . ."

"Of course it is blown out of all proportion. The police are handling it," Carlotta exclaimed in a high-pitched voice, almost hysterically. "To make a panic, this would be very bad."

Paul looked philosophical. "Carlotta," he said, "I've been meaning to ask you if you won't consider a small role in the movie."

Carlotta brightened. She raised a champagne glass to her crinkled lips.

"They say he *eats* certain parts," said Irma, in a languid voice. "How do you call them, the testicles? Balls?"

Just then, Luis Vasquez dropped the champagne bottle. It sprayed across the table like an explosion of carbonated semen.

Carlotta sprang from her chair. Maria jumped away from the table. Paul began sopping at the mess with his napkin, and Alex was suddenly all over Carlotta—did any get on her? "Oh *Mummy!*" he exclaimed, "your *Lagerfeld!*" Which was absurd, it wasn't any kind of Lagerfeld, Carlotta did not wear really good clothes; she was flashy. Luis Vasquez fled the table and returned with the maître d' and two waiters, who set about stripping the tablecloths.

Valentina sat frozen, clutching her neck. Everyone was squalling and screeching and switching places at the table, the ambiance turning very loose and wet and ungovernable. For a moment I detached and saw us all as monsters on a rampage in a foreign country. Ray scooped an orchid out of a bowl and threw it at me.

The waiters were replacing the tablecloths, shifting the ice buckets and bowls of flowers, clearing used glasses, setting down new ones: I suddenly saw everything through their eyes. It was something you could not avoid down here. These sudden, horrific illuminations, seeing yourself from *their* point of view. You would notice how robust and attractive even the poorest Colombians were, then feel like a form of cancer. We, the white plague.

Of course, just then the legend was current that the actual plague had traveled from Africa to Haiti and the rest of the Caribbean and from there to New York and San Francisco. But you had only to think of Pizarro, and Cortés, and the ravaging microbes they brought to the new world, the wake of mass destruction they left in their panic frenzy for gold, to realize that no bane, no scourge, no pestilence could come into the world as it now was except through the agency of the white race and the petty capitalist spirit. No one else had the means or the sheer criminal will.

Paul was telling Carlotta the story of Elizabeth Forster-Nietzsche: how as a little girl she collected every scrap of her brother's writing, and grew up almost as Nietzsche's consort, eager to ingratiate herself into the circle of Richard Wagner. For her Richard and Cosima Wagner were the *ne plus ultra* of artistic loftiness. Then, when Nietzsche broke with Wagner, Elizabeth, frantic to retain her welcome at Bayreuth and her status in the *haute monde*, denounced *The Case of Wagner* and married the unspeakable anti-Semite Bernhard Forster.

Carlotta listened, her strong face wreathed in distracted smiles, as if to an old, comforting fairy tale. Her twinkling Prussian eyes nestled in their sockets like poached eggs in spider webs. Irma sat beside me, ripping an orchid apart with her fingernails, and across from us Maria pestered Michael with little word games, little guessing games, brushing her fingers against his hands, her sing-song voice girlish and silly . . . On this occasion I saw more clearly than before the stunning narcissism behind Michael's humble, reserved manner, saw that his southern beauty was so extreme that it eliminated the possibility of normal social interaction, in the same way that a severe deformity presents an obstacle to be overcome . . . His beauty was enough to rip the veneer of civility off the raw desires orbiting around him, enough to make everyone around him regress.

With her new husband, Elizabeth Forster-Nietzsche traveled Germany raising funds to establish Nueva Germania in Paraguay. A colony of pure Aryan families, disgustedly fleeing the Jewish contagion raging in the Fatherland. In letters home, Elizabeth

painted an idyllic picture of an almost regal existence in Paraguay,
but in fact things began unraveling rather quickly . . . Forster did
not have a clear deed to the land, but had made a deal with the
Paraguayan government, securing leases that would be extended
if 140 families settled in Nueva Germania within two years
. . . Elizabeth was confident that even without meeting this figure,
the leases would be renewed. But her husband knew better.
Forster had sold the land to the colonists without really owning
it himself . . . if they failed their quota, he would become the
object of hatred and ridicule. And then the leases were, in fact,
revoked. Forster went up to Asuncíon to beg for an extension
of the two-year clause. Refused by the government, he shot
himself . . .

Paul wanted Carlotta to play Elizabeth in her later years, when
she had taken control of her disabled brother's copyrights and
turned the ravings of the "mad philosopher" into a minor publish-
ing industry, with herself the president of the archives . . .
manipulating one Nietzsche acolyte after another into running the
place, while establishing an exalted literary salon . . . writing a
biography of her brother, fixing her own three nominations for
the Nobel Prize . . . and at last (Paul was wired out of his mind,
with a little encouragement I'm sure he would've thrown himself
into the pool), at last, getting Hitler to extend the copyrights, by
dating them from her *editing* of the Complete Works rather than
the time of their composition *(was Paul actually going to say it?)*,
culminating in Hitler's visit to the Nietzsche Archives in Weimar,
and Elizabeth, age ninety, greeting the Führer at the door . . .

All the while Paul painted this garish picture, guests were
stretched out beside the pool, music blasted from the restaurant,
the sharp smell of chlorine mingled with broiled fish and alcohol,
and the sky was a carpet of stars, with a three-quarter moon
. . . I forgot the essential horror of it all. Luis Vasquez continued
to drag people into the garden, feeding them fat spoons of coke,

jabbering nonsense the whole time like a kid pissing his pants around celebrities.

Michael's sinuses erupted. He was miserable with the heat and everyone offered some consoling wisdom about drinking quinine or taking antihistamine pills or salt tablets or what have you. In all the solicitude, there was an unacknowledged, palpable satisfaction that the most beautiful person should prove the most susceptible to bad things in the air.

Carlotta regaled us, meanwhile, with stories of her epic vacations in the heart of Africa and Uruguay and Palma de Majorca, all those steaming places where old Nazis hang out, and in the middle of this she quoted Paul Bowles, Paul Bowles of all people, on the distinction between tourists and travelers, a distinction that could not possibly have any significance where Carlotta was concerned, for she was obviously someone who had absorbed everything and learned absolutely nothing, aside from petty details that distinguished one place from another. Alex egged her on, with a sadistic relish made more obvious by little winks and eye-rolls directed at his mother's listeners. "*Oh, Mummy, it wasn't Goa, it was Fiji, you dropped the camera from the balcony in Fiji,*" he'd tell her, and she'd say, "*Please, Alex, I'm sure I can tell the difference between Fiji and Goa, the camera fell right on a beggar's head and killed him, can you imagine? Killed him instantly, ha ha ha . . .*"

It was there again, the semitooth working its way out of my gums, I had brought my finger to my mouth like a child, and as I probed around I stared at Valentina, all the way down the table, the strong lights reflected from the pool haloing her face in ice blue, the curved red line above her lips appearing to wriggle on her face . . . remote, remote . . .

"If you are this stuck on making a period movie," Alex was telling Paul, "we should just raise money to make another film! All these concepts, it keeps adding to the complications . . ."

"No, no," Paul said, "these are very short scenes, very brief, narrated maybe by Irma to Michael, showing the history of Germans in Paraguay . . ."

That flawed mouth was moving down the table . . . Ray had gone over to sit with Maria, Michael was smoking a cigarette, Alex played with his fingers while Carlotta fingered her necklace and chattered at Hannah . . . and then Valentina sat in the chair across from mine, puffing tersely on a filtered cigarette, her voluminous body sweating in the brown dress . . . We hadn't properly had a talk, ever, now she was asking where I'd met Paul, how long we'd been friends, and when I said "Munich" she wanted to know if I had known Rudolph . . . which I had, only slightly, Rudolph had taken an instant and rather meaningless dislike to me, and I to him . . . I noticed her hands, which were actually . . . well, big, big peasant hands . . . Irma got up and walked into the garden with Alex . . .

". . . and the stories," Valentina was telling me, though she seemed also to be telling Michael—he crushed out his cigarette and looked at her with the same rapt, seductive expression he gave everybody, inwardly nodding out no doubt and flying away to a secret island of a million mirrors—". . . as you know, all kinds of wild stories have started, stories about me, stories about this one and that one . . ."

This theme—the wild stories about her, the bitter aftermath of Rudolph's death—carried over into the conclusion of the meal, into the taxi that took some of us back into the Gesemani district, Valentina even kept it up while we were body-searched by a patrol at the traffic rotary where Carrera 1 and Carrera 2 intersect. Others had taken a different taxi and still others were detained in Luis Vasquez's car. As I felt the adolescent soldier's light hand fluffing my trouser inseam, Valentina was saying that in many ways her worst mistake "was to go on that trip to Florida, when Rudolph became possessed by this urge to marry me . . ." Even though they'd kept the marriage a secret, thinking anyway it wasn't valid since no blood test had been taken, word got out, and then when Rudolph died the gossip ran that she had gone out and scored Mandrax for him even though she knew it might kill him, "because she was due to inherit everything," though this was obviously not true, she didn't even have the marriage license. But, she said, people could be cruel and vicious.

"You can keep your hand off my tit," she chided the inspecting soldier, looking him straight in the eye. This elicited a chuckle.

Michael said almost nothing. The soldiers took longer with him, I suppose because he looked young and virile and hip and they figured he would just naturally have some dope. And then as we drove off Valentina triumphantly drew a bottle of cocaine out of some secret compartment in her purse, spurring gales of laughter from the driver . . . Michael laughed as if laughing were a new and vaguely disagreeable experience for him . . . I wondered if the burden of his looks (which were so "real," and required such seriousness) had entirely robbed him of a sense of humor . . .

At the Arsenal, the disco lights were in full throb, but the room had a sparse clientele and an air of glumness hung over the place . . . As successive waves of our party arrived, the long, narrow bar took on a slightly more festive aspect. However, we knew that Nicky and Juan, the drag queens who ran the place, feared and despised Luis Vasquez, who Nicky said ripped them off year after year during the film festival, forcing them to throw huge private parties at their own expense for various movie stars and directors. And now Luis Vasquez was pressuring them to turn the place over to Paul for his movie. Because of the various language barriers involved, this minor issue had gotten locked into an intractible and negative configuration that Paul attempted to shift. He was more than willing to pay them some of Alex's money but Luis Vasquez insisted on their using the location free and Alex was split between doing the right thing and screwing them over. Screwing over a couple of piss-poor drag queens had a certain attraction for Alex—he was that kind of guy.

Nicky told me that Alex had offered them all parts in the movie, but that this didn't compensate for money down the drain. Luis Vasquez, Nicky said, had always conducted a brisk trade in white powder in the Arsenal, selling and scoring both, plus, he had long enjoyed the oral blandishments of Nicky and Juan whenever it pleased him, fortunately not often—and all because he was in the government and a well-known police informer.

They were happy to see the rest of us, with our dope and our pesos, especially Irma and her platinum aura, and Michael, who was any homosexual's image of perfection. A few couples were throwing themselves about on the dance floor. Alex, who came through the door with Carlotta (who was hardly unknown in the Arsenal) announced a round of drinks for everybody, an offer so uncharacteristic we all jumped on it before it evaporated.

If there was anywhere to feel centered in Cartagena, it was not at the villa and certainly not at the Bolivar, though both locales had a comforting decrepitude. And the Caribe, full of mass-produced "luxury" furnishings, gilded toilet fixtures and color television, was simply a bad version of home. The Arsenal, on the other hand, existed in the eternal present of Youth, connected via disco tapes and dance moves and magazine fashions to a network of sympathetic interiors and people. In another year or so, MTV would transform the last of local peculiarities into Esperanto.

After midnight Nicky changed into Nina, a raven-haired Indian temptress. Juan, still mustached, became Juanita, "the total blonde." A few deft strokes of the mascara wand, a slash of ruby lipstick, change of tank tops and a couple wigs, presto change-o. The den mother of these two queens was a buxom lad named Kiki who manned the bar while they waited tables.

We had met their sisters in Mexico City and Barcelona and

Rome and Paris and Miami, especially Miami. Muscular, tough, and feminine. The Arsenal boys were called upon to be many things in the course of an evening. It was never sure what sort of crowd would appear. Sometimes the bar was empty and they closed at one A.M. or midnight. Sometimes the drug heiresses and trainee pimps from Paco's took over, an unsavory pack of loud-mouths, as Nicky told us, stingy with tips, and all you heard was *maricona, bufo, concha, and puto,* as if the glittering scum from Paco's never took it up the *culo* themselves. Most often, it was gay. Gay and festive under the orange lights and demon masks and crepe paper streamers, though Nicky and Juan were anxiously certain that much gayer bars could be found in Nueva York and Miami, that the Arsenal was necessarily inferior to its *norte-americano* counterparts. It was useless to tell them that the Arsenal had, for us, a raw charm we could not find in our native cities, a hopeful hopelessness unlike the gelid, cynical opportunism rampant in any gay bar north of Havana.

It was useless to tell them that because they already knew it. And they preferred the heartless, profitable North to the slave conditions of the working class down there. Who could blame them? Us? In our cocoons of low-burning adventurism? More queens were pouring in. Tonight it would be gay. Many femmes from Santa Maria arrived, in skin-tight chinos and blouses knotted at the navel. Alex stood at the bar, basking in his own largesse. It was easy to see the disfavor Luis Vasquez enjoyed among the gay boys, who avoided his glances and only grudgingly filled his drink orders.

Nicky introduced some hustlers from Manga Island, some-one called Big Tony and his friends Clarence and Louis (Clar-ence and Louis "liked to make a sandwich," Nicky assured me) and for a moment I thought Paul was going to relax for a change and buy himself some entertainment, but instead he went to where Ray and Irma were settling in, opposite Carlotta and Valentina, who had slipped into a sort of mother-and-daughter configuration. The disco beat crept up in volume while Ray and Paul continued a desultory argument they'd started some hours before. Michael sat trapped between me and Alex on a bar stool. A fan in a rotating wire cage blew warm air into our faces. People were quite openly snorting coke at the various tables.

Behind the bar, Kiki was becoming fascinated with Michael Simard. He was talking to him in broken English and topping off his drinks for free. Nicky pointed out the gigantic lump in Tony's chinos, guesstimating its true dimensions by means of his own left forearm and fisted hand. It was a country where such things came large, Nicky said. Paul returned from the table. He put his arm across Michael's shoulders.

"Well, my friend."

Queens swirled around the cramped room, striking poses for imaginary millionaires and paparazzi. Alex came over and stared into my face.

"I have a proposition," he said.

This took me by surprise.

"Maybe Paul has told you, I am also a painter."

Paul had, in fact, mentioned Alex's artistic ambitions: "He makes these big faux-Fauve paintings, you know, the 'wild style' everybody creams over these days, only his are big realistic nudes of Carlotta, with her withered old tits."

". . . so, if you could help me get a gallery in New York," Alex was saying, "I'd be willing to give you a percentage of sales . . ."

". . . ?"

"I realize you don't like me," Alex added.

"Now Alex, what gives you that idea?"

"Well, you told me so straight out the first night you got here."

"I did? But look, Alex, I was drunk, and besides, I didn't even know you then. Now I can appreciate you a little better."

"I wish you would think about my idea."

"Oh, naturally."

"I'm very serious, you should give it some thought."

"Okay, I will. In the meantime, would you think about something?"

"What's that?"

Never kid a kidder, I thought. "Well, given there's a homicidal maniac loose in the neighborhood, I wonder if you'd consider putting us all in a hotel with better security."

"Ha—don't tell me you're afraid of the Vampire?"

"Of course I am: he kills foreigners—I'm a foreigner."

"Yes, but you're not a tourist. You have a work visa."

"Somehow I doubt if that's a meaningful distinction."

"Now, can I ask you a question? For the sake of curiosity? Why are you so certain this person is a man. Why couldn't it be a woman?"

Since Alex brought it up, I glanced significantly at his mother and Valentina across the room.

"Or two women. But let's be serious," I said. "Why can't you put us in the Caribe?"

Alex frowned, then brightened. "Because of Carnaval," he said, triumphantly. "All the hotels are booked for Carnaval."

"You just said an hour ago that they were losing reservations because of the murders," I said.

"Oh, but the Caribe is full, all the same. We were trying to get a room for a cousin of mine passing through."

It was time for Paul to put his oar in.

"I'm sure Michael would feel safer at the Caribe," he said. "Wouldn't you?"

The question caught Michael off-guard. He scrunched his mouth up to show he was thinking about it.

"They don't even know," Paul continued, excited, "exactly where or how the Vampire overcame his victims, but it wasn't far from the Plaza de Bolivar, this is sure. And where did he dismember them? He *boiled* some of their internal organs . . ."

9
Night

*T*he tapping noises woke me, the sound of a pick chipping at metal. I opened my eyes and tried to focus the vague rhomboid shadows on the ceiling, finally groping for my glasses. The shadows were like strangely tilted prison cells. Everything was deadly still except the chipping, which seemed to be happening in the street below the window.

The dark shapes of the room's furniture gradually stood out from the walls. I knew exactly where I was in space and time, yet my body felt all at war with itself, its various parts taunting and mocking the ensemble, so to speak, with little twitches and spasms and pinpoints of pain. These miniature pains reminded me of the cockroach dragging its shattered belly across the ground, which of course recalled the odd worm of flesh above Valentina's mouth, Jaybill's pile of artificial arms and legs, Michael's dark lips, the grille of the restaurant ashtray, and Irma's mouth, all mixed up and tossed together, and I thought of my own scarred cheek and my face lying there in the darkness.

I imagined that someone below was chiseling the wrought iron bars off a basement window, and with some audacity, too, since it had to be three or four in the morning and every stroke of the instrument echoed down the cobbled avenue. As I sat up in bed, another sound commenced in the hallway, a squeaking noise, like a rubber wheel rubbing against linoleum, accompanied by a hoarse intermittent whisper. Fear began spreading up my legs, climbing my lower back, suddenly my organism was unified in a soft ball of fear. I expected at any moment the telltale creak of the twisting doorknob, the rattle of a passkey slipped into the lock.

The pencil line of light beneath the door was obliterated by a large object. The object wavered, the light slithered on either side of its moving shadow, and then the line returned to normal. I waited, holding my breath, thinking of the sinister brothers who ran the hotel, three of them, all in their twenties, built like soccer players, given to darting glances and furtive looks, as if the hotel business were a front for some darker, clandestine activity. Could one of them be the Cartagena Vampire? Or, better still, all of them?

The chipping outside suddenly ceased: now everything was frozen in a kind of electric silence. I forced shallow, inaudible breaths, as if someone outside the door had his ears pricked for any evidence of movement. Although I was terrified, I was also quite drowsy. I closed my eyes and lay back and started to drift off, when the whispering resumed, full of gluey-sounding breath, and this time I crept out of the bed, my weight causing the floor to creak, and crawled, with interminable caution, over to the door. I saw myself crawling and thought of the cockroach again, venturing out from under the hedge with its elaborate but useless defenses at high pitch. Finally I peered into the hall through the keyhole.

Now the rustling sound of rain commenced outside, drowning whatever faint ambient squeaks and creaks might have issued from my own little movements or those of anyone in the hall. The circle of lighted corridor visible through the keyhole included the lower half of Michael's room door, the molding on either side of the door frame, and a small quadrant of the linoleum floor, a completely static composition that was also empty. Had someone been there? Did I imagine it? And what if they had simply moved to the small balcony overlooking the cathedral? There could, of course, be guests of the hotel drunkenly prowling the corridors, even this dead end, but the whole place had closed up so long ago that anyone doing that would have roused the night clerk.

I was wondering how long I could kneel in that position, probably wigged into paranoia by the epic quantities of speed and coke I'd been taking without even giving it a thought, when a figure entered the frame, a pair of legs, in black slacks, stood directly in front of Michael's door, wearing soft black Chinese slippers, paced back and forth a bit, the slippers getting wet from the glassy skin of water on the lino, tapped at the door, paced, tapped again, louder, over the seething rattle of the rain, until it was really a loud knock. A ruminant, angry voice from inside, a call, a cry, something muffled, then the door opened onto a black space, a ghostly view of Michael's bare legs in the blackness, the lower half of the other body entering the room, the door closing, and then, almost immediately, audible through the downpour, the chipping sounds resumed down in the street, followed by a horrendous thud from inside Michael's room, like a heavy object falling from a great height.

And then everything fell silent, only the rain continued lashing the walls and pattering crazily against the windows. I remained kneeling and staring through the keyhole, quite stupidly I thought, unable to compose the slightest meaning for what I had just observed, though the meaning was obvious enough, it was either Maria or Irma sleeping with him, though how whoever it was had managed to get upstairs, with the front gate locked after midnight—unless of course she'd bribed the night clerk, or made some such arrangement . . . But I had hardly any time to think about it before another set of legs came squeaking along the hall, which was turning glassy from the water pouring in at either end . . . Ecru trousers, with creases, gray suede shoes, a bit of magenta shirt . . .

The new arrival loitered outside the door, with his ear no doubt pressed to the wood, his clothing beginning to merge with the cream-colored door frame and pale walls. The colors wavered and seemed to float free of the objects in physical space. Eyestrain reduced the visual field to a broad smudge. And then, quite suddenly, the person outside dropped to a crouch more or less identical with my own, and stared into Michael's keyhole—it was Ray. This surprised me: he had manifested almost total indifference to Michael until now. Moreover, it was virtually impossible, at that hour, to move in and out of the villa and the hotel unobserved, since both places were policed by their staffs. So what was this strange nocturnal caravan up to?

Anyway, what could he possibly see? The room had been pitch dark when the door opened. Maybe they'd put a light on. Michael undoubtedly liked to watch himself making love. But that banging noise, what was that all about? It took me some minutes of further staring to realize that Ray's hand was inside the front of his pants, that his arm was moving up and down. I, too, aroused by imagining Ray's erection, had taken my own naked organ in hand and was pumping it in a desultory sort of excitement.

10
Empty Days

*T*he week before Carnaval passed more or less uneventfully, except for an accident with Luis Vasquez's Buick. Luis had taken Valentina, Irma, Michael, and Hannah up into the hills to meet Jaybill Hanratty, whose house Paul had decided to use: it would be the "jungle hideaway" of Alex's heart-of-darkness character, where he and Irma sometimes carried on their affair. According to Irma, Luis had helped himself to plenty of Simone's whiskey and on the way back down had decided to play chicken with a truck full of migrant workers. The migrant workers had not been amused and had finally tossed a melon at Luis's windshield, causing him to lose control of the wheel, spin off the narrow road, and hit a tree. Hannah's leg was broken and Michael had an ugly bruise on his forehead; everyone else walked away from it without a scratch.

I only had two or three scenes left, all of them scheduled for the end of the shoot. The fascination of watching other people act wore off in record time, and I was left with whole days of nothingness, walking all over the dusty town and its periphery.

The lower beaches of Boca Grande were a nightmare. Hundreds of deformed and insane people assaulted you one after another, sometimes in waves, begging, hawking Swatch watches and souvenir caps, carry bags, scarves, Pepsi-Cola. Big crazy women balancing trays of papaya on their heads, you couldn't hear yourself think with them screaming *papaya, papaya!* and god forbid you should buy anything, the whole beach would be up your nose ten seconds later shoving belts, kites, and suitcases full of sunglasses at you. The only way you could escape was to walk up the peninsula to where the water got warm and stinky from the Hilton sewage system and a Bidonville tucked between the seafood joints and cocktail lounges. It was like swimming in a toilet, but people generally left you alone.

You could rent a tent or a canvas parasol from a kid named Jimmy who ran the Caribe concession. He was a small thirteen-year-old who scampered around the beach in a white bikini bottom and a sailor's hat, patrolling his tents and lounge chairs, fetching beers and Cokes for the guests. A child, but something about his body, the way he planted himself on the sand, giving you a generous overall view . . . his eyes roamed over people with unnerving frankness.

I could find Carlotta there any day, languishing in her sheik's tent, swabbing her firm old dugs with coconut oil, though after three or four encounters we had nothing left to say to each other and kept politely to our own turf. At that point I needed the solitude of the beach, the steady cadence of small crashing waves and faraway Spanish voices, a little vacation from Paul and his manias . . . Quite often my tent had a prime view of her tent, and I watched her pretend to teach Jimmy German verbs, all the while patting his buttocks, squeezing his arms, massaging his toes . . . her fruity old voice warbling away as if her constant chattering would distract him from what she was doing.

Carlotta's obvious desire for this youth's body was chilling. And it brought him into focus as a possible source of obscene pleasure. Soon we were competing for Jimmy's attentions, in our respective tents, my English lessons nudging out her German lessons. We staked out our beach territory earlier every day.

Whatever her life had been, I thought, it was too late to change anything, and in a few years it would be over. The indecency or amorality or whatever it was that Alex wafted about himself came from her, but now she had nothing much to gain from her regal indifference to other people, her moral frigidity . . . And her advanced age was turning her into something generic, a senior citizen, with a hoard of tiresome stories and venal memories.

You looked at Carlotta and thought that the only things she had learned in her many decades had to do with managing money and flesh: what kinds of foods to eat, how long you should sunbathe, how many hours of sleep she needed. She put every-thing into holding off death. All her concentration, all her time, all her consciousness. She could lie there in her ridiculous yellow bikini, or play canasta with the retired Nazis she picked up in the restaurant cocktail lounges, or price goodies in the emerald shops, and every action was nothing except the refusal of death, it had nothing "in itself." Like Marilyn Monroe slapping away those diamond bracelets in *Gentlemen Prefer Blondes*. It gave her every move a grotesque, forced quality: when Carlotta did something, it was not so much because she wanted to, but because it proved she wasn't about to die. If she grabbed Jimmy's foot or rubbed his little behind, for all her decrepit sensuality, it only meant she'd drag him into the grave with her before she'd go by herself.

The Vampire of Cartagena stayed quiet in the week before Carnaval, probably content to hear himself discussed everywhere in breathless voices full of fascinated horror. Everyone had his own theory. If you wandered the streets alone at night, which I rather stupidly did, you encountered plenty of jumpy people. However, the initial tourist exodus did not continue, and festival chaos gradually claimed the city.

Gusty weather promised headaches and canceled shooting days. The Bolivar doubled its occupancy, filling with strangers, solid-looking citizens from North America, revelers from Barranquilla, Riohacha, Maracaibo. Too much energy for that sleepy town, but the town was also on a jag. Even the languid Bolivar staff snapped into something like friendly efficiency.

The tourists tore through the old city in cabs and horse-drawn carriages, swarmed through the market arcade around the cathedral. This new energy reminded me that nothing remains fixed. The city was shrinking. Its attractions were being used up in a frenzy and turning a dull gray.

A storm brewed in the mountains. I felt it in the air when I opened my eyes, one day when I'd promised Irma and Ray to go to the beach. My nerves jumped along odd patches of my body. I jammed my face into the pillow, determined to outlast the nausea and blackness that overcame me when I took pills for a while and then stopped. Valium would have smoothed the transition, but nobody had any. Calmatives were alien to this city of drug merchants.

For several days I had been aware that the thing growing inside my mouth "didn't feel right," and caught myself fingering it compulsively. It now felt more like a foreign object than any sort of tooth, however deformed, and that morning I dug at it more ferociously than usual, managing to pull the whole thing out of my gum. What I brought out between my fingers was something I could not identify. On one side it resembled a chunk of vitreous rock, smooth and white and shiny, while the other side had all kinds of pores and little bubbles, rather like a grayish lump of sea coral . . . Whatever it was, I did not think it was a product of the human body. How it had become lodged in mine for such a long period was something I didn't especially want to think about. And the object itself . . . frightened me. I opened the bed table drawer and threw it in.

Michael was eating breakfast on the terrace. I spotted him from across the busy dining room. I didn't see Hannah until I was outside. I sat down anyway—it would've been awkward not to. Hannah smiled the way she always smiled, like a snake examining an edible rodent. She wore big amber sunglasses and smoked an unfiltered cigarette with angry concentration. I thought she had a black eye. Her crutches were stacked conspicuously against the table.

She was a very unpleasant person from whom we were all obliged to collect our weekly salary, a process she made as tedious and humiliating as she possibly could. Like many line producers, Hannah acted as though she were paying out her own money to people who were not really worth it.

"You could have saved yourself and stayed in bed," she said. "We won't shoot today."

Her voice blamed me for the weather. I didn't know what to say, my hands shook—I hid them under the table. Michael looked moody. He hadn't shaved. His hands kept going up to his forehead to hide the bruise there, a habit that plainly annoyed him when he caught himself at it.

"I'm not really spending that much time on the set these days," I said. "That's not why I'm up. I generally get up early."

"I see," said Hannah, feigning a reproached air. "Not interested in the film?"

They were the only people eating outside. The eggs on Michael's plate looked abnormal. Like dwarf eggs. Michael spread guava jelly on a toast slice and offered it. I shook my head.

"Oh, I'm interested," I countered, nodding, aware that Hannah despised me and wanted some verbal faux pas she could drag to Alex between her teeth. "How's that *leg*, Hannah?"

The stony face went stonier. Michael covered his mouth with his napkin.

"You can imagine, can't you? I'm supposed to send telexes, I have to hobble down to the bank like this. They're probably closing early, too, for the holiday. Stinking town."

She then scraped back her chair and hoisted herself upright. She tucked one crutch into her armpit and swung herself away from the table, positioned the other crutch, and stumped off into the dining room, the plaster-wrapped leg cleaving the air in front of her. We heard the rubber crutch tips thumping and squeaking across the linoleum, distinct amid the din of voices.

"I hope she breaks the other one," I said.

"You dieting?"

"This heat spoils my appetite." A few hours of bad sleep and the absence of a morning amphetamine were enough to twist the day into hopelessness. Down in the plaza, the daily throng of shoeshine boys and *tinto* sellers had swollen with the holiday influx. A greenish infusion colored the clouds. Wet wind churned along the pavements.

"It's not even hot," Michael said. He was looking at my face with unusual interest.

"I can never eat in the morning. Why don't you come swimming with us."

"Who's us?"

"Me and Irma and Ray. Maybe Maria."

"Maria's gone out of town."

"Oh, yeah."

"Gone down to Cali for the Carnaval."

"Huh. She didn't even mention to me she was going."

"She just went on a sudden impulse. I took her out to the airport in a taxi."

"How odd."

"Not really," Michael shrugged.

"Are you and Maria, like, a thing?"

Michael poured himself another cup of coffee.

"Not really," he repeated.

"So come swimming with us, you gorgeous hunk."

"Give me a break."

"Well, you *are*."

"Yeah, sure."

"Michael Simard, don't sit there and pretend you don't know you're practically the hottest thing anybody's ever seen."

"Now you're being ridiculous."

I continued to torment him, knowing it would get me nowhere and possibly alienate him. The fat purple bruise above his left eye made him look even sexier. There was some relief, at least, in speaking this pent-up and constant attraction, even as a joke, for it seemed to make everything less "real."

"Come on, come with us. You can swim here in your *jock strap*, you know we'd all crawl over broken glass to see that."

"Look at this sky, it's gonna pour!"

"So? We can hang out in the beach restaurant."

Michael yawned expansively.

"Think I'll skip it," he said.

I smoked a few of his cigarettes and watched the listless circus of unemployment in the plaza. Men wearing sandwich boards covered with lottery tickets paraded back and forth through the park. In front of the Palace of the Inquisition, a cement mixer had been mounted on a wheeled wooden platform, amid a lot of other metal and equipment.

"Anyway," I said, casting about for something to say. "How are you doing? Is this working out like you expected?"

Michael thought about that. "I didn't really have any expectation," he said. "I guess everything's okay. I'll tell you, though, I've been getting really strange sensations in my stomach. You know? Kind of low down, right above the groin. Little stabbing sort of pains, nothing major, but a real noticeable discomfort. I can't tell if it's the food, or maybe I've been drinking too much. See, I've never had any problem there until now. But it feels strange."

"Kind of a kidney pain, or what?"

"Your kidneys are here, right? So it's not kidneys I don't think. It's more right in the middle, here."

I knew that Michael could go on for an hour about it, so I blew out a conclusive-sounding sigh and told him he ought to see a doctor. There was another patch of silence while the wind got stronger through the trees.

"Doesn't it bother you," I asked after a while, "that they lock the gate out front at midnight?"

An odd look came over his face.

"Well," he said carefully, "sure. Sure it does." He scratched his head. Then nervously lit a cigarette. "In case of a fire, we'd all be trapped like rats."

"And the mosquitoes in this place," I said. "I'm just bitten to pieces every morning."

"You can buy those coils for mosquitoes."

"I really think Alex should put us into the Caribe. You and me, at least. We're actors, we ought to be treated—you know, with some deference."

Michael listened, nodding, chewed his lip, puffed on his cigarette.

"I only acted this one time," he said. He ruminated for a bit. "See, the thing is," he finally said, rubbing the fine black stubble on his chin, "I actually don't want to move to the Caribe. You know, Boca Grande, it's like one big shopping mall in some crummy suburb—"

"Even so," I said. "There's air conditioning, a pool, you don't have to wake up the desk every time you go in or out—"

Just then, Alex stuck his head out, looking for company, though obviously not ours, and hesitantly came to the table; instead of sitting down, he leaned against the railing. He was holding a folded newspaper that he tapped against his pant leg.

"You're missing the elections in America next week," he said.

"What a tragedy," I said.

Michael shook his head.

"If you like," Alex told me, "I have a book of transparencies I can show you some time before we leave Cartagena. Maybe you'll join me and Carlotta for dinner at the Caribe some evening soon. In fact, you could take the transparencies back to New York with you."

"Yes, well. Okay."

Alex stood there for another minute, grinning rather stupidly. We were all at a loss for words. Then he started back into the hotel, pausing to squeeze Michael's shoulder "encouragingly"—a little producer's squeeze, evidently.

At that moment I realized how much I wanted the film to be over with, that I could not endure much more daily contact with anyone there. Back in the room I lit a joint. I opened the shutters and watched clouds gather over the back streets. Thunder rolled up in the hills, firecrackers spluttered in the alleys around the cathedral. The grass made the room wobble. I lay on my back and stared at the churning fan and thought of monkeys in cages picking fleas off each other.

The cameraman and the cameraman's assistant were eating sandwiches in front of a shop along the arcade, a place with three scrawny tables. I thought it would be prudent to eat even though I had no appetite, so I made my way down and out to where they sat. They told me what kinds of things the place had. There was a milkshake made of pulverized mango and pita bread sandwiches with chunks of pork slathered in salsa. The two men pointedly locked me out of conversation by speaking German. As I chewed, I imagined getting worms from the pork and had to put the sandwich down.

The sky had gone black by the time I got to the villa. A parade of little soldiers was trooping at the distant end of the street. I ran my hand along the ancient wooden door like a blind person reading Braille. I felt a cold, heavy object in my hand: a hand-shaped brass door knocker, relic of a Spanish galleon. Hector Luis, bleary-eyed, swung open the door panel cut in the massive portal.

Thleeping, he declared, leading the way through the foyer. He waved his arms. *Everybody thleeping.* The green parrot, liberated from his perch, nestled in the crook of Hector's neck and the shoulder of his red jacket.

Wind swayed the vegetation. Ivy fluttered on espaliers against the courtyard walls. Hector babbled to himself, dragging the two pagoda-shaped monkey cages into the shelter of the foyer, the metal bases scraping on stone tiles. The monkeys clung to the bars, little fear-frozen faces staring out accusingly. I started across the patio. Lightning strobed overhead. I turned around. Hector crossed himself, then fled to the kitchen, the parrot clinging to his sleeve.

I waited in the spectral dining room for the rain. The house, open to the winds, looked gray and moldy, a vast decaying sponge. When the rain started lashing the garden, pulses of lightning strobed through the clouds. I thought about flooding in low areas, fishing parties struck by lightning. It was suddenly quite cool in the normally too-warm house, and Paul appeared like a fogbound spirit in a Bergman movie: "Look at this weather in this weary world! Want some coffee?"

The rain clattered on the barrel tiles sloped along the second-floor roof. Dead fronds were snapping off the palms and crashing into the flower beds. Paul went out to the kitchen. I was annoyed to think his company wouldn't relieve the unpleasantness in my own brain. I had fastened on the thought that I wanted to be somewhere else, and now it would take over my mind.

"Alex says the city will be full of gangsters and beauty queens," Paul said. He sipped coffee at the oak railing, wiggling his fingers in a stream that gushed from a roof gutter. "I thought we might film at the jungle house, what do you think? You know that during Carnaval the drug dealers show up from all over Colombia and shoot each other in the streets? Everything sounds like fire-crackers."

"You look sort of overworked."

Paul held his face under the drainpipe flow, swabbing water across his neck, into his hair.

"Think so? I'm losing my kindly-SS-man look. Soon I'll have to play Mengele. Depraved, evil . . . well, it's a stretch, but I've given it a lot of study. I can't believe the Americans will elect this cowboy actor again."

"Sure."

"But *why?*"

"Because we're like ants in an anthill, how should I know? You're the one that's from Germany. Anyway, Alex is completely on my case about his paintings now."

"How stupid. Get him to give you a lot of money and tell him you'll do all these things for him. What about Michael?"

"Well, I don't think you're going to get anywhere with that one."

"No, I don't either. *She's* curious about Jaybill, though." Paul yawned. He repeated his ablutions under the storm drain. "Irma would fuck a horse out of curiosity, I think."

"Maybe so, Paul, but maybe not *your* curiosity. What do you really want?"

Paul looked at me over his coffee cup and shrugged.

"When I look in the mirror here," he said, "I see that I'm disappearing. Losing little pieces of myself. One day it's my sense of humor. The next day my libido. then there's my intelligence, less and less of it. My memory, kaput . . . And I'm losing my feelings, too. I used to feel everything intensely. An opera would move me to tears. Now it all looks stupid."

"I felt so buoyant when I got here," I said.

"Right now? Or you mean down here?"

"Well, the whole situation—I mean, don't take this the wrong way, but I'm not really an actor anymore, and I'm starting to feel . . . I don't know, Paul, I'm thirty-four, I have to begin thinking about how I want things to be."

Paul made an annoyed face. He moved to the sideboard and flicked a light switch behind a bowl of painted plaster fruit.

"Power's off. This is only an interlude. You can think about things down here. In New York right now there's ten inches of snow."

"I mean, I haven't worked, I haven't studied, I just don't know what is going to happen to me."

"This is everyone's theme lately," Paul said. "All day I am considering what I'll do if Ray leaves me and I'm all alone again."

He flicked the useless light switch a few times and paced over to the railing, struck a thoughtful pose, and folded his arms. I joined him at the balustrade, but faced the garden, vaguely aware that my movements were all wrong for the moment he was trying to have with me.

"If Ray leaves you you can move to New York. Anyway, he's not going to. You love each other. Where is he, anyway?"

"Oh, he said to say since it's raining he's going to sleep all day. You think we'll stay together?" Paul sounded doubtful. His face strained forward. Without his glasses on he looked haggard and vulnerable.

"That's what I assume," I said.

"This is such a sleepy house when it rains. Just think if we both had money, how we could live. Life would be a dream, a virtual dream. You know, I have great hopes that we can do more projects together. But that's probably not enough for you to go on. Money, money is always the killer. I have to go on acting, and you, I suppose, must write things, yes? Yesterday," Paul said, flicking his glasses from his shirt pocket and arranging them on his face, "I saw a man with elephantiasis, of the *foot*, can you believe it? It was all bloody and he had it up on a bench in the esplanade. Some of these people give themselves diseases just to have a gimmick. Or the mothers swallow things when they're pregnant, to make the babies deformed."

We were moving, a few feet at a time, down the gallery of the dining room, with the rain drama crashing down in the patio. I felt hungry, suddenly. I explored my pockets and pulled out a twist of paper. I thought, "what the hell," and swallowed the two Obitrols in front of Paul.

"What are those like?"

"Very smooth. Irma gets them from her pharmacist friend in Berlin. What do you think about the film?"

"So far? I think I'm very happy so far. What would make me happiest, though—well, wait a minute."

Paul went to the end of the gallery, into the sitting room near the steps to the pool, and came back with a stack of loose papers, among them the clear plastic folder where he kept each day's shooting pages. Inside it were photos that he'd showed me early on, images he kept referring to: there was a snapshot he'd obtained from a Cologne artist showing two strapping blond youths and a tame deer in a shadow-dappled northern forest. One boy buggered the deer, while the other boy buggered him. The special thing was the dreamy look of animal innocence on all three faces. A police blotter photo of a male corpse with its head blown off—parts of the jaw, a fragment of one ear, and other bits made the thing recognizably human remained. The missing area had come off so cleanly it might have been sheared off with a scalpel. The killers had arranged the body in a wing chair, a shotgun propped between its legs.

Finally, there was the torture photo made famous by George Bataille, of a man killed in the Boxer Rebellion, his arms and legs and both breasts hacked away, hoisted on a wooden stake, his viscera dripping between flayed ribs. The face pointed to heaven with a look of ecstasy. Paul laid it on the table:

"Him, with her, but with Michael behind him, holding him—so that Michael would be his arms and his legs, if you see what I mean . . ."

"Mmm, yes, but you know he won't. It isn't something he would normally want to do, and what can you offer him that would motivate him? You know, Paul, I have a feeling that sexually, Michael is the most conventional person working on this movie."

"Perhaps that's so. Perhaps you're right. There's no point in asking him to do anything sexual, really."

"Give me a cigarette. Thanks. What is it that has you so worried with Ray. Why do you fight."

"Well, these . . . separations, it's like he has a whole other life in Sydney where he's not seeing me for long periods of time."

"And he's fucking other people . . . ?"

"And he's fucking other people, though I don't especially care about that."

"These days you probably should, you know."

"You can't control everything in a relationship. I just worry, that's all."

"You worry he'll find someone else he wants to be with."

"It's possible. And I've really come to rely on Ray. Over the years. I don't know that I could just start over again."

"You know you're very lucky to have someone."

"Yes, and you should have someone, too, I really don't know why you don't, we really ought to *find* someone for you—"

"The trouble is, I'm only interested in people who look like Michael."

"That *is* a problem, unless you have a great deal of money."

A haze of blackness and fear was sifting down, along with the rain. If Paul was abandoning his fixations, taking a "mature" attitude in order to worry about Ray and him, this meant that the distance between us was widening again, and I would soon be left alone, once the film was in the can and we had all flown off to our respective cities. But what could I offer him, to make him more interested in me? Anyway, why did I *want* him interested in me? I suppose I had fantasized that this movie would lead to another one, maybe one that I could write . . . For a minute or two I hoped that he would leave Ray, or Ray leave him, so that Paul could become neurotically dependent on his friends. Then we would have the chance to really do things together, really make things happen: because, I thought, the "old" Paul would've been clever enough to get the two actors together sexually with Jaybill Hanratty, would have found the will to exploit Michael Simard in all sorts of ways.

But of course it was better if none of that came to pass. Realistically, it was stupid to pursue these fantasies when a stable, caring, monogamous relationship was boringly ready at hand— for him, at any rate. That there was someone loose in Cartagena enticing strangers into some dark place, strangling them with a bit of rope, and cutting their corpses into soft chunks was argument enough for the joys of normality and staying in at night.

11

Carnaval

I'm afraid an entire series of things is jumbled up in my recollections. This is not, after all, the story of what happened to me, but in telling what happened to Paul, I am obliged to drag in all sorts of peripheral characters and marginal incidents that only have a sort of half-life in his story. I confess that since my meeting with Robert Scheib I've written down several versions of all this. It is always at this point that the narrative shatters and the resulting shards turn opaque . . . Events crowd in on each other, and I no longer can say with any certainty what order they happened in . . .

It may have been an overdose of Obitrol, or too many rum drinks, or simply the phantasmagoria of the fiesta, the streets full of goblins and small explosives going off, that got me thinking about the thing I'd pulled out of my mouth and the queer way that Maria had taken off for Cali without telling anyone and the odd hours I heard Michael coming and going—but as soon as Paul seemed to abandon his designs on Michael, relegating him to a "secondary" interest, the boy took on a different sort of fascination.

I am talking about extremely subterranean currents, the sly language of postures, glances, movements of the hands, a way of abbreviating one's attention, traveling from Paul to Michael and mirrored in my own cooling attitude toward him . . . which isn't to say that either one of us became unfriendly, quite the contrary, we were now positively unctuous toward Michael, unctuous and at the same time perfunctory, unmistakably indifferent. And this feeling spread, rippled out among the others . . .

On the set, too, little things . . . Additional dialogues between Alex and Irma, another love scene . . . while one of Michael's interviews with the prefect of police, played by Luis Vasquez, was lopped out of the script . . . Alex, sensing a turn of the psychic screw, behaved as if some high-octane gas had been pumped into him. Between shots, we heard him describing his future plans, his big projects . . . more film producing, definitely, but he had other irons in the fire, he told the crew, for instance, another novel he was writing . . . also a show of his art work coming up in New York—still in the discussion stage, but virtually certain . . . As Alex waxed, Michael wilted. Within a day or so, the handsome youth betrayed little signs of irritation and confusion . . . I know that this happened during the period of Maria's absence, because that, too, became a slightly submerged motif of set talk. Maria's Cali boyfriend had called, asking for her, and claimed complete ignorance of her plans to go down there for Carnaval. And this led to swift, sadistic panic on the part of Alex, who wanted to notify the police that she was missing, implying that Michael might know something about it . . .

"The facts are that boy is strange," Alex insisted one morning, while we were shooting a scene at the Presidential Palace of him and Irma arguing about her part-time work as a chanteuse.

"No stranger than you," said Paul good-humoredly. "You think he's done away with her?"

"He must know where she is," Alex pressed. "I mean he's fucking her, isn't he." I gathered that Alex had had some ambitions in that area himself.

"You mean even now," Paul joked, "after he's killed her? That's sick!"

Carlotta had come along in the Cadillac. She was standing behind Alex nodding her agreement. Carlotta had on silver lamé hot pants and a blouse of green silk. As she gaped at the goings-on, she chewed an enormous sugared donut. Michael was "unhealthy," she chimed in, confectioner's sugar coating her mouth like the residue of some arcane sex act, apparently basing this conclusion on Michael's frequent allergy attacks.

"So," Paul asked me later, "what do you think? Think Michael Simard is the Cartagena Vampire?"

"He can suck me until I'm undead any time," I said. "But where do you suppose she's gone?"

Paul made a sarcastic mouth and shook his head. "She'll be back," he promised.

At the villa, lounging around the pool, Irma remarked that she thought Maria had gone somewhere "with a third boyfriend, from Bogotá." Valentina, in Olympic form, breaststroking back and forth in the water, added her observation that Michael was now technically available. This was a broad nudge to Irma. Valentina had been encouraging her for some time to "find out how he fucks."

"I somehow think he must be wonderful," Valentina sighed.

"For that lucky girl who wants to see her own head on a stick," Ray quipped. He was reading a paperback about mass murderers. Since the first bodies were discovered in the canal, Ray had scoured the town for cheap books on serial killers, and now posed as an authority on the subject. "*I'd* ask him about his childhood," he went on. "Especially his relationship with his father. There's usually something funny there. Depending on your sense of humor."

The jokes about Michael were never shared with him, and of course this naughty buzz caused him further alienation from the rest of us. He didn't realize why we giggled and traded loaded glances when he showed up, only that we did, and it unnerved him. A new side of Michael emerged. Where before he had been laconic, aloof, and democratically friendly without sharing much of his inner self, Michael now started clowning around, assuming an overly familiar, back-slapping sort of camaraderie. He began giving us his "feelings" in bursts of obsequious sincerity. He had seemed precociously sophisticated, now he was becoming oafish. He yearned, it seemed, for the uncomplicated, carnal-minded attention we had all given him in the past.

At the jungle house, shooting a scene with Irma, Michael volunteered to play it with his shirt off, stripping down to the skin. He bared his tanned, well-pumped musculature in an exhibitionistic trance.

"Nice bod, right?" he announced, looking all around. He wiped his long hands on his pectorals, sliding them slowly down his torso, over the rippled abs. It was as if he had known all along that this was what we wanted from him, the almost tactile sight of his naked flesh. And he was willing to offer it to us, as a bargaining chip of last resort. Later, during a break, still bare-chested, he grabbed Irma around the waist and waltzed her frantically across the terrace, like a man in love. He was surrendering the prize of his sexuality: if we would just adore him again, maybe he'd fuck all of us. Paul and I looked at each other in bewildered amusement.

Carnaval Saturday happened to coincide with the American presidential election. As far as the Colombians were concerned, the selection of Miss Colombia at the Hilton was of far more pressing importance than the rulership of the noxious empire to the north. I went with Ray and Irma into Gesemani, the part of the old town outside the city walls, where the Miss Colombia floats were lined up along the esplanade.

The sky was a brilliant blue color, with square white clouds set in it at intervals like chessboard pieces, almost mathematically regular. There were hordes of people jammed into the streets, a ferocious din, and a wild feeling in the air. Irma strode along in her white shorts and pink halter top like a sultry Hollywood apparition; she had borrowed a black leather motorcycle cap from someone, and peered out from under the visor with a raptor's acuity. Ray, dressed in a sailor blouse, shorts, and sockless loafers, was beaming with contentment. His face had color, and his hearty, easy demeanor had returned for the first time in weeks.

Some of the queens were already enthroned on their decorated truck beds: Miss Cali, Miss Medellín, Miss Azufral Volcano. All covered in flowers, giant topiary teacups, shamrocks, and zodiac symbols, floral jungles with stuffed parrots and plaster monkeys, papier-mâché leopards, the queens in diaphanous, shiny gowns, in bathing suits with satin sashes, flanked by little costumed orchestras, tinny-sounding bands, and all the while children darted between the legs of the crowd, tossing balls of flour, smacking everyone with caking white powder, and chucking firecrackers under the floats.

"This is good," Irma decided.

The esplanade smelled of gunpowder and roasted peanuts. We walked down to the spraying fountains in front of the Centro de Convenciones and watched the crowd of transvestites and teenage hustlers thicken in front of the movie theater. They assembled on the steep pyramid steps like crows or sparrows on telephone wires, hovering above the pedestrian crowd. On the other side of the marina, revelers dressed as devils and gauchos joined the general stream of the assembling parade. A starburst fountain sprayed jets of water through the air and rainbows floated on the mist, dissolving and reforming, and meanwhile we talked about everything that had happened in Cartagena.

Ray seemed keen on dispelling the racist curmudgeon image he'd established, with me anyway, in the previous weeks. He had forgotten that I already knew another side of him. He talked about Foucault, about an E. M. Cioran book that he was reading.

"Really interesting on death," Ray said. "Death of the person and death of civilizations, too."

With a sort of artful humility, Ray managed to remind us of his long tenure as Rudolph's assistant, a job that had obviously demanded special sensitivities as well as an intellectual dimension. While he talked his hands did a fantastic dance in the air, moving great imaginary obstacles from his path, stacking ideas in invisible blocks, rolling his own thoughts through the air like a ribbon of pastry dough.

It was inevitable that we compared Paul's directing techniques with Rudolph's, and speculated about just what Paul hoped to draw out of people. Irma was too tactful to say in front of Ray what she thought about the movie, but I could tell it had disappointed her, she didn't like the work she was doing in it. As for me, the minor character I played seemed completely unnecessary to the story; I was there because Paul wanted me around. We complained, but without the savagery we would have used in Ray's absence.

"At least you get to play the piano," Irma told him.

Banners swirled around us, Santeria effigies swinging on long poles. Men in skeleton outfits strummed guitars while nuns and bandits moved their mouths around sticky mounds of cotton candy, twirled rosaries or pistols, danced, roller-skated; swarming through the crowd were dozens of beggars from an Ensor painting, beggars without noses, without feet, beggars sawed in half pushing themselves along on skateboards, beggars that sang, beggars that shoved their afflictions under your nose so you got a good whiff, beggars wagging their stumps in a provocative manner, and next to them souvenir vendors with the evil eye, coke peddlers flashing cellophane packets, trumpeters with missing teeth, whores rattling tambourines; a tidal wave of noise, bodies, faces, death masks, pickpockets, kids.

All at once it started moving, sweeping everything along with it. At first we strolled casually in the crowd, and then it caught us in its own rhythm, its march-step, until we were trapped in a dense insect wedge of humanity, behind an army truck with a canvas tarp that a soldier untied as the parade surged onto the coast road into Boca Grande, releasing thousands of blue and yellow balloons that floated up above the palm trees and drifted lazily toward the bay.

"This is insane!" we all kept shouting to each other over the roar of the crowd, laughing, smiling at complete strangers, cruising people in bizarre outfits, catching the startled and delighted looks of people surrendering themselves to a manic fantasy. On the varicolored floats the heavily painted beauty queens of Colombia waved their elbow-length gloves at the multitudes, at the bathers gawking from the broken sidewalk in front of the Capilla del Mar, at the boy soldiers posing against their jeeps beside the weedy, rubble-strewn vacant lots, at the polyester tourists behind the side gates of the Caribe. I felt an onrush of goodwill, even love, for Ray and Irma: that we were together in this strange place, having this absurd, brainless experience. And it continued, of course, right through the sentry gate at the Hilton, hundreds of people pouring into the lobby and through the ground floor of the luxury hotel, the beauty queens descending from their floats and migrating to the stage of a vast chandeliered ballroom, a stage where what looked like army generals and cardinals of the church and numerous other officials sat under a gigantic flag of the republic and its presidential seal.

As various announcements and introductions were made through a deafening sound system, we wandered back into the lobby and picked our way through the crowd to a big modernistic terrace built directly over the surf. This was where the committed drinkers had established a beachhead and were knocking back huge tropical drinks, and a sort of burial mound of food had been built up in the middle of the place. We found the bar behind an incredible crush of people and then went to the far edge of the terrace, right above the rocks. An announcement was being made, in Spanish, inside the Hilton, carrying out through the ballroom windows.

"Can't make out a fuckin' word," Ray said. He rattled the ice in his glass.

Irma assumed the keen-eared, frozen pose of several other people who were straining to make out the announcement. She frowned, perplexed, and turned to face the sea.

"Who is Miss Colombia?" she wanted to know. "It sounds like they are saying, but which one . . . ?"

Owing to some vagary of acoustics, the next part of the announcement reached the jigsaw cement terrace in sharp, clear tones, I couldn't catch or interpret every word, but a man inside was telling the crowd, ladies and gentlemen, Ronald Reagan has been reelected president of the United States.

12
Mala Hierba No Muere

*B*ut in fact . . . in fact, the whole business ended in an onrush of foolishness . . . more inanity, more petty rivalries, more circumspection . . . as things will, on a film. With nothing resolved, really . . . well, what was there to resolve? Paul seemed satisfied with what he was getting, not that he'd really managed to maneuver things—between Michael and Irma, Irma and Michael. And then, when I thought it might turn into something . . . well, there was always that strange bit of tooth or whatever it was in the bedside drawer, I took it out and stared at it, but you know something, I felt distinctly nervous about that little clump of matter: it reminded me of bad things in science fiction movies . . .

It seemed entirely possible that Jaybill Hanratty would turn up again, with "Simone," in some kind of configuration . . . And then Alex, with his book of transparencies, which he pressed on me two days before we left, at the end of a "business talk" where I got drunk and agreed to everything . . . There was, of course, a strange evening at the villa—Maria had returned, just when we'd begun to suspect that someone really had done away with her . . .

"Poor Hannah," Valentina sighed. "Poor, poor Hannah."

"What a curious sentiment, poor Hannah." Paul folded his hands above his plate, probed his teeth with his tongue.

"Poor Hannah my arse," Roy grumbled, slicing his chicken cutlet into little squares. "Poor us that poor Hannah's here."

The other plates had been cleared . . . There were mixed sentiments about the chicken. Maria declared it delicious. Michael had eaten his with great appetite. The thing that had been there between them . . . seemed to have evaporated during Maria's absence. She never said where she'd been . . . Irma puffed her cigarette . . . in the candlelight, the spark of a match, Paul lights a cigarette, the flame reflects in his glasses . . . Hector Luis moves between the chairs, pouring coffee and brandy. We've all just finished our dinners. Numerous porcelain birds, blue jays, finches, yellow canaries, perch on painted branches in a straight, close line running down the center of the table . . .

Irma and Michael pass a joint between them as I listen to Maria enumerate the contrasts between Carnaval in Cartagena and Carnaval in Cali—not that she's actually saying she's been in Cali all this time, but just as a general thing . . . Cali, she insists, is more truly festive, the parades more "authentic" . . .

"Authentic in what sense?" I ask.

"I think it's awful we don't *invite* Hannah," Valentina is telling Paul. It's hard to know if she's serious. Everyone at the table has developed a habit of undermining any earnest utterance with comic movements of the face . . . subtle displacements of the gaze . . . a manner that belies meaning, just a fraction or so, signaling depths of private irony. "A woman alone at the Bolivar," Valentina stridently continues, cheeks flushed with incipient hilarity. "And with *the leg broken*."

Valentina tries not to laugh when the others start, but the

effort's too much. Irma barely follows the conversation. She's in another world. No doubt she's playing her own favorite game, imagining what we all would've been in the Third Reich. I look at Paul across the candlelight. Paul looks at me. Together we look at Irma and Michael, their heads framed in a fuzzy halo of light against the darkness, as night noises from the patio create a sort of unfortunate Joseph Conrad feeling, and it seems to me that the two of them, in some ineffable manner, passing that joint, for example, fingertips brushing, her glancing into his eyes, him glancing into her eyes . . . with Maria determinedly focused on what Valentina and Ray are saying, Valentina and Ray and Paul, and Paul's telling Valentina, "She isn't *alone* at the Bolivar, she's got Vale to look after her . . . anyway she's a miserable person."

"She's from a very good family, Alex told me," Valentina counters, as if this would make any difference.

"Pacific people are more free," Maria says ethereally, resuming her speech on Carnaval. "In Cali, we have the big ocean, it's more cosmopolitan. Here everyone stares at you, if you're a European."

"Which you're not," Michael murmurs under his breath. She looks at him sharply.

"Sort of like rural Italy," says Paul.

"But here you had all the beauty queens," Ray says. "You wouldn't see Miss Santa Marta in Cali."

Paul stands up. He moves down the table and sits next to me. Irma stands up, picks up her coffee cup. Her hand drifts over Michael's shoulder.

"We have better things in Cali than Miss Santa Marta," Maria declares, ignoring Michael as he stands up and joins Irma at the balustrade. "Those beauty queens are all mistresses of army generals."

Paul looks at me. He touches my arm in the darkness. Irma and Michael are moving with their coffee out into the patio. Something is taking its course . . .

"You don't believe me?" Maria says.

"Of course we believe you," says Paul. "Alex says that after her coronation at the Hilton, the winner enters a special room. There, the president of the republic sodomizes her. Only then does she truly become Miss Colombia."

"Now it starts," says Valentina from her end of the table. She cradles a brandy snifter between her middle fingers.

"No," Ray's saying, "first she sucks off each member of the parliament. They dip their cocks in cocaine, and she has to get them all off while the national anthem plays."

"You guys," Maria says. "You wouldn't say that if Miss Colombia was a *man*."

"I'm sure she was a man, not too long ago," says Paul.

That night . . . the moon hung stupidly in the sky. I could see Irma and Michael dimly, crossing the patio, Irma throwing her cigarette into the stone fountain. The monkeys were scrabbling around in their cages. Darkness and silence were flowing together, darkness and silence . . . So they would: him and her, her and him . . . his mouth with her mouth . . . after all this time, despite all our efforts to bring them together—that is, to bring them together "for us" . . . and then, out by the pool . . . recumbent on a chaise, Valentina tosses ice cubes into the pool.

"It's not really obvious," she says, "that things are ruled by terror . . . when you go into the streets, sure you see soldiers and guns, and *quelque chose*—but you see poor people laughing, smiling . . . that too. Almost everyone does the cocaine, they dance, they make love. No one's starving."

"*Quelques choses?*" Paul screeches incredulously, dragging a plastic lawn chair from the storage shed at the end of the pool area. "You certainly do see *quelques choses*, Valentina. So glad you noticed."

Maria, pacing the pool edge with a tall gin and tonic held like a beacon, pauses for a long swallow and says, "If you look close,

Valentina, you'll see the resignation and fear behind all the laughter and dancing. If you ask anyone here about the government, they clam right up. Betancur's picture hangs in all the shops, right next to Christ. Why do you think they take coke all day and live in a dreamworld? Unless you're from an important family, the men have to serve in the military, nobody can leave the country without a lot of cash in the Banco de la Republica—and people disappear here, you know."

"And *quelques choses,*" Paul says.

Is she reacting to the idea that Michael and Irma . . . off in Irma's room . . . Valentina shakes her head sadly, conveying her disappointment at oppression everywhere.

"Yeah, Valentina," Ray quips. "Why d'ya think they sell cock for a dollar? Just naturally horny all the time?"

"I'm sure," Valentina smugly observes, "I wouldn't know about all that." She pesters the ice in her drink with a fingernail.

Ray leaps into the pool. He's wearing all his clothes. The clothes balloon out around him as he floats to the surface. His head splashes up and he spits an arc of chlorinated water in the direction of Paul, me, Valentina, Maria, all ranged along the tiles, everything ghostly and reddish in the wobbling glow of underwater lights. Around us the muted, variform darkness, climbing plants, potted ferns, a palm tree higher than the roof, everything evokes the primordial forest the neighborhood was carved from four centuries ago.

Ray propels himself to the metal ladder near the foot of Valentina's chaise. He sloshes out, dripping copiously, staggers to the steps that go down to the patio, retrieves his drink, tastes it, then starts shedding his sodden clothing.

Valentina stands up. She walks three paces and lies face down beside the water, plunging her arm in.

"Of course you're right," she says. "There's plenty of misery."

Maria presses on: "Have you seen the children sleeping under the benches in the Plaza de Bolivar? And the kids in the doorways? On this street? They crawl under the chicken wire at the schoolhouse and sleep in those demolished classrooms, curled up around their shoeshine boxes."

"See?" Paul chides Valentina. "Ask Mother Teresa here."

"Well, really," I said, unfolding a metal chair. "It's appalling. On the other hand, if I'm gonna feel ashamed about being here, logically I should feel the same way about living so near to East Harlem or the South Bronx. These people do thrive on tourist money, after all . . ."

Paul, distracted, says, "Tourist money in East Harlem?"

"No, what I mean was . . ."

"We went to the South Bronx," Valentina sighs, gazing in Paul's direction. "What was that place called that had the rappers? Fashion Motel?"

"Fashion Moda," Paul says impatiently.

"Well, there."

Just then Michael comes out to the pool. He yawns. It is quite dark except for the glow of the pool lights.

"I've seen terrible poverty," Ray says, drawing attention to the fact that he is now stark naked. Maria announces that she is going to her room to fetch something. She walks past Michael, while Ray steps out of the shadow of the palm tree, holding his glass, staggering over to us. Swinging between his pale thighs, his long, dark member is a compelling sight. "In Rangoon," he said. "And Jakarta. Back in the merchant marine. People knifing each other over bits of rotted food, same sort of climate. Takes the starch out of people."

Now, to everyone's mild surprise, Michael begins to disrobe, stands beside an empty chaise lounge, pulls off his shoes, pants, and shirt, his tanned body buffeted by dancing needles of light from the pool. His white underpants glow as they would under a disco UV.

"Ray, for heaven's sake," Paul's saying, delighted and appalled by Ray's nakedness. Ray struts up behind Valentina, whose spread-out body, swathed in an invincible white dress, is pointing to the far end of the pool. She raises herself, cranes backward. The sight of Ray's nudity makes her giggle uncontrollably. She spins up into a sitting position, her back to the pool, but keeps her eyes averted. Now Michael dives into the pool, swims a lap, swims another lap.

"Look," Paul tells me. "Ray has a big surprise for you."

"I saw it," I say. "Why don't you make it bigger and *really* surprise me?"

Hector scuffs up the steps from the patio, a tray laden with fresh gin and tonics balanced in one hand. Paul has tipped him royally for working late. He's out of uniform, in a pair of gray twill slacks. He pays no attention to Ray's exposed dong. He heads directly for Paul, then performs a quick circuit of the rest of us, finally offering Ray the last drink. As Ray takes it, Hector makes an ironic bow. Valentina howls.

"This is a pleasant moment," Paul opines. He settles on his lawn chair.

"I wouldn't go that far," Ray says.

"Neither would I," says Valentina, her voice weak, unable to control her giggles. Michael steps out of the pool, his underpants plastered to his flesh, the dark volumes of his groin vaguely visible through the clinging cloth.

"A nice break in a really tiring project," says Paul. "Don't you find? Everything seems to go along on schedule from day to day, but I'm extraordinarily worn out by it. But here we are in our little island of *la dolce vita*. Even if we are surrounded by a sea of misery."

Ray dives gracefully into the pool, thumbs linked above his head. His body is strong, well-proportioned. He seems very small compared to Michael.

"People *aren't* happy," Valentina declares, her manic star fading, as a brisk, hot wind flaps the palm branches. Alcohol is creeping up on her brain. "Perhaps one day," she says portentously, "we'll have a world where people can be. We must hope, no?"

"A brighter world," Paul exudes thoughtfully. "Yes. Where men can be equal. Full of bright voices and happy laughter . . . what a *great* idea! Michael, is that not a great idea? I'm surprised, darling, that no one ever thought of it until this very moment."

Michael opens his mouth as if an opportunity to appear intelligent has finally opened for him, but I am much quicker.

"You realize," I say, "in a brighter world, we'd all be swinging from lampposts in front of the Casa de la Candlearia."

"Maybe you would," Paul says. "I'd be sucking el presidente. I know which side my brighter world is buttered on."

Valentina's reservoir of empathy has clearly been drained by this discussion of local conditions. She now finds herself alone with three drunken homosexuals and Michael, with whom she's never been particularly friendly or unfriendly. She's been waiting all night for Luis Vasquez to take her dancing at La Piragua. They've been seeing each other . . . But it's already eleven—she announces her retirement. And if Luis Vasquez arrives, she instructs us, we must tell him that Valentina is very, very disappointed.

"And very, very disappointing," I add once she leaves.

"Oh," Paul says reproachfully. "Valentina's charming."

"She's very *chic*," says Michael. "Isn't she?"

"You just aren't used to her," Ray tells me from the pool. Paul watches Ray swimming halfhearted laps.

"Since you are," I say, "I think you should be the one to tell her that Luis Vasquez is the biggest queen in Cartagena."

"Not after *you* arrived."

Michael stretches out on a chaise. He crosses his long legs, the white bulge of his groin creating a kind of seething lump of matter in the shadows. I force myself to "casually" get up, stroll around the pool, look at Ray swimming, circle around to sit on the tiles near Michael's chair. I look at his flesh in the darkness, the long-muscled limbs, his black hair, his strong fingers gripping his glass . . .

"I told you the one about the kidney," Paul's dark silhouette says from several feet away, crossing its legs in the chair.

"No," I tell him. Michael is staring at the pool, not reacting very much to what's said, and his body is close enough that I could, if I dared, reach my hand out . . . I could even touch him in a "friendly" way, put my fingers on his fingers . . .

"A man went into a bar in New York," Paul says. "He's having a drink, a woman sits down next to him and starts talking. They have a few drinks and then they leave together. The guy's married with kids, he doesn't go home that night, the next night, so the family gets the police out. Four days later, the man wakes up in Central Park. Terrific pain in his side. He staggers off to the nearest emergency room. There, they make a strange discovery."

Ray clings to the pool ladder from inside the water, listening.

"Cheap suspense," he says, pushing himself backward back into the middle of the pool.

"They find that his left kidney has been surgically removed."

". . . ?"

"The strange part," Paul says, "is that they're not surprised. Apparently a lot of this goes on these days."

Well, yes, it's a good story—but I notice Ray's body in the pool, Michael's body sprawling on the chaise . . . one body "against" another body, Ray kicking up waves in the water . . . one of Michael's feet rubbing the bottom of his other foot . . . Paul sitting in darkness, a black shape—and then, rather startlingly, Michael speaks:

"I heard something interesting, too . . ."

His voice trails off. He sips his drink and puts it down on the ground.

"Yes?" Paul uncrosses his legs. Ray glides underwater. Now he comes up, breaststrokes to the ladder, hoists himself up, a great dripping shower.

"Oh, I don't know, it's nothing," Michael says. "I mean I did hear something, but . . . never mind, really."

"Bloody hell," snorts Ray, examining his shriveled fingertips.

I am watching Michael's fingers as they stroke the aluminum arm of the plastic chaise, migrate to his thigh, and briefly stroke his large groin, returning to the chair arm a moment later.

"Well, I shouldn't—but anyway, I was talking to a room service waiter at the Caribe the other day, I met him on the beach. A guy named Julio. So I was telling him why I was down here, and telling him, you know, the producer and his mother are living in this hotel—and I described Alex, and Julio knew who it was, he says, 'Oh, sure the tall man with the sunglasses.' 'Yes, exactly,' I tell him, 'and his mother, you know she lives here in Cartagena.' 'Oh,' he says, 'yes, I know which man you're talking about, but he's not at the Caribe with his mother.' 'Oh,' I tell him, 'but he is, he's with a very old blonde woman, his mother.' 'The blonde woman, yes,' Julio says, 'but you're very mistaken. Señora is not his mother.' 'What do you mean,' I said. Julio said, 'Mr. Gavro visits the Caribe with his wife.' "

Somehow I knew what was coming, and moved a little closer to Michael's chaise, watching Ray drip water on the tiles, and the wavering liquid shadows cast on the ancient brick walls running up behind the pool. Michael moved the leg closest to me, swung it over the edge of the chaise and planted his foot on the wet tile. I looked at the foot, inches away from me. The toes were rather long and bony and had fine little black hairs on them. As Michael talked his toes flexed and then arched outward. The longer I looked, the more Michael's foot took on a life of its own, the more it became an erotic object, the locus of all his nerve endings . . .

"Now I get confused. 'Mr. Gavro isn't married,' I tell Julio. Julio gets a knowing look on his face. 'Ah,' he says. 'I see. They are not really married.' 'No, of course they aren't,' I tell him. 'It's his *mother.*' So Julio laughs and says, 'That's quite impossible.' Because, Julio says, he delivers breakfast in their wing of the hotel, and one day last week, he came to their suite and found the door slightly open, and thought maybe they were on the terrace, because he knocked and there wasn't any answer. So he took the tray in, and found them, he said, *together in the act of love.* 'Surely,' I said, 'Mr. Gavro was with a girlfriend or something.' But no, Julio won't hear of it. Then he describes Carlotta to a T. And, he says, 'Mr. Gavro's old wife, she looks like she is enjoying it very much.' "

The silence resounds around the pool. Weather happens. I move myself still closer to his body, to his foot, thinking of the prosthetic legs on Jaybill Hanratty's veranda. Somewhere between the moon and the villa a cloud shaped like a long, poisonous turd hovers in the balmy air, blue as a fatal contusion. I think of how the Bay of Naples looked in moonlight. Ray shivers, scampers to his heap of clothes, pulls out his underpants and slips them on. He stands for a moment in the dense shadows and then takes a running dive into the pool. His body becomes a gelatin of concavities and convexities flickering underwater. Paul looks at Michael, I can't really see his face but I know his expression is one of total rapture. Michael, acutely self-conscious, says, "I *knew* I shouldn't have said anything."

It was the most Michael Simard had ever said all at once, and though it would be hard to say exactly how, we each in our respective dim corners of the pool area understood from the way he told the story that Michael Simard was as gay as a jewel, even if he'd banged every woman working on the movie. (I did not think he'd had Valentina, but you never know.) He was coming out to us, and Paul wasted no time in pulling his chair closer to Michael's and revving up the conversation. It was a pretty unmistakable impression, but Paul had to be sure.

Next it was dope, another round of G&Ts, some joints from Ray's stash, lines of coke on a little compact mirror. Paul stripping down to his underpants, diving in the pool, climbing out, tossing off the underpants, getting Ray to do the same with his, more drinks from Hector, who, from what I could see, looked bemused by developments. And then Paul was telling me to come in swimming, I looked about to melt in the hot night air . . . so I took off my clothes and jumped in. The water was cold, we thrashed around . . . more gin, more joints . . . and by the time it started to happen, we were all fairly drunk—no, we were all completely drunk.

Paul ran back into the house, upstairs, and came flying down again, crossed the inside hall, went down through the dining room. He came back holding a bottle of poppers and a fifth of brandy . . . Ray was standing behind the inclined back of Michael's chaise, talking about . . . Berlin, I seem to recall, in a casual, steady voice . . . clubs in Berlin, places to eat after midnight in Berlin. And I noticed his hands were on Michael's bare shoulders, squeezing them . . . Paul squatted down beside the chaise, uncapping the bottle and holding them under his nostrils, while I, sitting on the tiles on the other side of Michael's body, began stroking his calf, lightly, with my fingertips . . . After a few minutes, we had all moved closer to the pool, Michael lying on an inflatable raft, Paul kneeling beside him as Ray knelt between his legs . . . sliding several fingers in and out of Michael's . . . Michael groaning commands: "oooh, yeah, baby . . . that big powerful . . . take that . . . all the way in, yeah, baby . . ." I ran my tongue over his chest, taking occasional hits off the poppers and flying out of my skull into some other universe, water lapping the edges of the pool, the underwater lights casting giant bobbing shadows along the walls . . . "That's it, take that . . . lick . . ." Then the configuration changed, Paul got on all fours on the inflatable with Michael kneeling behind him; Ray moved over and squatted down before Paul . . . angling his . . . into Paul's mouth as Michael entered . . . while I buried my face . . . between Michael's . . . Now it was "give me that nice tight . . ." to Paul, and "eat that . . ." to me. The sound track of this particular orgy tape was becoming a bit of a camp: ". . . get that . . . in the air . . . pump that . . . with your . . . ," and several more variations ("Now I'm . . . your tight . . . with my fingers, man, feel those fingers . . . feel the . . . of that . . . in your . . . man . . . suck the head of my . . . suck it, lick it . . ."), lasting for two or three hours, far into the night . . . And the odd thing, as far as I was concerned, was that everything was about us having him, him having us . . . that is, I didn't really do anything with Paul or Ray, they didn't do anything with me—a few caresses, an occasional lick of each other's organs and holes, scattered unfeeling kisses . . . but nothing, nothing significant. And Hector Luis spying from between the potted plants inside the house, watching the gringos making sandwiches . . . I felt the whole preceding period had been leading, inevitably, to the taut bud of Michael's . . . on my tongue, as I slathered it and sucked it into my mouth, licking it open . . . The other odd thing was . . . now that we were having him, all unexpectedly, it was as if it was someone else . . . in other words, now that I could wrap my . . . around his . . . and give it a nice long . . . it no longer seemed like "Michael Simard," but just any good-looking boy we'd picked up. Someone passed the poppers . . . I inhaled twice in each nostril and handed the bottle back . . . His flesh was everything. I thought of Jaybill Hanratty and his four stumps jiggling on his torso . . . and that thing she'd pulled from his shorts like a tube of whale blubber . . . and the wire mesh of that ashtray, and the weird rock or whatever it was I'd dug out of my mouth . . . and Irma's lips and her crossed eyes and the sunglasses she wore and Michael's serious Balkan-looking lips and now the tight aperture of his . . . against my teeth . . . while the oily shaft . . . of his . . . squished in and out of . . . A faint whiff of . . . coming from the junction down there . . . I angled my face further down and licked at Michael's . . . loose in their sac, easy to roll with the tongue . . . they tasted anti-septically of chlorine. At about four in the morning it was my turn to get . . . offering my . . . like some futuristic bathroom appliance . . . Well, you get the idea . . .

Our orgy with Michael notwithstanding, we'd all been getting on each other's nerves for weeks—in fact, a tremendous inventory of shit had gone down, and a day or two later we got some rushes from Miami that were not so wonderful. Some of the acting was incredibly wank, there were times when we all looked like we were in different movies, although . . . there was something funny about it, too . . .

Alex arranged through Luis Vasquez to screen the rushes at the art museum. The museum director even made a little cocktail party out of it . . . There was no sound track, so we sat there looking at random footage while Paul explained things. We weren't supposed to deal with drugs or the army or the govern-ment, so Paul made up an entirely original story line. Carlotta invited various local snobs, old queers and dried-up party girls putting on an air of culture. Like a third-rate embassy party. One suddenly got a taste of Carlotta's regular life in Cartagena: vulpine middle-aged and elderly right-wingers, with that touch of insanity they all have . . . jungle vivisectionists, retired army generals, motor scooter sales and rental people, Prussian lunatics from hill stations, plus the usual local bohemians, college professors, aging nymphomaniacs . . .

After that there was an excursion out to the Rosarios, where

Carlotta packed a big picnic lunch, and Valentina got a rash from some island plant, and Alex complained about the budget . . . and a wrap party at the villa, where some of the transvestites from the Arsenal came, and Michael got into an argument with Maria, Irma ripped her dress on a nail in one of the chairs, Paul bought several grams of coke from Luis Vasquez, and we all took turns snorting it in one of the upstairs bedrooms . . . And around two-thirty in the morning, when everyone was thoroughly wrecked, Jaybill Hanratty and Simone showed up, her pushing him through the house in the wheelchair . . . And the next day I caught the morning flight to Miami.

PART TWO

the space
of death

13
Puzzle Pieces

"*O*f course," Robert Scheib said, "you have the imprisoning logic of the whole situation, the way reality shifted on its axis—and that's why the story's really jarring. We lived a certain way six or seven years ago and then things changed."

I did not think this was entirely accurate, but we were on our fourth or fifth tall glass of vodka and soda and veering, I felt, away from the whole truth and nothing but. It was a real effort not to become histrionic, sentimental, emotional. We were two men who did not know each other very well, both in early middle age, making pleasant masks for each other in the starlit dreamtime of the Chelsea roof, while all around us the world we had known all our lives moved inexorably toward a gray homogenized blankness. There was the time with Paul and the time after Paul—that's what I now realized. Too late, as always, for knowing a thing to make any difference.

"There was the Berlin Film Festival," I remembered. "I had some kind of awful fight with Ray for getting in a brawl over a restaurant check. Paul came to New York a few times. When they were editing *Laughter in the Next Room,* in fact, I went to Munich. Ray was at the apartment, this was wintertime, there was lots of snow. He gave me an address, Danzigerstrasse. Where the editing room was. So I took a cab there. Valentina was cutting the movie . . ."

Valentina was cutting the movie, and Paul was sitting beside her, hunched forward in an office swivel, joking, laughing, Valentina laughing . . . I had a sharp memory of her, wearing brown corduroy slacks and a big yellow sweater. I had never registered before how truly statuesque she was. Maybe it had to do with her sitting at the Steenbeck in the temple of her art, with the canvas bins full of splices all around her, and a big fur coat draped over her chair.

"A fur coat?" Robert's expression sank into a kind of fixed bemusement. His little cigar was burning a deep scar into the redwood table. Yes, a fur coat—funny, the things that stick in your mind.

"Silver fox or something. It was tawny brown and white, the kind of coat you see everywhere in those coffeehouses in Vienna, you know? The places with the string quartets and gigantic pastries."

Paul had had her run the first assembled reel through the Steenbeck, and as I watched her Valentina became, for the first time, a creature all her own, with her own strange internal movements, that queer linear scar above her upper lip a spur to memories of Cartagena and the somewhat regal way she had distanced herself from various internecine intrigues. I remembered, too, the persistence with which she'd presented the "facts" of her relationship with Rudolph Bauer.

"That documentary," Robert sighed. "The one Paul did. We go to interview Rudolph, this is some months or weeks after *Tarantella* is all edited and shown at Cannes, Venice . . . anyway, we go with our equipment to the apartment where Rudolph is living with Valentina, and . . . he's coming into the living room with the leather vest and the leather pants, lighting one cigarette from another, his face is all bloated, his eyes have become piggy little slits, puffing and puffing his cigarettes through the Chinese beard—and the cruel thing, of course, is that he can barely speak, his voice and his breathing are all destroyed from the drugs, the drinking, the five packs of cigarettes a day—Rudolph always mixed up everything all together, sleeping pills and uppers, tranquilizers, stimulants . . . Well, he gave us his answers, which were, like always, quite intelligent though it looks very odd in the movie, that interview, as if a very ancient turtle or a pile of moss had elected after centuries of rocklike stasis to speak, in words of one syllable . . . And, as you know, six or seven hours later, Rudolph was dead."

"And she found the body."

"Yes, he was holding a cigarette that had burnt down and gone out against his fingers. It's odd how she knew to go into his bedroom and check his breathing: the TV was on, and he normally flicked back and forth with the remote, but she could hear that it stayed on the same channel."

"What exactly was the scandal all about?"

Robert hiked up his shoulders and pointed his chin at the sky, his left-hand fingers held a little cigar, his right fist was planted in his left armpit.

"The main thing was he was in such terrible shape. She'd tried to get him off the various pills he was taking, making him promise not to do them. Well, you can imagine how effective that was—as he looked worse and worse each day. But then, that night, in a rather contradictory fashion, after he'd taken a lot of sedatives that didn't do any good, and drunk about a quart of cognac, Rudolph insisted that she go score some Mandrax for him. With Mandrax he could usually get to sleep. According to her, she said no, and he pleaded and begged and badgered until she relented and made him promise if she got the Mandrax he would go to a clinic for a sleep cure.

"So she goes out, cops the Mandrax, brings it back, and leaves again to join some friends for dinner. And gets back, according to her account, at a little after three in the morning. That's when she finds him . . . You know, at first she tried to have Paul's documentary stopped with a legal paper, claiming it was exploitation. She especially hated the narration that I wrote, which treated him as less than a total saint. But you know, until this minute, it didn't occur to me that what she felt threatened by was that interview. Because anyone could *see* what scary physical shape he was in and draw the conclusion that giving him drugs at that point was potentially lethal."

"How did Paul deal with her anger over the film?"

Robert laughed. "Oh, he went to her and said the interview was all my idea, which it certainly wasn't, and that after Rudolph croaked he'd wanted to remove it from the film, but *I* had insisted on leaving it in. So they made up as friends while she went on hating my guts for some years."

"That is so like Paul, deflecting that anger onto somebody else."

"Paul had a genius for that sort of thing."

"But you couldn't really get mad at him."

"Some people could. He liked to see people squirm when their nasty little secrets got laid on the table, and some people didn't find that amusing. I always thought what attracted Paul to Rudolph was that stone cold malevolence Rudolph could get into, which was so much more extreme than anything Paul could really allow himself. But he liked to watch it in action."

"He was fascinated by power."

"Yes, his whole thing was to be the *valet* of power. The henchman standing off to the side, watching."

I remembered that January afternoon in Munich again: as we

prepared to leave the editing room, Valentina began straightening up her things, putting reels into tins, sticking labels on them. Paul was on the phone to Ray, reporting that Valentina insisted on catching a flight to Berlin that afternoon, despite his efforts to keep her there. Then she went out to the lavatory, and Paul hid her purse. She had a huge vinyl bag with her whole life stuffed inside it, and a suitcase.

There was another editing room next to the toilet. Paul put her bag in there. Valentina took a long time primping in the WC. Paul made a phone call. Valentina came out, got her coat on, and then got that sudden panicked look people get when something they need is missing. She looked all over for the bag; meanwhile Paul was on the phone, and she kept asking him if he'd seen the bag, and Paul was such a convincing actor that he got her believing she'd left it at his apartment . . . I could see that she knew she hadn't, but once he got off the phone she called Ray, just to check. But Ray had gone out and turned the answering machine on.

In the end, Paul had to relent and show her that he'd hidden the bag. It was obvious that Valentina was touched by his childish attempts to delay her departure, like a kid hiding his mother's purse so she won't leave him alone. But when I thought about it later on, it bothered me. It wasn't simply that he played tricks on her to keep her around him, but this frightened need for her company I sensed in his distraction once she left, his fretting at dinner that night that she might be away in Berlin longer than she'd promised—and Ray, too, seemed peculiarly focussed on Valentina's itinerary. It was as though her movements influenced not only their social life but the emotional equilibrium between them. There was something bizarrely juvenile, not to say freakish, in the way they talked of her, she was a wondrous, magical creature for them, full of wit, goodness, and occult good judgment. This had not been the attitude in Cartagena and I could not account for it now, except by supposing that the realm of lack between Paul and Ray had grown so wide that a third person was necessary to dissipate tensions.

After that he paid more visits to New York, phoning up out of the blue. We would meet for dinner. Paul was never in New York for more than three or four days at a time, he had business in Chicago, business in L.A. In the year after shooting *The Laughter in the Next Room* he seemed to be on a plane every minute. Ray spent most of that year in Sydney. Even though there was a sort of reunion the following February at the film festival, and Alex duly showed up in New York pressing me to bring his slides around to galleries, I lost any sense of Cartagena as a time that had really happened, and felt that I had dreamed up all the people down there. They were becoming ghosts . . . Some were literally ghosts. I heard from Paul that Luis Vasquez, for example, died from AIDS, and some months after that, strange to tell, Hannah Slausen, the line producer, threw herself out a sixth-story window in Berlin. Paul said that Hannah, after breaking up with Vale, the cameraman, resumed an old affair with a policeman, who apparently brutalized her, beat her up all the time, the details were unclear. At any rate, out the window she went.

New York was a city with its own growing ghost population. I can't talk about all the people who died that year, and the next year, and the year after and the year after, except to say that what had been a nebulous and ill-understood menace became the main thing on practically every person's mind. In the ordinary course of my week, I often walked past a building just off Union Square where a dead friend had briefly lived, in a small tenth-floor apartment, which I had only visited once; and every time I passed this building, or passed near enough to remind myself that it was near, an hour's conversation with that particular ghost replayed itself, the stark New York efficiency decor of that apartment sprang into my memory, the black-and-white octagons on the bathroom linoleum, the pinkish light in a tank of tropical fish, a phone call he'd taken during my visit, a call from another junkie. Even though I have an ample memory file about that person, a single afternoon of his very brief tenure in that obscure location has come to dominate all my other memories. The city was becoming mined with these architectural *aides-mémoire*, structural residue of vanished lives; the route to the Chelsea itself took me past the studio of a photographer whose disintegration I witnessed in close-up over a three-year period.

One day, in a science fiction bookshop and novelty store on Broadway, I ran into Michael Simard. He was browsing through Japanese slash comics, dressed for the gym in a strappy undershirt and workout pants. His hair had grown almost down to his shoulders, which gave him a "French hippie" look. His body, his face, stunning as ever. It is hard to render the exact attitude I picked up from him. He talked about Cartagena with a certain air of bemused disillusionment, as if it had happened in the long-ago past, though at that date the film wasn't even finished (Paul filmed two added scenes in the Munich zoo, I believe). If he had been carried away by the thought of becoming a film star, it seemed that he'd since realized that *The Laughter in the Next Room* would not be the vehicle for his discovery.

But I'm getting this wrong: Michael's expressions weren't specific to his feelings about the movie, or at least I can't say so with any certainty. Perhaps that night beside the pool he had revealed himself in a way that he hadn't intended. Maybe he'd gone down to Cartagena with the plan of presenting a wholly invented, "new" Michael Simard to a group of complete strangers, and had almost made it through as that mysterious laconic being, and then, at the last minute, afraid that we were all losing interest, he turned himself into a complete whore. Looking at him in Forbidden Planet, against a backdrop of gorilla and android full-head masks, I could not quite believe I had ever had sex with this man. The connection had meant nothing: he'd fucked with me and Ray and

Paul out of sheer boredom, or maybe to curry favor with Paul. But here, in the northern hemisphere, on a warmish day in early June, the thought that I had once had my tongue in this person's rectum struck me as preposterous and even a little sad. Desirable as he was, Michael had nothing in common with me, nothing to do with me, and I realized then that I scarcely existed in his mind. For him I was boring, powerless and therefore boring. I had nothing to offer him. As we chatted, I noticed he wore a beeper hooked to the elasticized waist of his workout pants.

No, everything was losing its reality . . .

"Ray bought a house," Robert said. "Just before you all went down there. Near Bonday Beach in Sydney. He rented an office in King's Cross—you know Sydney?"

"No, I've never been to Australia."

"It's interesting. It really is."

". . ."

"He'd set up a distribution business for art house movies, independent movies. He really did quite well."

I nodded. "Yes, and then I remember, when we went to the Berlin Festival, he met that couple, Ned and Claire. I've got their address written down. They're living now in Rome. But at that time they were the other independent distributors in Australia."

"Right. Some big company went in and hiked the rentals up and so on. But at the time Ray made a lot of money. That was a strange time."

"Well, he was out from under Rudolph," I said.

"The fact is he couldn't really work in Germany at that point, not without Rudolph. After Rudolph, everything fell apart. So he went there and set up his company and then, I think, he started thinking over his relationship to Paul. That was the only real long-term relationship Ray'd ever had, and, you know, Ray was kind of the doormat."

"They seemed so . . . together."

"Sure. Hey, Ray was a simple guy. He worked for Rudolph all those years, and you know what Ray liked? To play pinball in a bar, drink a few beers, hump a trick or two on the weekends. Other than that, he had his life with Paul, very domestic, they had their book collection, their tape collection, it was normal, and the relationship quite open. Paul said when the sex wasn't great anymore that he got off on watching Ray do it with others. Right around when coke became a big thing in Paul's life, that was when the fisting craze really hit. He could get off in a big way to see Ray with his arm up somebody's can . . . Of course that was Rudolph's thing, too.

"There was always a rivalry between Paul and Rudolph over Ray—and there you really had two men who could drive somebody crazy, but somehow Ray managed both of them. You had on one hand Rudolph, an impossible person whose self-loathing exploded in all directions, his body growing fatter and grosser every year, with his uppers and downers that he washed down with quarts of cognac and weisswursts and schnitzels and big plates of carbonara spaghetti, Rudolph was like, total oral city. That was one person who never truly relaxed for a single microfraction of an instant. And being the assistant, Ray sits next to this time bomb for eight to sixteen hours every day. And then he'd come home to find Paul ablaze with cocaine fantasies. The insane projects he dreamt up, requiring Byzantine global manipulations . . . financing from Saudi sheiks and Texas heiresses and floating bits of international white trash Paul managed to hypnotize in the course of his endless travels. Paul spent *most* of his time wondering how to get rich people to give him money, you know.

"Somehow, Ray let it roll through him without ever getting crazy. He just had a real calmness about him. After Rudolph died and he went to Australia, he made that little movie—"

"Oh, the sheep film! Yes, my god, Paul showed me a tape of that."

"And imagine, it won a prize! And Ray did it all by himself, I really believe it was the first time that person had anything of his own going for him."

"So that . . . kind of gave him a leg up."

"Well, precisely, and then he got sick. He went very quickly from feeling independent and making money for the first time in his life, to getting very, very sick."

14
Munich

*R*obert said that Paul hardly ever talked about his childhood, but his childhood started coming back to him the minute Ray was in the flat again—he'd had a brother who died at home from some hideous childhood disease, Robert wasn't clear what it was, encephalitis possibly or TB, one of those wasting diseases that drags on for years and never gets any better. Ray had pneumonia, there was nothing to treat that type of pneumonia at the time, except conventional antibiotics, which were basically useless. But he had to go right into hospital a week after he arrived from Sydney, and Paul believed it was all over, because people were popping off overnight from pneumonia then. If they had KS or shingles or what have you, they lasted a bit longer.

As soon as he checked Ray into the hospital Paul said, He's so wasted I don't see how he can last another day. But then Ray went into some sort of spontaneous remission, he came out very weakened, but Paul figured they could manage him in the apartment—except that Ray had other things going wrong, he couldn't always walk, in fact he was bedridden most of the time. Paul put him in the main bedroom, and he also slept in there with Ray at first, but Ray got these terrible sweats, great gallons of fluid seeping out of him, the sheets had to be changed several times a day and besides that he couldn't control his bladder or his bowels quite often, and furthermore he had some type of internal bleeding. He disintegrated very rapidly in Munich, and Paul, who was never exactly Mother Teresa in the first place, became a total nervous wreck; for one thing the doctors didn't have the slightest idea how to treat half the problems Ray was experiencing. There were all kinds of theories flying around—you'd hear about special things they had in America or France, but mainly the medical profession acted as if the plague had broken out, forget the Hippocratic Oath, the average doctor was strapping on masks and gloves and space suits before he'd lance a pimple.

There were still debates raging in the newspapers about quarantine and special laws that allowed the police to arrest people who might be harboring the virus. Bavaria. There was quite a lot of hysteria, even from some of Paul's friends. He said it was absolutely demoralizing the way certain people shunned him, not phoning up, or if they did run into him, acting as if he'd get some of it on them. By that time, Robert said, a number of people they knew were sick with AIDS in one form or another. Paul, of course, wasn't sick, but managing Ray from day to day began making him sick. That was where, Robert said, Valentina, maybe to her credit—although there are two ways of looking at it in retrospect—came through for both of them quite remarkably.

People get used to anything, of course, Robert said, and I'd love to say Paul adapted to this situation where someone he loved, someone he'd had a great physical passion for at one time apart from everything else, inspired extraordinary sacrifices—well, Paul did do what he was able to, for all his cynicism Paul had plenty of human compassion, he wasn't a shit. On the other hand, after this had dragged on for a while Paul developed an abstracted quality that made you wonder what was passing through his mind. He'd relied for so many years on that sardonic merciless humor of his, he really didn't have a separate mode with which to deal with the new situation. Because, you know, Robert said, Paul despised self-pity—he wouldn't allow it, not from himself, anyway, and he lacked the ability to accept anything resembling pity from another person. So he kind of got stuck in a constant effort to regain that steadying comic despair he'd always had as a defense against the grandiose emotional exhibitionism of certain people in Rudolph's circle, Rudolph included. And this self-deprecating need to be trenchant and witty and aloof about his real feelings took on a kind of demonic edge when he talked about Ray. Ray started losing a bit of his human status. He was becoming this difficult lump of matter in the bedroom.

Valentina spent a great deal of time at their apartment; so did Robert. So did Irma, who happened to be acting in a Schiller play in Munich at the time. Irma sometimes sat with Ray in the afternoons or dropped off groceries to save Paul a trip to the supermarket. Everyone maintained the fiction that things would "improve." Meanwhile, Ray had tremendous difficulty holding anything in his stomach. He lost an incredible amount of weight. The doctors had him on an intravenous drip hanging from a metal rod beside the bed. When he could actually sit up or shuffle out of the bedroom, he'd always want a cup of coffee or something perfectly unhealthy which he'd throw up immediately and then have a coughing fit, where he'd lose his breath and have to be pounded on the back for half an hour.

Valentina worked out a routine. She changed the sheets and cleaned the shit off him, the things Paul couldn't bear doing very often. Ray had started to smell funny. He gave off kind of a close, gluey odor. Paul said, The whole house smells of death, it's unbearable. Sometimes if he said things like that, he'd go into a laughing jag right away, as if he really couldn't credit what was happening. First thing every day he looked in on Ray, they had these rambling dialogues for hours, Ray's conversation had become a little weird, as you might imagine, his mind wandered . . . Meanwhile Paul was petrified out of his wits about his own health, Ray was getting weaker by the day and it was like, "I'm next."

Ray had good days and bad days, but every good day was a little worse than the one before and the bad days were a lot worse. He had an intolerable amount of pain and the doctors were overcautious about painkillers. They never prescribed enough, so Paul and Valentina began overdosing him, which would put him out for days at a time when he didn't have any nourishment except the drip. Sometimes the medication made him constipated, they'd have to administer an enema, other times he pissed and shat in his sleep, and they'd have to clean that up with him unconscious, hauling and heaving this naked dead weight around the bedroom while Valentina stripped the bed and freshened the sheets, and sometimes he woke up screaming in the middle of all that, screaming and weeping, *Just let me die, I want to die.* Naturally, they did consider sending him into the next world, plenty of times, if he'd agree to it, and when he was lucid, not out of his mind with pain, they discussed exactly at what point they should cop enough Dilaudid to finish him off. Unfortunately, that seemed always to be followed by several days of fairly tolerable peace and quiet, where he just lay there suffering, or stoned on medication. He couldn't read or concentrate on anything, couldn't follow TV except for the soccer matches, which did seem to take his mind off it. But his body was just this big disaster area by August. He really couldn't talk very much. It was often impossible to tell if he was awake or asleep, he slept with his eyes open sometimes.

Paul left the flat as often as possible, said Robert, half the time walking down to the Chinese Tower in the English Gardens to get drunk. Robert said he forced Paul to join him at a health club for a sauna, or to take in a movie. Paul had stopped snorting coke, Robert believed, but he would do a line or two when he thought he might absolutely go crazy otherwise. At ten in the morning, every ashtray in the flat was overflowing with cigarette butts, Paul couldn't put his mind on anything, though he did force himself to look after money, at least to the extent that the bills got paid. And of course, said Robert, any catastrophe that drags on too long begins to look normal.

Paul took a quickie acting job at Bavaria Studios, an American coproduction, playing a Nazi officer as usual, he merely had to open a door for Himmler at the Wannsee Conference and salute. I remember, Robert said, that the director knew Paul's situation and gave him a line, "Heil Hitler," which turned it into a speaking role, so Paul was paid a lot more for it. Paul told Robert he had never felt quite so much conviction in a line of dialogue before, since he figured "Heil Hitler" would be paying for his lover's euthanasia. You know what his humor was like, Robert said, I began telling you the childhood business, Robert said, oh yes— why it came up, he told me he grew up in a house full of gloomy kitsch, this kitsch proliferated all through the hunger years and the economic miracle, all these thousands of hideous knicknacks his mother collected and arranged all over every shelf and windowsill. Little elves and trolls and Santa Clauses and toadstools with frogs and ceramic squirrels. Robert said that Paul said that he now felt he was being buried alive in his own kitsch. First he'd been suffocated by the mental kitsch of the Third Reich, and the kitsch of his mother, all her painted dwarves and Hansels and Gretels and what have you, every sort of mass-produced horror, and now, thirty years later, his grown-up adult life began to look as empty and desperate and terrible as theirs. He suddenly saw his antisentimentality, that "nonstyle" of the apartment, as a form of sentimentality. The Warhol painting in the hall, the tasteful little handicraft gewgaws from all over the planet, the modular furniture, the psuedo-Aubusson carpet, the semichic café just under his third-floor balcony. And then, also, the kitsch of his feelings, the code of sentiments, which Paul said were exactly reproduced in all the "moving" accounts that were coming out about the same catastrophe. Paul said that even his homosexuality had turned into *soẓialkitsch*, because this nightmare which was so particular and moving to himself was happening to thousands of other people at the same time, and being treated as a "social problem," or a political cause, and therefore his entire existence was becoming leftist kitsch or fascist kitsch, depending on the vantage point. He cited in particular a dreadfully insipid "AIDS memoir" written, Paul said, by some hack Hollywood screenwriter that someone had sent him in the mail. *Even the worst sort of people*, Robert said that Paul said, *are dragging out the violins*—Ray can't even have his own death as a personal tragedy, Paul told Robert. Instead, Ray is having a kitsch death, *thanks to sentimental morons and fascist monsters*. Paul could not envision any real life for himself after Ray, and he said that somehow the *generic* nature of Ray's demise was transforming the time they had already had together into a chimera, a retroactive hallucination or a dream that had continually promised an entirely different outcome and now made no sense at all.

All the same, it was also something concrete and intractible involving hospitals and doctors and a private-duty nurse at one point, before Valentina took over things—Ray looking less and less like Ray, Robert said. Ray aged about fifty years between July and September, which became, somehow, even more disturbing when he did recover slightly and dress himself and stagger out into the living room. There were a few occasions when he even felt well enough to take a drive, Robert said. Paul took him out a number of times, to a bar, for example, never the Eiche or Harry's where they'd run into people they knew, but places like Philomar Bar, which wasn't popular then, except with Turks, and other times to restaurants, where Ray typically had trouble eating anything. Whenever Ray made that type of exertion, the relapse was more or less instantaneous. They didn't have AZT, or rather they had it at one hospital but only were giving it to a limited number of experimental patients—and they were giving huge doses of it that produced pernicious anemia. Paul kept trying to get Ray into one of the treatment protocols, but whenever they went for evaluation, Ray had some new pathology, for example, Robert told me, a green fungus he started getting in his mouth, also some rare type of tissue degeneration in his rectum, so he'd have to be treated symptomatically, with whatever drug the doctors had any vague intuition about. Actually, Robert said, what they gave him did seem to help, but then he developed KS lesions, either in August or early September, Robert couldn't recall exactly, the soles of his feet first of all—so that affected his walking, he said that when he walked it was like stepping on cockroaches with your bare feet. Then the lesions spread across his chest and down his left arm, a big one right in the center of his forehead. They were growing into his internal organs as well. You can picture it, Robert said, like an endless horror dream. Whenever they thought it couldn't possibly advance to a worse stage, it did.

Naturally, there was so much stress in the flat, Valentina and Paul both needed to blow off steam. There were arguments, nothing too dramatic, but intense scuffles over who should look after him, during which hours and so forth. Valentina had taken it on herself, but this was a little bit different than frying up schnitzel for Rudolph at three in the morning after he'd ODed on Mandrax or drunk a quart of Rémy Martin. The whole thing was taking its toll. Valentina had made such a brave Florence Nightingale thing out of her role in it that she couldn't then back out of it and, Robert said, as you probably know, this other situation developed out of the blue.

It started one night when Robert stopped over at the flat. There had, he said, just been some unbelievable episode of Ray falling out of bed and crawling down the hall puking out his guts. They'd cleaned him off and given him some heroin—that was another point, Robert said, Paul had started copping heroin from a dealer named Billy Sauberman who hung out in Harry's New York Bar. Sauberman was a joke name, Robert said. It was like what people say about the Germans, that they're "Sauberman," you know, "clean," like the typical German has a floor you can eat your dinner on. And Billy was called Billy Sauberman because he never used any of these drugs he sold. Paul was giving Ray a little chip of heroin every once in a while, on top of his hospital medication. Anyway, Valentina was on her hands and knees scrubbing puke off the hall carpet, they were both laughing, a little hysterically, at the horror of it all. Robert said that Paul was amazed that Ray could still be alive and this kind of gothic household pathology had become absolutely routine. Paul said that they were so accustomed to cascades of body waste, they could probably become Red Cross nurses in Lebanon when it was over.

In any case, it was a typical evening chez Paul. They went to the beer garden at the Chinese Tower, where they had those long church basement tables with paper tablecloths and on the bandstand a little orchestra of variously plump and scrawny ladies blowing on wind instruments—which reminded Robert, Robert said, of Joseph Conrad's *Victory*, and the innkeeper Schomberg, and those tropical islands that Germans particularly tend to languish on. Just think how many dreams we Germans focus on the south, Robert told me, all that yearning for Capri and the bright sun, just to run away from Shitland.

All the fairies and bum boys and punks of Munich, Robert said, were cruising the pagoda. The tables were crowded with Paul's actor friends, director friends, they paused to chat here and there. Paul told Robert, Robert said, that he could feel the *wave of horrified sympathy* rippling through the English Garden, *sympathy and revulsion* . . . There were so many in those days, Robert told me, who believed they could cheat death by turning away and pretending that the people who had it, the AIDS bug or whatever it was, had done anything different than they'd done—fucked the wrong kind of people or shot drugs or what have you.

They found a place at the end of a long table and ordered a pitcher of beer. It was a balmy evening, Robert said. Paul, he thought, had taken a little sedative pill, or a little chip of heroin, Robert didn't know what, but Paul's blood pressure seemed to have dropped during the brief walk from the apartment to the English Garden. When Paul was not in the apartment he tried to put Ray out of his mind entirely. He had even come out of his depression slightly, as if he knew the end could not be far off. Bear in mind, Robert told me, Ray no longer resembled Ray very much, although he still had his mind, intermittently at least, but he was so fogged with medication, and he seemed to withdraw more and more inside himself—at least that was how it seemed. And, Robert said, Ray had come to hate his body: it was a fearsome enemy making him crazy with pain. And Paul, at that point, needed some relief from everything, including Valentina, because he was starting to feel the two of them were married and had this dying child in the main bedroom.

We sat there, Robert said, under the spreading elms with the bandstand lights casting a greenish haze on the tables, just enough light to pick people's faces out of the darkness as they moved around, and we talked and talked, scraping our minds for things to talk about that didn't lead back to Ray and the apartment. I remember, Robert told me, Paul saying he'd been listening compulsively to Glenn Gould's recording of *The Goldberg Variations.* Paul maintained, Robert said, that Gould's *Goldberg Variations* were his supreme aesthetic experience. The more he drank, Robert said, or the more whatever he'd taken kicked in, the more insistent Paul became about *The Goldberg Variations,* specifically Gould's performance of *The Goldberg Variations*—Paul's mind had fixated on *The Goldberg Variations and everything that kind of mathematical clarity and perfection implied*—for Paul *The Goldberg Variations* represented an ideal condition of human temperament. At that moment, Robert said, Paul believed all the troubles of the world, including Ray's illness, resulted from a collective failure to appreciate the purity of Bach and *The Goldberg Variations*.

A young man came over to the table. The branches rustled overhead. Robert said he felt little drops of rain, the type of rain you get on warm summer evenings. The young man introduced himself as Chris, as a friend of Mutti. You remember Mutti, Robert told me—Mutti is even now after years the bartender at the Kleist Keller, one of Rudolph's first Munich boyfriends. Mutti who was so adorable at seventeen, when Rudolph discovered him selling vegetables on Leopoldstrasse, at the corner of the Münchener Freiheit station. Rudolph put Mutti in film after film, and gradually, said Robert, of course, Mutti has gone all beefy and bull-necked and fat-assed like they all did. Mutti Flatface as he's now known. Anyway, Robert said, this Chris, friend of Mutti, knew Paul from seeing him at the Eiche, he jogged Paul's memory, he gave the impression of a quite pleasant youth, rather graceful, with a nice open face and depthful eyes, he sat down and fell into some deep conversation with Paul, Robert said, possibly about *The Goldberg Variations*—and I, Robert told me, drifted off into my own head, which at that time was full of tiny little problems, an offer to ghostwrite the memoirs of a gangster on the Riviera, for example, which has now, Robert said, taken three years, and whether I should stay some further months in Munich, helping Paul through this difficult period, or go back to Paris . . . and if I would keep the relationship with the woman I was seeing then or if it was finished, all these urgent boring thoughts and problems. And a little puddle of beer was soaking into the tablecloth, it looked like a continent, Robert said, and if I tipped the tablecloth a little this way the stain looked like a comet with a tail, and the way the veins stood out on the back of my hand struck me for the first time as a sign of middle age, and so forth.

Chris told them of his bartending job in a local disco. He was a student of literature, preparing his doctorate on the influence of something or other on Samuel Beckett. Also he had attended the Cordon Bleu, he drove a motorcycle, he hadn't known he was gay until his nineteenth birthday when he found his will in the men's room of the Bahnhof, with a Turk, et cetera, et cetera.

Signals flared back and forth, a sweet erotic tension between Paul and Chris that lingered in the air. Needles of rain fogged Robert's glasses, he said. He could hardly follow what they said, but something was developing, they drained the second pitcher of beer and sent Chris for another, and Paul asked him what he should do, meaning what was the right thing to do, with a lover dying in the flat and so on, and Robert told him he ought to go have sex with Chris and relax for a change, and Paul decided he would. He asked Robert to go back and tell Valentina he wouldn't be home, she should stay in the flat that night, so they drank for a while longer and then Robert walked back to Paul's flat, where he found Valentina in a mildly inebriated funk, watching TV. What's up? she says, Robert said. What's he doing? Oh, Robert says, he's actually found himself a date. I see, I see, Valentina says, Robert said, as if she'd been expecting this kind of thing all along. Why on earth should she care, I wonder? Robert said.

She's never been especially friendly to me, Robert said, but on this night she's Miss Congeniality. A little drunk. Well, she says, why not have a little wine. I'm not wild about this idea, Robert said, but I think, if she's decided we should be friends I can't very well refuse. Ray's asleep. He's much worse, she tells me. I think his brain's going, she says. She says Ray has been talking about going to Nepal, expedition climbing. Delirious.

We sit at the table with the balcony doors open. I can hear

people eating and drinking in the café downstairs, Robert told me, and some music coming up, and on the TV they're showing a dubbed version of *North by Northwest*. The rain stops. The sky is a true Prussian blue, even though we're in Bavaria, blue with dark ink clouds in it. Valentina pops open a bottle of burgundy. I hate burgundy sometimes, Robert said, pouring himself a little more vodka. It's too heavy for summertime, he said, and besides, that big severe face of hers, serious, beetling, like it takes a week for an idea to form. *Quite a pretty evening,* she says; Robert said, *it's these nights Rudolph loved sitting in the English Garden,* and I'm thinking, Robert told me, *Please, let's not start in on Rudolph, Blanche*—and then she says, The only time I get to breathe is when Ray's sleeping, and so on, and then asks about Paul's date, does Paul know the guy or what? It's a friend of Mutti, I tell her. Luckily I don't say Mutti Flatface, because her eyebrows shoot up suddenly, she takes a big swig of wine and says, *I suppose you know I've been seeing Mutti for a while.* Well, I was not current, Robert told me. I can't keep track of everyone's *erotischer* life, can I. Oh yes, she says, he's such a good person, a pure soul. I doubt if people understand what a special person he is. Her voice is a little spacey. Oh, I tell her, Robert said, he's the salt of the earth. Everybody loves Mutti, he's a sweetheart. Thinking, Robert said, that he was way too much of a sweetheart for the likes of her, actually. Oh, sure, she says, all the fags in the Kleist Keller adore Mutti because they're in love with him, except he doesn't swing in that direction anymore. This, Robert said, sent a chill up my back, I could hear this note of bitterness and resentment, and I thought, now we get the inner narrative at last. Don't take this the wrong way, she says, but really, with this AIDS, it makes you wonder: I don't judge people, but look how they don't control themselves. Paul runs off with someone just for fuck, she says, Robert said—even now that we know what can happen.

There were further reflections of that general stripe—liquor talking, Robert said, Valentina didn't fancy being alone if Ray died in the night. I didn't blame her, Robert said. Anyway, she puffs herself up with a little more booze and delivers her sermon on the situation, and I figured, Robert said, that could change 180 degrees in two seconds flat. The Germans are crazy, Robert told me—for good and bad, both. During the war, the most popular song was the "Spring Song" of Mendelsohn with words by Heinrich Heine, a one-hundred-percent Jewish product, they tried to suppress it but they couldn't. People liked it too well. And when bombs were falling on Dresden and Hamburg, Zara Leander was singing, *because of that the world doesn't crumble, tomorrow the skies will be Himmelblau*—heavenly blue. Completely crazy.

As I listened to Valentina talking, Robert told me, I began almost unconsciously to detect an "influence," if you see what I mean. I had never known her to have a single idea of her own. When she lived with Rudolph she talked exactly in his vocabulary and parroted his ideas, word for word. If Rudolph told you it was healthy to fart forty times a day, she farted. Then again, with Paul, monkey see, monkey do. And on this night I hear another voice coming out, and sharp opinions about things, decisive, well-informed. She speaks about the epidemic: it's just common sense, she tells me, Robert told me, these doctors must be taking the wrong path with this multifaceted illness. I know, Robert said, that she doesn't have phrases like "multifaceted," she's got to have picked it up somewhere—next she's citing new theories about how the virus attaches to the cells, how "progressive doctors" working with AIDS now believe there are more causes besides just the virus, cofactors, and so on. Perhaps the virus theory itself is a hoax—have I thought about that?

What I think, Robert said, is that she's had a generous dose of someone else's rap, though I can't imagine whose. So then she says, some cousin of hers has become friendly with a Dr. Zryd, who's running a clinic in Bad Endorf, near Rosenheim. *Ironically enough,* she says, this clinic is in a mansion once owned by the Bechstein family. There, she says, in the 1920s, the Bechsteins had a literary salon. And Gottfried Benn was coming there, and Thomas Mann, and Elizabeth Nietzsche, all very posh, she says, I'm thinking, yeah, and tomorrow the sky is *himmelblau*—and now, she says, *ironically,* according to her, this Dr. Zryd, a vital young researcher ("on the side of life," as she puts it), Robert said, is having tremendous success with AIDS patients. Her cousin So-and-so has introduced her to this "dynamic" doctor, at a little informal dinner—as if anybody we knew went to any other kind of dinner, Robert weighed in, informal dinner as opposed to state dinner or god knows what other kind of dinner?—and Zryd, the doctor, Valentina says, Robert said, "has a revolutionary concept," she says, that the immune system failure everyone has chosen to call AIDS might actually be the result of syphilis that was left untreated.

I had already heard about Dr. Zryd and his revolutionary concept, said Robert, it was in the *Suddeutschen Zeitung,* I used to zoom in on any article having to do with AIDS, especially to do with treatment, because nothing seemed to be working anywhere. There were rumors that Zryd had "cured" one man we all knew who'd evidently been at death's door the previous winter—and now, thanks to Zryd and his revolutionary concept, was going around Munich extremely fit, giving blowjobs in various lavatories. On the one hand, the whole thing sounded like a pile of horseshit; on the other hand, anybody involved with this health debacle was willing to grasp at straws. The Zryd concept did have a certain plausible ring to it, especially if you knew nothing about medicine. I mean, Robert said, when somebody starts yammering on about the blood-brain barrier and etiology and mutation of enzymes and Christ knows what else, you tend to glaze over and believe they know what they're talking about. That was definitely the case here. What Valentina wanted to know, Robert said, was whether I thought Paul would consider putting Ray into this Zryd Clinic, this place in Bad Endorf near Rosenheim, even if the treatment were highly experimental and possibly unsuccessful. Well—at that point, Paul would've taken Ray to a faith healer. Valentina knew that already, but she wanted reassurance, said Robert, so I said yes, I think so, yes.

15

The Crazy Place

"*T*he evening shadows fall," said Robert Scheib, drunkenly, on the Chelsea roof, introducing the events of October and November 1987, most of which occurred outside his immediate ken, and which therefore had the oblique quality of "the laughter in the next room" that Paul so often attributed to Edith, rather than to Osbert, Sitwell. Paul himself was the source of these stories, which were, Robert said, invariably confessional, expiatory, but also illustrated what Paul called "the cosmic irony" of the situation.

Ray was moved by ambulance to the clinic in Bad Endorf. Over a period of several days, during which it had become clear that some form of neuropathy was erasing Ray's awareness of who he was, it was agreed that the Zryd penicillin therapy couldn't be any worse than the untreated degeneration. Paul later averred that he initiated this move "with a bad conscience," that he had "desperately needed to believe" in the Zryd approach, the Zryd methodology, that Dr. Zryd "inspired complete confidence," mainly (or so it seemed in retrospect, said Robert) because "Zryd is our age, he doesn't view this disease in a moralistic light." One could "talk to Zryd as to a friend, rather than a doctor."

Paul and Valentina both remarked on Dr. Zryd's "immense personal charm." The incredible confidence inspired by this young doctor was later enlarged upon in newspaper accounts when the Zryd method and the Zryd clinic were investigated by the health authorities. Valentina said that Winfried Zryd was "shockingly handsome, for a doctor." Paul told Robert that Zryd "looked like the young Belmondo." It was as if Paul and Valentina were inclined to trust Zryd because he looked like someone they would cast in a movie about a brilliant young physician. Paul confessed later that if Zryd hadn't looked so much like a movie star, his, that is, Paul's habitual skepticism probably wouldn't have escaped him so readily, especially after Zryd cut off Ray's painkillers.

The long and the short of this story—this is the narrator talking now—the truth or untruth of particular details, are distinctions no one is really qualified to make, because much if not most of this story is hearsay: I heard it from Robert and Robert heard some of it from Paul and even more of it from other people who heard it from people who heard it from Paul, but we will proceed with what we have. The painkillers were cut off, according to Zryd, according to Paul, according to Robert, because the efficacy of the "enhanced penicillin" crucial to Zryd's method, the blood-brain barrier–crossing penicillin, being injected twice a day into Ray's arm could not be measured properly if there were opiates in the bloodstream. Robert said that Paul said that Zryd told him that sedative drugs interfered with absorption of the superantibiotic Zryd had developed. The trouble came when they withdrew the narcotics, Robert said, because besides the Percodan and Darvocet that Ray had prescriptions for, Paul and Valentina had been continually upping the dosage and supplementing it during spells of intense pain with small doses of junk—so by this time Ray was, for all practical purposes, a junkie, and manifested withdrawal symptoms so acute that he started screaming like some animal in a slaughterhouse, bellowing for minutes at a time and then passing out from his own pain, waking up in even deeper withdrawal, screaming, pissing, shitting, and of course hemorrhaging. When Paul and Valentina returned to the clinic on the afternoon of the second day, Ray's bedclothes were spattered with blood, they'd put him back on a maintenance dose of morphine, with the idea of lowering the dose gradually until he kicked the stuff. Robert said Paul reported that Ray's face scarcely resembled anything human: the eyes were full of animal panic and fear. At times he'd only react to stimulus by screaming. Ray's room was adjacent to Zryd's office, so they could hear him screaming whenever they went in to discuss Ray's condition.

Over the following week, Paul and Valentina, Robert said, developed a social relationship with Zryd, apart from the professional connection. This, Paul said later, lent a surreal piquancy to their meetings with Zryd. The doctor projected powerful confidence. He assured Paul that even though Ray had a lot of pain, the pain would lessen once the superantibiotic took effect, the "viral necklaces" as Zryd called them would begin cracking apart (Zryd's phrase) and expelling themselves through the urine (Zryd's phrase), all the while unendurable shrieks of misery bled through the walls (Paul's locution), interrupted now and then (Valentina said) by fits of inane sobbing. The nerves of Ray's brain (Zryd) were affected: he seldom knew where he was (Paul), even when he remembered who he was (Valentina). Incredible as it seems, Robert told me, quoting Paul, Zryd sat at his desk tapping his fingertips on the blotter or slapping his palm with a stethoscope, murmuring this soothing drivel about viral necklaces, and then a char came in with a silver tea service and poured them all a nice cup of tea. Then they discussed (according to Paul) the latest Botho Strauss production, and a Burmese restaurant that had just opened in Schwabing (Valentina related), and finally they took a "quick look in" on Ray, who'd just nodded out from his morphine shot.

Valentina had resumed sleeping at her own apartment, though Paul often called her begging her to stay the night whenever his new boyfriend was working at the disco. Paul depended on Valentina in myriad ways. He couldn't bear going to the clinic every day, he couldn't face it, but someone had to go, so Valentina went, reporting on Ray's progress, such as it was.

She also began fretting about Zryd, Robert said that Paul remarked at the time. Valentina voiced the worry, Paul told Robert, that Zryd was "working hours that would even have killed Rudolph," that Zryd seldom left the clinic, even though he had "a magnificent penthouse" across the river in Au, that Zryd had become "obsessed with curing these patients," working round the clock in his laboratory, staying awake on speed, gazing at cell envelopes and protein chains through a microscope, checking blood samples, running tests, all the while debilitatingly understaffed and frenzied because, as Valentina put it, "the poor man needs to have a little fun for a change."

Paul's affair with Chris intensified in proportion to the crisis (Robert said). Now that Paul had regained possession of the master bedroom (Robert said), Chris tended to be there four or five days a week, most of the time (Paul told Robert sardonically) with his legs in the air. It had reached the point (Paul confessed) where all Paul wanted to do was (in his phrase) "make sex," because (he said) "I'm trapped in this horror trip," and the only thing that took his mind off it was the sight of Chris's asshole hanging over the side of the bed (Paul's crude phrase), and that was another thing (Robert said), whenever you went there, you felt they couldn't wait for you to leave, even at ten in the morning (Robert said) certain areas of the flat had a distinctly raunchy odor. All this lubricity (Robert said) had an air of doom about it, because Paul said that he and Chris had both tested positive for HIV, and had therefore dispensed with any kind of protection. "We're just fucking ourselves into nonexistence," Paul told Robert, Robert said.

Chris spent more and more time at the flat. Eventually he started cooking large, intricate meals. Others were invited over, "precisely as if Ray were already dead," Robert said, a remark later echoed by Irma. As an added treat, Robert said without irony, Chris played the accordion, a Scandelli accordion with Lurex-covered bellows and mother-of-pearl inlay, first they'd serve osso bucco or paella for seven and then Chris would trot out the accordion and play "La Vie en Rose" or "Lili Marlene" or "The Boulevard of Broken Dreams" (a big camp), and the guests found themselves singing along like lobotomized idiots, or else Paul forced them to watch his videotapes of Maria Callas rehearsing at St.-Martin's-in-the-Field, or the clips of his interviews with Leni Riefenstahl, Chris meanwhile rolling fat joints until everybody was drunk and stoned. Paul always invited the guests to rummage through the drawer of a built-in hall closet next to the bathroom where he had a whole pharmacy of prescription drugs. He was never happy, Robert told me, unless you did a Tuinal or a Valium or a Mandrax. And things, Robert said, would eventually move into that queasy hyperspace of too many drugs and too many drinks and too many voices talking at once, voices tearing across each other in a room—contentious voices, reminiscent voices, all the past history of everything raked over with a razor blade, everyone wearing his suit of public emotions and attitudes and semiprivate feelings too. And sometimes, Robert said, there would come a moment of true awful gut-wrenching terror at what the future was likely to bring to every person in the room: either death or an endless piling-on of losses until one's entire context, the whole human frame of reference that had made one's life what it was, had been erased line by line, down to a blank slate facing nothingness.

One morning Irma got a call from Valentina, who said she had to talk to her about an urgent manner. Irma had been at the flat a few nights earlier for dinner, Robert said, she had later phoned Robert to ask if he didn't think the situation at Paul's was "a little weird," since everyone had ended up arguing all night about nothing. Irma later told Robert that she had, eerily, been expecting a phone call from Valentina, even though they weren't friends. Valentina had come to see Irma in the play she was doing and left the theater without coming backstage, which Irma interpreted as a slight. But Irma had also had a dream, she told Robert, in which she and Valentina had been obliged to scale a glacier, somewhere in Greenland or Antarctica, the two women roped together. And in the dream, Robert told me, there was a passage involving freezing water, where they had to climb into the sea, wearing heavy clothes, clinging to the side of a raft made of hollow barrels. Irma didn't know what the dream meant, but said there was a horrible kind of "aurora borealis" effect in the sky, with sheets of leaden gray instead of rainbows.

Valentina expounded the problem at a café on Leopoldstrasse. She was dressed emphatically, Irma told Robert, in breezy youthful clothes, this somehow made her look old and wily and suspect, with that unhappy face, Irma said, always so grave and overwrought; Valentina reported that she'd been spending all her free time at the clinic, went into Dr. Zryd and the great work he was doing and how it was making him a virtual prisoner amid all that hopeless suffering—"though we must always hope, mustn't we," Irma says Valentina added quickly, Robert said—and from what she could see, the man was beginning to lose it out there in Bad Endorf, his nerves were all shot, Zryd had told her, Valentina told Irma, that if he didn't get laid pretty soon he would soon have a nervous breakdown. "So of course at first I thought of a prostitute," Valentina said, "but it's so old-fashioned, and then I thought, why not I offer myself, you know? He's terribly attractive, he's young, like us, very hip . . ." Robert said that Valentina enumerated various reasons why she felt she didn't interest Zryd in that way, but it came to her, all of a sudden, remembering they'd shown Zryd a video of *The Laughter in the Next Room,* and how much Irma's performance had interested him, that there might be some chemistry between them—well, Valentina said, the thing is, he's really going nuts. It's just too much tension.

Irma didn't immediately perceive where having sex with Dr. Zryd would benefit Ray, which was somehow the pretext of this meeting, but then Valentina explained that Zryd was the only actual doctor on the clinic staff, and if he fell apart from stress, the clinic might close, and Ray would have to be moved elsewhere, to a hospital probably, or, worse, back home, causing unbelievable problems because Paul now had another boyfriend. And gradually, Irma later told Robert, the weirdness of the whole thing became less weird, began in fact to strike her fancy. She had been asked to do a great many strange things in her life, not just beginning with her discovery in movies, either, and as a general rule, she told Robert, she had done them, mainly out of a bored desire to flout convention. She considered the whole thing for a while and finally agreed, *As long as he knows I'm not a call girl,* she told Valentina. *Tell him we'll just get together without talking, he takes his clothes off, I take off mine, we do it, no discussion.*

The clinic surprised her. Irma expected a chrome-and-glass, Frank Lloyd Wright type of place in the middle of a garden suburb, full of modern fixtures and opaque glass interior walls, a space center control room reception desk, patient and nursing traffic rolling across shiny floors under bright fluorescent lights. Casa Zryd, however, was set back hundreds of yards from a narrow country road, isolated from the town, in a conifer forest, the property line drawn by a high fieldstone wall, pale sodium lights capping the gateposts. A tree-lined avenue of whitewashed gravel led to a two-story Palladian layer cake, the kind of house some superannuated prince might inhabit with scores of bedfast and senile relatives.

Ray had stabilized, Paul told Irma in the car, though his breathing was erratic. Also, he seemed to believe he was in the process of casting a remake of *Quo Vadis* for Rudolph. Ray flickered in and out of the reality picture, Paul said. The last time he brought the clinic into focus, Paul told her, he asked me to read to him. So, Paul had brought along an English edition of *The 120 Days of Sodom*, figuring it wouldn't make any difference what he read, and it was one of Ray's favorite books. Paul had another inspiration as well. You know, he told her, Ray loves to watch. I mean, he said, so do I. He might not know what he's looking at, but what do you say?

A stout nurse in a navy sweater and hospital whites carried a bedpan from Ray's room as they went in. The clinic looked deserted. The whole place had an air of desuetude, like an old-style nursing home. Ray's room in the rear section of the ground floor had tall ornate windows overlooking a neglected garden of box hedges, stone crop, and Japanese hydrangea bushes, all gone to rot, a big boring landscape rolling away behind it with farms tucked in corners of yellowed valleys.

Ray was propped up on pillows. His arms lay at his sides, outside the sheets. Irma noticed the lesions on his arms and face. His head looked as brittle as a Mexican sugar skull. The features were shriveled up into a network of crevices, the brown eyes sunk deep into gray craters, like charred eggs. Paul went around the bed near the window and peered into Ray's face. Irma could hear his labored breathing, and then noticed the ribbed translucent tubes running down from his chest into some large plastic cannisters. The tubes were moving slightly, like bellows, and in the plastic cannisters some kind of fluid was accumulating.

"Here is Irma to visit, Ray," Paul told him.

"Vicinius," Ray muttered. "You pee in the unctorium."

"Does he see me?" Irma asked Paul.

"I wonder."

She marveled that anybody that far gone could still be said to live. The ribbed tubes were sucking fluid out of Ray's lungs, making a regular, frictive, rubbing sound. She told Robert that he showed no sign, just then, of being there in the world in his head, just the dull paralytic gaze, and then she stared into the sad autumn garden and realized the hushed, morbid building was exactly the kind of environment she herself expected to die in. An American army plane roared across the landscape at low altitude.

"Bombs away," said Ray.

Paul walked out of the room. He came back with Zryd, who shook hands with her, looking slightly bewildered and shaggy. They looked each other over, ridiculously, like actors playing a scene.

"You are a very talented woman," Zryd said fatuously.

"No words," she instructed. Paul switched on a bedside lamp. He sat down and opened his book. Irma pulled the doctor to her by the lapels of his lab coat. She kissed his open mouth, running her tongue inside. He started to speak, she put her hand over his mouth. She unzipped his pants and reached inside. She pulled his lab smock off his shoulders and let it drop to the floor. She pushed him against the wall. She hiked her skirt up and yanked her panties down.

"The Duc," Paul whispered into Ray's ear, "Curval, Hercule, and Bum-Cleaver penetrate his ass ungreased."

She rubbed her cunt against Zryd's penis. Paul looked up from his reading and smiled.

"He is whipped very lustily, Messeurs extract four of his teeth . . ."

Irma slid down the doctor's body, crouched before him, took his penis in her mouth.

"As always, each friend has a share in the despoiling of the victim, and Durcet crushes one of his balls between thumb and forefinger."

Zryd seemed passive, she told Robert. She liked his face, his body. It was like acting. She mounted herself on his penis and threw back her head. His pants were bunched around his ankles. Now he slid into her with a vigorous sense of purpose. He lifted her by the thighs, pumping her, as though pride in his physical strength gave him greater pleasure than her body itself. He bit her nipples.

"All four gentlemen soundly flog Augustine. Her glorious ass is soon washed in blood."

The vegetation outside swayed in the wind. Ray sighed. Zryd reached orgasm swiftly, withdrew, wiped his cock with a pocket handkerchief. Then, unthinkingly, he wiped his sweating forehead with the same handkerchief, smearing semen across his brow.

"Fantastic," he said, quickly retreating to his office.

"He's a great man," Paul told her in the car.

"I've had greater," Irma said. "But he's all right."

She was thinking it didn't mean anything, and the more it didn't mean anything, the more it seemed like something out of one of Wieland's movies, or better yet, one of Rudolph's, the scenes where he piled on the horror until you had to laugh. She got off on it, too, as she did in her own films when the man making love to her became confused about what was real and what was acting. That happened a lot in Wieland's pictures because he used so many Turks and other nonactors. They sometimes believed if they touched her breasts or climbed on top of her pretending to screw, that something could actually be happening between them. But Irma immediately understood that the clinic thing was a movie, Paul's movie, and soon it was the same hard work as any movie. They performed variations every afternoon, Paul reading from *Quo Vadis*, or the Bible, or a cookbook, or the Munich telephone directory—it didn't seem to matter. Sometimes Valentina came along. She would go into Zryd's office and open the communicating door and move one of his wing chairs over to an angle where she could observe, Irma didn't much care for that really, but in for a penny in for a pound, she told Robert. Sometimes Ray became lucid, asked them to move this way or that way, he wanted to see Zryd's scrotum pushing at her from behind, or Irma's ass when Zryd entered through the back door, or Zryd's hands squeezing her melons as he mounted her, these specifics were all reported to Robert by Paul, and a little differently by Irma. After the first day, they stripped completely if Ray wanted that or seemed interested; on one occasion he asked the doctor to just leave on the lab coat, and a few times, according to Paul, Robert said, Ray's prick became hard and Paul jerked him off without losing his place in Macaulay's *History of England* or *Jude the Obscure,* but mostly Ray was on the mysterious Planet Debby.

So Paul, Robert said, gave Ray a unique going-away party. Whether it relieved Zryd's stress at all or merely suggested an alternative career in the cinema, who could say. It did seem to make the death a little easier for everybody, including Ray, who expired quietly one afternoon during a recitation of *Mein Kampf,* just as Irma was rimming Zryd over by the window. Ray had been planning aloud the sets for the burning of Rome in *Quo Vadis,* oblivious to the words of Adolf Hitler gently issuing from Paul's lips, when he shut up suddenly and then asked Paul, in a croaking voice, *What were the last words of Veronika Voss?*—and by the time Paul remembered them, Ray had already dropped his body.

16

Where the Railway Meets the River

*T*he next thing, Robert told me, was an acting job Paul took on a shoot in Malta, and after that he traveled around to Paris and London, looking up friends, avoiding other friends. Valentina was left with the chore of notifying the other friends about Ray's death. She did this in rather a perfunctory manner, despite the aggrieved voice she used on the phone: she told everyone about Paul going to Malta and his being too upset to talk and said he would get in contact eventually. A long time passed, Robert said, with no word from Paul whatsoever. Meanwhile, Robert heard that Chris had died, carried off with remarkable speed by pneumonia.

One day, apparently by chance, Paul did pick up the telephone when Robert rang the flat, and before he could make an excuse to hang up Robert insisted on meeting him somewhere. They met in the café on the ground floor of Paul's building. Paul looked like he'd been sleeping in his clothes, distracted, pallid. He chain-smoked and ordered coffee after coffee. He fidgeted with a paper napkin and tore it into tiny pieces. Terrible overwrought silences stretched between bursts of disconnected chatter. Paul groped for words, ideas. His hands gestured strangely, as if fingering an elusive ectoplasm. He talked of going to America. He mentioned hooking up again with Alex to make another movie. He said he had an idea for a comedy set in India, about two servants running a house owned by Greta Garbo.

"Guests arrive, wanting to see Miss G., and the servants make it impossible for them." He said he'd had Ray cremated. The ashes were in a little urn, he said, a stainless steel urn that looked like a cocktail shaker. When spring came, he said, he and Valentina would fly with the ashes to Australia, stopping here and there along the way to visit friends.

Paul rubbed his unshaven jaw with his dirty fingers. Robert told him the important thing was to work through his grief and somehow go on with life. Paul nodded agreement but without conviction. Lighting another cigarette, wiping his smeary glasses on a napkin, he glanced around the crowded café and said he was deathly tired of life and of looking at the same streets, the same restaurants, the same dreadful people—and anywhere else was worse, or the same, a complete trap. Paul remarked, according to Robert, if you begin to take an interest, pretend that tomorrow begins a new day, *then you've really had it.* Robert saw that Paul struggled to inhabit the moment rather than cave in under awful feelings. Paul took a little pill, he noticed. A while later Paul said, "Do you know, after all these years I at last made a little pilgrimage to Dachau?"

This recent memory seemed to focus his thoughts. As he described the trip, he became more himself. Paul said that he had arranged a little trip to Munich for Michael Simard, "who is working as a rent boy," Paul told Robert, offering to pay him something like a thousand dollars for the weekend. But before Michael Simard arrived, Paul looked up Billy Sauberman and copped several doses of Mickey Mouse blotter acid. He sent

Valentina away (she was half-living in the apartment by then) and prepared himself for a weekend of heavy sex. He had an idea that had come to him, Robert said, as most of Paul's ideas came—that is to say, marching in heavy boots through his brainpan—and when he left for the airport he took the acid along with him.

Michael Simard looked even more like a GQ layout, having pumped himself relentlessly at the Chelsea Gym, and stepped off the seven-hour flight flawlessly groomed, in a green trench coat, black hair slicked back in a fashionable ponytail, the composed beauty of his face impassive as an executioner.

"Welcome to Germany."

"It's been quite a long time, hasn't it."

"Here, darling, put this under your tongue."

As they drove on the autobahn, Michael talked. He talked about his job. He now serviced many famous people, and they all had little kinks.

"Many clients?"

"A lot of regular clients. Some days I do a lot, sometimes only one or two a week."

"How many have you ever done in one night?"

"Oh, I don't know, three or four; if it starts early in the day, it could be as many as six."

"And you spend an hour with each one?"

"An hour, or sometimes less, sometimes a little longer."

"When you do so many, how do you manage to get a hard-on each time?"

"Well, the best thing is if you don't have to come. If someone sucks me I can usually manage a boner."

"But then it goes limp when you try to fuck them?"

"Very rarely. You get used to the condom."

"Do you advertise in the gay papers? Or just go to hustler bars?"

"If clients drop off, I run an ad. I mean, look, Paul, this isn't my vocation or anything. But it's good to make a thousand dollars in a couple days, it makes you feel you have a stake in the economy."

The padded steering wheel beneath Paul's fingers began to exhibit an organic tension, like the evenly muscled flesh of a boa constrictor. They talked about a famous murder case.

"I told him," Michael was saying. "I said, I *know* Andrew, I've *done* Andrew. He *does* enjoy piss, he *does* get into whipping. But no way would he have shot that Norwegian kid . . ."

The leafless branches overhanging the road were faintly haloed in Freon blue and green against a dense, lavender gray cloud bank, as if they'd been dipped in water and laid against pillows of litmus paper.

"But they say the other guy shot him," Paul said. "While Andrew screwed him."

The clouds sparkled with pink energy. They churned into blocky shapes of crabs and dolphins. Michael's American voice reached him in scratchy wriggles of sound he could barely make sense of. Paul clenched his jaw to keep the road focused.

"I know the Filipino," Michael said. "His father works for the UN. He's a shit queen."

"The Filipino's father is a shit queen?"

"No, the kid, the kid. Ties you down, shits in your mouth. I don't get into it at either end unless somebody's really special, and that kid isn't. *Andrew* on the other hand likes to give pain, he likes to humiliate, but he knows where the limits are. It wouldn't surprise me if the Filipino snorted too much coke and went out of control."

Light traffic on the motorway consisted of noisy motes of chrome, gusts of exhaust, salt-crusted car windows. Indistinct faces framed in tinted windows. Paul moved his hand across the foamy ridges of the seat, over the firm casing of Michael's trouser leg, lodged between Michael's thighs. Michael shifted on his spine, thrusting his crotch closer. As Paul fondled his heavy penis through the fabric, Michael's expression remained bright, neutral. His brittle fingers, lower joints sprouting vivid black hairs, brushed the back of Paul's hand. The pyramidal roofs of the Dachau guardhouses drifted into view.

"Could you do that?" Paul wanted to know. "Just shoot somebody?"

"Me? Fuck, man, not my scene."

"If somebody made it sexy for you? And the guy wore a leather hood over his face?"

"Hey, I don't believe in that shit."

Paul steered the car into the parking area. "What if there were no consequences? If you could absolutely get away with it?"

Michael thought about it and smiled.

"Don't put ideas in my head."

There were five other cars in the lot, where rain from earlier in the day had puddled and begun to freeze. The cold surprised him as they got out. The drug danced on his nerve ends. His teeth clattered uncontrollably. Michael hopped eagerly on the pavement, vapor streaming from his nostrils. They walked along the slick path, crunching parchment sheets of ice, over a thicket of spidery plane tree branches reflected in splotches of congealing water. Ahead was a sliding gate, half-open, maple branches entangled in loops of accordion wire. On the inner grounds, small groups of visitors walked along the edges of a concrete embankment, separated from the flat gravel walk facing the entrance by a ditch and a barbed-wire fence.

The fence was strung between concrete pylons. On the side of each pylon a metal-shaded floodlamp was trained on the rock slope and the concrete ditch. Hooked iron rods poked from the tops of the pylons, supporting the top strand of barbed wire. Across the ditch at the edge of the slope, a margin of grass massed in electric green profusion.

The tourists moved around the corner of a reconstructed barracks. Paul forced himself to walk in that direction. His innards vibrated. He touched Michael's fingers. He thought he felt Michael's fingerprints, hair-thin ridges of identity merging with his own. The vibration in his body was overwhelmingly pleasant and a little sickening. He felt colors on his skin, mauve and yellow on his arms, crawling over his chest. Panels of ultraviolet light jumped through the air. Looking at Michael, he saw blood seeping from the soft parts of his skull. The air glued a breath of sap and decaying leaves to his nostrils.

Three tourist groups ranged irregularly between the ghost spaces of the barracks that had been razed after the war. Their figures wobbled in and out of sight, at times merging with trees and earth. Michael's face became a collection of squirming sea life, minnows and smelts and crayfish, pulsing under a cellophane skin. The fish mutated into parts of birds, leaves, vegetable roots. The pale yellow sweater under Michael's trenchcoat cupped his chin, holding the bits and pieces together, preventing his skull from snapping apart and disgorging his brain. Reptile lips slithered in worm motion. The nose sucked air into red cankered lungs that billowed under layers of flesh and fabric. As they reached the barracks, Paul devised a little mantra to organize the chaos in front of his eyes. Not so bad, not so bad, he whispered. Not so bad.

The fact that it wasn't so bad rubbed at his brain. The building resembled a subway car, the insides sanitized and solemn as a Lutheran chapel. A grid of bunks looked like vegetable bins. Here they slept. He looked for brain matter and shredded convict uniforms in the pinewood architecture of precise diagonals, calibrated shadows, a place as lacking in horror as Heidegger's cottage in Todtnauberg.

Something yelled inside him that he didn't want to know about. He and Michael entered a reconstructed washroom. Paul later told Robert that at this point he recalled an account of Auschwitz-

Birkenau about a trench so fetid with blood and maggots and corpses that prisoners, faced with the prospect of cleaning it out, preferred to be shot. Here all was clean. Two massive metal washstand saucers, mounted on pedestals pierced by fat hydraulic pipes, caught dull light from four contiguous windows in the far wall. The washstands and windows were insanely symmetrical: "like everything," Paul later told Robert, "in this roaring disease of a country." A thought danced unavoidably into his brain, announcing itself as the terrible secret of Dachau: "This is kitsch."

He felt phlegmy tar from a million cigarettes cling to the soft lobes of his lungs. He scanned Michael's face, which was growing a crust of weariness from travel and spectral dabs here and there from thousands of Jewish ghosts. But the fastidious room had never contained any victims, some professional atrocity memorialist had supervised its reconstruction. The ghosts had seeped into the ground, the air. At the end of the room a door led to a lavatory with eight ceramic toilet basins lining one wall, symmetrical, lidless, the repeated form suggesting a mold for plaster casts of the human face. Paul imagined millions of human faces gazing up out of a million toilet bowls.

Grimy bands of magenta and blue vibrated in the air like bands of exhausted confetti. Paul summoned images of pissing and shitting prisoners, heads shaved, forearms tattooed, emaciated, haggard, walking dead. But the pictures crumbled, leaving the single brittle image of an artwork for mass guilt. Not stark, but "stark," not moving, but "moving," like everything arranged to stir the dead conscience of the world. And all the dead abandoned by God seemed doubly abandoned by the implacable transformation of emotions into kitsch.

Michael's skin was becoming translucent. He would soon turn to stone, Paul thought, to mica, or devolve into a poisonous green lizard, black tongue flicking, or a great smelly cheese oozing oily moisture. They said nothing. They sensed when to move from the shifting quality of the silence.

Outside, a concourse lined with skeletal poplars ran the length of the former concentration camp. The sites of vanished barracks were marked off with stubby plywood borders. The earth inside them was raised, mulched with debris. Their shoes crunched on the gravel. A rift in the clouds revealed a streak of liquid turquoise. A band of Scotch pines and pin oaks fluttered like a feather boa draped across the horizon. Michael asked hoarsely:

"Did you eat today?"

"Don't tell me this is making you hungry."

"I had something on the plane."

"I would like a cigarette, though."

Paul laughed and shivered and Michael laughed at his shivering. The laughter fell like an act of vandalism in the freezing gloom.

"This is where they killed people?"

"It was more like a work camp. The big killing places were in Poland mostly."

Michael shook his head. "I should know more about that stuff than I do. I always meant to read up on it."

The path continued over a canal to the crematorium. They paused on a blunt narrow bridge and stared at a dense growth of birches and pines along the canal bank. Strands of barbed wire extended above the bridge railing. The silver-black water, shirred by a strong current, flowed over the knotted roots of dying locust trees. Michael's expression was intense yet unreadable, Paul later told Robert. He remains completely mysterious, Paul told Robert, as if he had no real existence as a person, but were only an ideal of beauty.

When they came within sight of the main crematorium, a somber parade of foreigners were marching away from it, heading back over the bridge. The area appeared deserted now. The acid would peak very soon, Paul realized. The bricks of the crematorium breathed and expanded and shrank back into their grooves. Paul marched close to the wall, running his fingertips over the bricks. Michael trailed him, hands stuffed into his trench coat. Paul felt the grass slither underfoot. He lost his place in the story. Once upon a time, there was a little boy whose mother lived with him all alone in a contaminated forest. He froze and threw his back against the wall and stared at the chill sky. In his head he spoke to the emptiness behind the clouds and wished for a primal moment, as a strong wind surged up from the south. Once upon a time, there was a mother and a boy.

They walked across the rolling lawn behind the crematorium. Once upon a time, they went to the witch's house. And there the wolf who had eaten the old grandmother, but they left a trail of crumbs. And then a sparrow came and ate the crumbs. Only the prince can find the pearl in the bottom of the sea, only his lips can wake the princess. They approached the smaller crematorium, near a trimmed bare arbor vitae hedge. *Thank God that no one knows my name is really Rumpelstiltskin.*

It was a plain garagelike building with a peaked tile roof, its walls brushed by frostbitten quince bushes. We're coming to the end, Paul thought, he later told Robert. His mind jumped its tracks again. He was twelve years old, with his friend from school, a boy named Peter Seitz, fetching a rake from the potting shed where the dust held the sharp smell of fertilizer. They piled leaves from the elm tree, raked bales of leaves into tall mounds and ran skidding into them and touched, he touched him through the crackling leaves, later the leaves were burned. Smoke on frosty afternoons gone long ago today tomorrow and then gone forever.

"You can still get a boner?" Paul asked.

"Are you kidding?" Michael said. "I *have* one."

A wreath affixed to the oven. Bare cement floor. Two metal grates set into it at the base of two brick kilns flanking the main oven. It was never used, he recalled. Fire is not your friend, he thought. The middle oven resembled an altar: two arched chambers, like cartoon eyelids, oxidized doors yawning open on corroded hinges. Bring me your poor, your tired. Small rectangular openings below. Chimney pipes ran from the crest of the brickwork into the roof. There was an empty space behind the incineration area, barred by a wrought iron gate.

And then, Paul later told Robert, as everything unfolded, the scattered lyrics of a dozen sappy songs whistled through his brain, kitsch for the kitsch-hearted, he said. *If ever I would leave you,* Paul climbed over the gate, *it wouldn't be in summer.* A dank, empty space between the ovens and the wall. *There's a place for us, somewhere a place for us.* Michael swung his leg over the railing. *Pardon me boy, is this the Chattanooga Choo-choo?* They wouldn't be invisible from the main room, but it did provide a modicum of privacy.

This is a good space, Paul thought. A wasted space. A space that would have been used for stacking corpses, clean as a German floor. *Take one fresh and tender kiss.* He unbuttoned his shirt, shucking off his parka. A drizzle of colored atoms congealed in the chamber. *Add one stolen night of bliss.* One boy, one girl, functioning incinerator, memories are made of this.

Orange light exploded in the room. Memories. War photographs. Soldiers caked with mud. Rotted boots. Smell of carbolic acid, cinders speckling the air. He sank his fingers into Michael's face. It came apart in soggy clumps of fat, bloody muck plopped onto butcher paper. Squids in a metal bin. Jagged hole opening. Veins stitched across a sticky membrane that covered wet fragments of bone. Inside the blue hole, the skinned head of a ferret. Alien life form sucking gristle from the walls of the cavity. Blue fingers wrestled off Michael's clothes. The sweater came away with a gout of hair and scalp attached.

Green vapor and the smell of disinfectant swirled from the

ovens. Red pinpoints strobed in the billowing fog. Michael pulled off his shoes. He slid off his belt. Flesh melted from Paul's body as he shed his clothes. Sirens in the camp. Boots thudding over frozen earth near the perimeter fence. Bursts of submachine gun fire.

The crematorium shook with the concussion of an antiaircraft barrage. Fleshless fingers tugged off Michael's jockstrap. Paul gripped Michael's inflamed penis. *There's no business like show business, like no business I know.* Their torsos collided. Skeletons raked through soft flesh. *Everything about it is appealing!* Their ribs fused. *Blue moon.* Paul pulled at Michael's hair and unfastened the ponytail. *You saw me standing alone.* His eyes. His throat. Michael shoved him against the oven. His tongue darted into the hole between Paul's lips. *I want you. I need you.* Paul's teeth fastened to the slimy gland. *Am I blue? Am I blue?* Blood, salt and thick, coursed into his throat. He felt the armature of Michael's body convulse. *Do you know how to pony? Like bony maroney?* Michael flipped him around, smashing Paul's chest into the wall.

Paul's cardrums fluttered as the sirens rose again. *It goes like this it goes like this.* Paul flattened his hands against the spackled cement. He bent forward with his legs spread. *Up there, there is a sea,* Michael crouched behind him digging fingers into Paul's hips. He lubricated the anus with his bleeding tongue. *St. Louis woman, with all your diamond rings, drag that man around by your apron strings.* Michael dropped one hand to jerk himself off. Green smoke rose between their bodies in the blue crematorium. *If it weren't for powder and all that store-bought hair.* Paul heard the troops marching like thunder, past the incinerators, motorcycles revving up, exhaust furrowing the highway yards away. *I've got you under my skin.* The flower of Abyssinia was opening. The sky was raging. The Lord is my shepherd, I shall not want. Michael's spitwet member slid into the opening. He maketh me to lie down in green pastures. The hole opened like the Red Sea. He leadeth me beside the still waters. *Fuck my hole, Mr. Death.* He restoreth my soul. Arteries. *You do something to me.* Scent of rectal mucous. Faint nauseating tang of roasted flesh. Yea, though I walk through the valley of the shadow of death, I will fear no evil for thou art with me. Michael's arms wrapped around him. His nipples were changing color. The limbs of a preying mantis encircled him.

Slice me up. The tongue bleeds over his shoulder. His organ is wet. His balls. The rectum gyrates around the stone-hard penis. In between. Two mineral beings freeze in the bleak diorama. The bodies turn to stone as pictures of skyrockets pinwheels flaming cities flash. Phosphenes. Anemonies palpitating under the cement floor. *Kiss me feel me kill me.* Paul flattened himself against the oven. He merged with the oven. They locked like dogs. The cock inside him spurted a cold acrid kerosene odor that permeated the room. They stagged away from the ovens locked together and collapsed after a grotesque waltz. Paul's face hit the floor. Michael's hips continued shaking. Fucking him face down, Michael swept the floor with his arms, grabbing up socks and underwear and jamming them under Paul's face. *Smell me.* His smooth buttocks translucent globes in a Bosch painting. Paul's come spurted on the cement. *What God has joined together.* Michael pulled out of him. He pushed Paul over on his back and stood over him, squatting over his face. He pumped his cock while the crematorium echoed his heavy breathing, gasped as he released a jet of opalescent semen, splattering Paul's eyelids. He squeezed the last drops of come into Paul's open mouth and uttered a cry of bewildered ecstasy.

The cold woke him, twitching, a pain in his side bringing the room back together. Pale light from a high window. Veins and bubbles in the wall plaster. They dressed with heavy, awkward movements, breath forming weak trails of varicolored vapor. Over the gate. The touch of metal on his palms sent a sharp metallic taste to his mouth. He watched the grim architecture settle into an old picture frame. Michael glazed over, wrapping himself in his coat with crisp, methodical movements. Paul felt for a marking pen he had in his jacket and wrote HIV on the glass door of the oven.

After they crossed the funereal esplanade of withered trees and entered the parking lot, Michael made a troubled face as if he expected something to come and punish him. Then he began to laugh. As Paul later told Robert, it was just another weird scene.

17
Greenwich Street

*I*n April that year, Rita Stone phoned me to say that Paul and Valentina were arriving in New York the next day. Rita Stone was a friend of many years who had met Paul in Australia, during the period between the filming of *The Laughter in the Next Room* and its premiere at the Berlin Film Festival. They had shot a small film together in Sydney, at Ray's house, that ended up being shown with the longer film—in other words, they became friends, Paul and Rita, and this time, on the occasion of Paul's first visit to New York after Ray's death, he would stay with Rita instead of staying at his beloved Gramercy Park Hotel.

I did not hear from him upon his arrival, a change from all previous times, and when he did call, on Tuesday, he proposed that we meet on Saturday, several days off, again a change from all previous times. I surmised that he was putting me off until the end of his stay, arranging things so that we would only meet once. It was all quite different than any previous time.

The buds were bursting on the trees that Saturday. I walked to Rita's old place, in one of those warehouses near the river, with a loading dock sticking out in front, paint-caked door buzzer dangling from wires on the door frame. The sidewalk under the loading dock's caved in, with weeds sprouting in the cracks, the usual mess of crushed take-out containers, cigarette packs, bits of glass, the floorboards under the door rotting, trucks full of Mafia-controlled upholstery backing in and out. As I told Robert, all the buildings on Rita's side of the street have that geriatric riverfront look. The street runs from the World Trade Center up through Tribeca and SoHo, almost flush with the river, and then it changes into West Street after that mess of streets around Canal and the Holland Tunnel. On the other side of the street, there are three high-rise towers put up in the early 1970s, a municipal experiment in mixed-income housing.

It is an area, as I told Robert, thickly polluted by memories. I remember dozens of parties at Rita's loft, as I told Robert—1978, 1979. In 1980, Rita gave me a birthday party, a joint party with someone born on the same day, whom I haven't seen in ten years. In 1980, half the people I knew lived in lofts in that part of town, and there were always parties. To give you an idea, I said to Robert, these were massive, drugged-out saturnalias of artists, writers, filmmakers, musicians. It was quite a fluid mix, I told Robert. We were all young. That communal feeling we had then dried up pretty fast, I said, what with careers and marriages, deaths and failures. Time and fevers, burn away.

When you go down there now, I said, the sidewalks are mined with embittered individuals. These relics from the old days, not Rita and her set, but art world types, painters and so on, who never made it. Strange, fuzzy persons who have finally figured out that nothing is going to happen for them. Those artists, I said, still have those cheap lofts and probably an NEA grant or two, and that's about it. Then too, I pointed out, there are the ones who were famous twenty years ago and lost their fame in stages. The minor conceptual artists, the earth artists, that sort of artist. These people, I told Robert, wander around those streets angry and muddled, unable to figure out exactly what has happened to them. It must be intolerable, I said, to realize that your best years are behind you.

The sky was brilliant blue, with little clouds the shape of teapots floating in it. Still chilly in the shade. That Saturday had the slack feeling of early spring, when the weather will no longer switch back into winter. It's the only time, I told Robert, that New York is really nice.

I squeezed the doorbell. I knew that Paul had to come down, because the door doesn't buzz open. He had mentioned, I said, that they were taking Ray's ashes to Australia, and yet, for some reason, I kept imagining that Paul would be the same as he always was. I had recently gotten over a horrible love affair that made me insane for two years, and getting over it had created an illusion that one can recover from anything. Somehow I had assumed that Paul would emerge from his grief in the same way, and start his life over again.

I stood outside for twenty minutes. I pressed the bell again. I paced around on the sidewalk. I smoked cigarettes. I looked at the apartment complex across the road. I once knew a friend who lived in one of those towers, on the twenty-second floor, with a stupendous view of New York Harbor and the Statue of Liberty. It was an awesome view, I told Robert, and I have often thought that if I had had such a view, such a commanding, effulgent, transcendent view of my surroundings, my life would have been very different. But the fact is, I said, I have never had such a view, far from it.

The bottom deck of the towers is a one-story plaza that contains a delicatessen and a video store and a locksmith shop. Various people were grazing the sidewalk, black ladies in hats and bulky cloth coats, pallid white girls with stringy hair pushing baby strollers, skinny teenage boys of both colors in leather jackets, kids on skateboards, kids with Walkmen. I saw that this tissue box plaza was really a self-contained little world. It would gradually connect itself to the World Financial Center in the distance, and the landfill condominiums around the World Financial Center, and other brand-new buildings going up along the riverfront. A ribbon of dismal middle-class normality was spinning itself out right across the street from the sagging row of warehouses, two distinct worlds, a world of bright mediocrity and a world of festering obscurity and spiritual pain.

There are times, I told Robert, swirling the ice in my glass, when a look or a shred of conversation from twenty years ago comes back to me with intensely concentrated ferocity, when a gesture or a sudden noise throws open a doorway at the end of a long narrow corridor of the faraway past, and then you can make out shapes and faces, forms, colors in the distance, at the threshold of recognition. What you really remember isn't what happened at a particular moment, I told Robert, but what you thought about yourself and the world you were living in back then, what you expected or dreamed that the future might be, how you interpreted reality at the time. What happened last week or last month, I said, sometimes settles into such remoteness you can't reclaim the smallest fraction of it, because it's still consistent with your picture of how things are. But once the picture changes, I said, the past stands out differently.

I only noticed how long Paul was taking because I saw all the cigarette butts I'd squashed out on the sidewalk. I buzzed again. This time, he immediately opened a window up there, and said he'd come down. I got a quick look at his face. It was an unusually perfunctory moment. His face was the face you give the delivery boy.

"You'll have to come up," he told me when he opened the door. "I've lost the keys. I can't find them, I've looked everywhere."

He had more lines around the eyes, but otherwise, I said to Robert, the actor look had come back, the actor face, with that poreless skin. He wore a black sweater and jeans and a pair of Nike sneakers, which wasn't his usual look at all. I thought, "This is how he dresses now." I thought this meant he had relaxed his terse, chipper business style, or else given up. Before, he'd always worn The Suit. The look. The Rolex. That owlish expression, as though he were always taking notes. So people would know he had irons on the fire, I said, meetings to make, planes to catch. I connected this new, slouchy look with Valentina, and with something Paul had told me on the phone about "flying first-class around the world on stolen credit cards," he'd mentioned lifting valuables from purses on the flights, pilfered emeralds or something. I don't know what it was all about. Paul always inflated little stories, Robert said. Maybe they pulled some scam or other that gave him a romantic fantasy of the two of them as jet-set pirates, or jewel thieves. In spite of the melancholy nature of their journey, and for that matter the wintry bleakness of Paul's whole existence at the time, the plain fact is that even in total hopelessness we go on hoping for things, Robert told me, spinning out narratives, casting ourselves in imaginary movies. And Paul, Robert said, had cast himself and Valentina as a "wild couple," willing strange and crazy things to happen to them. His stakes, Robert said, had been pulled up for him by other people's deaths. And hers—well, Robert observed, pouring himself another drink, *her* stakes always seemed firmly planted in other people's backs.

Rita's building has that endless Tribeca staircase effect, where you just keep climbing and climbing.

"I was all prepared for us to spend a lovely day together," Paul said, "and now, you see, we really can't leave the house. Valentina has gone to look at the Statue of Liberty. Rita has gone to Long Island for her nephew's bar mitzvah."

"I haven't been here for a while."

"It's a beautiful day out, too, isn't it. You're working hard on your book, I hope? I wonder if it will ever be finished."

Finally you come into an enormous living room, varnished wood floors, sofas, desks, bookcases, bicycles, a few potted cacti and leafy plants.

"When I started that book so many years ago," I said, "it began with a description of staying in an apartment a few blocks down the road from here, right next to the Trade Center."

"Oh yes? And was it still called *Burma* even then?"

The middle of the loft is partitioned into bedrooms with walls that don't quite reach to the ceiling. A narrow corridor leads down to the kitchen at the other end: industrial sink, cupboards, coat-racks, a big oak table covered with newspapers, coffee cups, magazines, et cetera. Homey as a potholder.

"Even then," I said, "it was called *Burma* and there was nothing in it about Burma, I think now it was about wanting to go to these perfectly preserved pockets of the past, Albania or Burma or Prague or Bucharest. So you could escape all the negative motion of accelerating time. I remember that the Trade Center made this horrific hollow ringing noise all night, and the streets were extremely desolate. I remember it began by evoking a sense of loss, and just think, I hadn't even begun to lose anything yet."

"Well, as you're such a bright person, you knew it was coming."

It began, I thought, with a scraping sound. As soon as we came into the kitchen I spotted the keys, in plain sight on the table. Paul had been rummaging everywhere as he talked, searching through dishes in a drying rack, even in the refrigerator.

"Look, they're right here."

"Oh. So they are. My God—you come in and find them like that."

I knew why he hadn't found them. I recognized that dread of

the next minute, the next movement. The fear of putting one foot in front of the other because everything beyond the front door will remind you of things you don't wish to think about. So to keep things suspended a little while longer, you lose your keys, or decide you have to change your clothes, or clean the apartment before you go out.

"Let me make a cup of coffee. Want a cup of coffee? Then we can go somewhere for lunch? Where would you like to go? We could go near your house, or down here, or the West Village . . . ?"

Everything, I told Robert that night at the Chelsea, everything that afternoon was jangled, brittle, even though it was warm it was also cold, cold like northern Europe is cold, that kitchen was cold the way flats in Amsterdam and Berlin are cold even when the sun is shining, and the mess of newspapers on the table, and the coffee rings on the wood, and the smears of brown instant coffee on the spoon, and Paul's black sweater, a turtleneck, and his hair and his glasses, in the beige plastic frames, and there were little moments within moments, moments when a little upsweep of yesterday's high humor wafted through the pale northern cold of Paul's depression. He filled the kettle. He lit a gas jet on the stove.

"Amazing," he said. "You walk in and lay your hands right on them. Amazing."

"I've missed you, Paul. I'm really sorry about Ray."

It was already almost a year. Somehow, as if he doubted my capacity for empathy, or was making a deliberate effort to abstract himself from his feelings, he began to compare his loss to the devastating love affair I'd had two years earlier, and cited similarities between what had happened to us—a comparison I myself had entertained in my head, but which on further reflection completely trivialized what had happened to Ray. It seemed a grotesque way of "equalizing" our different experiences, and I wondered, in my paranoid way, if this reflected a deeply entrenched pattern in our relations, in other words, that one of us couldn't lay claim to an experience unless it was mirrored in that of the other. But maybe, I thought, I told Robert, by casting it in miniature, Paul is attempting to climb out of his despair and take a renewed interest in life.

". . . and, worse, all the time he's dying, can you imagine, I get into this insane sexual obsession with a completely different person, and now *he's dead, too,* from AIDS . . ."

What do you say then?

"If it wasn't for Valentina, even if you don't like her, I assure you, I'd never have survived any of this, really, she's been incredibly loyal, all through. If you need Valentina, she really sticks by you, she really takes charge of the situation."

I thought about Valentina taking charge, I told Robert, even then, it seemed she had taken charge where Paul was concerned, because he mentioned her every five minutes. He seemed like himself, I told Robert, but he wasn't himself, and the more he seemed like himself the less like himself he really was. He told me about the clinic, I said, about putting Ray in the clinic and he said Ray had allowed that to happen only to spare Paul having to take care of him, and to let Paul have the idea that Paul was perhaps going to save him. Because, Paul said, I told Robert, Ray knew perfectly well he wasn't going to make it. And then, I said, Paul told me he was HIV positive and scared stiff of going out the way Ray did, and then he said, I remember precisely:

"The worst that could happen to me has already happened, and now the only thing left is the intelligent planning of my suicide."

The odd way he said it, I told Robert, made us both laugh. I had an absurd faith that I could talk him out of this idea. Anyway, I said, we take a cab to the West Village. In the cab, Paul wants to hear everything I know about AIDS: are things worse now, or better, has there been any progress, what are people saying? I see the trend of his questions and tell him that people survive much longer now with a good quality of life. Now, I say, there is AZT. Of course, I told Robert, I'm lying a bit, the AZT is completely poisonous and the best it can do is keep you alive a couple of years in and out of hospitals, but it seemed, at the time, the beginning of progress against the disease, I said, of course we know now, it was never a priority or intention of the government here to actually cure this disease, I told Robert, but rather to keep it confined to certain despised groups, here it is 1991, I said, and no more real progress has been made since then, in 1987, though of course there are all sorts of little stopgap treatments for specific kinds of opportunistic illnesses.

I told him, I said to Robert, that if he did start getting sick he absolutely had to come to America where Rita and I could take care of him. I did believe, I told Robert, we could get much better medical care for him here than in Munich. I now realize, I said, how much money it costs to save your own life in America, a malignant tumor of a country where having any serious illness amounts to financial ruin. This pestilent country, I told Robert, lives by the philosophy of kill or be killed, your money or your life, I suppose it would've ruined me and ruined Rita, I said, if we had had to take care of him. However, I said, I secretly believed that nothing really bad could happen to Paul. I don't know why I believed that, I said, especially since something bad had already happened to him.

I don't remember, I said, where we ate, or what we talked about at lunch, I can't retrieve it, I've tried a million times, what was our small talk on such an occasion, knowing that at least one and possibly both of you will be dead in the not too distant future, at least in all likelihood. At the time, I said, there was still a belief that only a certain percentage of persons with HIV infection progressed to full-blown AIDS, there hadn't been enough studies . . . Now, of course, it's thought that a hundred percent sooner or later succumb. At any rate, we went to a different place for coffee, and he ate a slice of carrot cake. I would like to know, I said, why I happen to remember that. Carrot cake. Memory is so capricious.

Then we went to Boots and Saddles, a bar where the sadomasochist cowboy look has always enjoyed a great vogue. It was full of tall people with unattractive facial hair. I told Paul that I would go to Greece in July. I had rented a house in Santorini. I had come into some money. Years ago, I had filed a lawsuit against the surgeon who did my face, it had finally come up on the court calendar and the doctor's malpractice insurer had decided to settle.

I felt it was important to tie Paul to some definite plan in the middle future. Keep hope alive, and all that lark. So I told him I would pay his ticket if he came to Greece, and rather than make a big portentous statement about what he should or shouldn't do, I tried to make it sound slightly wank, as if by coming there he'd be getting away with something—cheating the inevitable, maybe.

"We can seduce young Greek boys," I suggested.

We finished our beers and walked around the corner to a news shop. Paul rummaged through some porn magazines, commenting on the models. It's strange, he said, isn't it, what a variety of us there is. He bought a few magazines. I'm going to buy some food for the house, he said. I thought it was time to say good-bye, but something stopped me. The way the street looked, or the traffic, or the hopeless inane little bits of conversation I heard as people moved past us on the sidewalk, a fire hydrant somebody's pit bull was pissing against. I stood facing him at the curb, and behind him, out of a manhole cover, a plume of thick gray steam rose and spread through the air, as if hell were throwing up a fog in which to whisk him off. I was suddenly overwhelmed by a sense of total chaos in the world and the feeling I would never see him again. And I tell you, Robert, I said, Paul was one of the few people in my life that I could talk to, one of the few people who understood me. I never had to explain anything to him, he already knew.

We went into the corner grocery, a mom-and-pop store. Paul took a shopping basket and began tearing through the place. He threw in a bottle of orange juice, then a bottle of grapefruit juice, a six-pack of Heineken, a jug of cranberry juice. Cheese. Cheddar cheese, brie cheese, blue cheese, provolone. Sweet Italian sausage. Hot Italian sausage. More cheese. A head of lettuce. A dozen eggs. Pretty soon the basket was overflowing. He picked up an item, looked at it, threw it in, then mumbled, "Oh, what if Rita doesn't like this kind," or "Valentina likes these," dropped two or three more items in, and I looked at all these packaged goods, all this shit, in one tiny store, in one little neighborhood, full of so much plastic and glass and cardboard you could pollute a whole country with it, and I thought, there are millions of these stores, millions of these cheeses in boxes and milk cartons and Styrofoam egg containers and millions of assholes shitting it all out, chewing it up, shitting it out, but of course you can't keep this kind of idea in your head for very long.

Paul's got one basket on the checkout counter and now he's filling up another one, I told Robert, which is ridiculous, he's leaving the next morning and Rita and her husband never cook at home, and then I realize, I said, that he doesn't want to leave the store. First he didn't want to leave the house, now he doesn't want to leave the store. Once he's done the shopping, that will be the end of something, and something else will have to start. So we spent another forty minutes picking over all the shit in this convenience store, sifting through the same shelves and refrigeration cases, piling up jars of pickles and cocktail onions and tubes of anchovy paste and capers and tubs of cottage cheese until there wasn't another thing Paul could buy without looking like a complete maniac. This is not a supermarket but an overpriced convenience store, nobody buys four bags of groceries in that kind of store. We had a real job loading it all into a cab, and then Paul got in, and neither of us wanted to make a big deal out of saying good-bye, but it really was too perfunctory, in the end, and then he shut the door and waved out the back window. I tried to hold a picture of us wrapped around a Retsina bottle on some terrace in the Greek islands as I walked home, but the picture kept dissolving, and I knew it was never going to happen.

Gone Tomorrow

*H*ere's how it was, said Robert: long before he even came to New York, he told Valentina what he was going to do, he was afraid to do it really, and first he wanted to take Ray's ashes to Sydney and stop everywhere that he knew people and take a last look around, say his farewells—even if he didn't come right out with it, most people figured out that Paul was saying good-bye, either figured it out at the time, said Robert, or figured it out afterward. That final year, Robert said, she said she'd stay with him, but he'd have to put some things in writing. So he did.

Paul needed her to keep reality at arm's length, send the checks to pay the bills, answer the phone calls, take care of business. There were residuals and percentages and other bits of money floating around, and Ray's estate had to be settled. That's what they did in Sydney. Sold the house, liquidated the business, dealt with the lawyers, took the ashes up in a helicopter over the bay and poured them out.

She took over his private life as well. She kept him from getting too involved in things. She became like his mother, his wife, advising him on this, on that: this was a person who had given up, Robert said, and you know that a great relief spreads over someone who has finally given up, a terrific sense of relaxation—Paul didn't have to be a magpie anymore, he didn't have to be witty or funny or tell gossip anymore, he could be like a convalescent on sedatives, or someone who's been through an earthquake or a plane crash. And of course, Robert said, the queer thing was, he wasn't really sick, he didn't show any signs, he was all there and he wasn't there, all at the same time.

In exchange for the paper, the will, whatever it was, Paul was to leave her everything. The car, the flat, the paintings, Ray's money, all the exemptions from the bankruptcy. It all comes to something like three-quarters of a million, Robert said, not a bad little fee for a year of baby-sitting.

In any case, after Ray died she started turning up at night in Harry's, the Eiche, in her green coat with the fox collar (never in the fur), weary-looking, her hair yanked back in a bun, eyebrows arch as ever on that glabrous forehead, Robert said, still with her naïveté, her girlishness. But now, Robert said, she played the "woman of the world," the weary soul braving her tragedies. She would sit at a table full of Rudolph's old familiars, order a white wine, laugh courageously at other people's jokes. After the first glass, Robert said, she hurled the occasional sigh, after the second glass the tongue came loose. Always, Robert said, the plebeian house wine the others drank, never champagne, never French, Valentina fancied herself one of the little people, full of peasant wisdom and peasant innocence. She was positively *manly* in this new persona, Robert said, a worker bee. She was never pretty, Robert said, but she had her largeness and her pointy features and a face too big for them, and that gave her stature.

And then she would talk. In aggrieved cadences. Whispering. The terrible strain, her and Paul, the sadness . . . losing Rudolph, and now Ray. But, as a solid plebeian sort of person, she now realized that every hit must make you stronger, she said, Robert told me. *These are life's lessons,* she sighed with an improving air, *for life, one must be strong, one cannot become one of the weak ones,* she said, time and time again. *I only can have my heart broken once,* she said, *and then I must be hard and strong.* You could hear Rudolph in her voice, and Paul, sometimes even Ray made a little guest appearance in Valentina's soliloquies. She had patched these men together and made a personality for herself.

There was Zryd, too, whose clinic had been closed by the authorities, Robert said, and there were rumors flying, that not only was she sleeping with Mutti but also carrying on with Zryd, who later went to jail for a time . . . Whenever the topic of Zryd and the Zryd method and the Zryd clinic popped up in a conversation, Valentina defended the doctor with unusual ferocity, Robert said, thereby defending her own part in putting Ray in there. You can just imagine, Robert told me, this large girl with her strict schoolmistress face and her silly gravity. Some people who had known Valentina for years, Robert said, but had never had any curiosity about her began to take notice of her now. She was like a rebuke, Robert said, to their own cynical acceptance of the death spreading all around us. Half their friends, Robert said, had been wiped out by the plague, and here they all were, still growing fat in Harry's Bar, chewing over old times, fomenting little intrigues. Among a certain set, Robert told me, sympathy for "poor Valentina" became a sort of cult. It tended to preempt consideration of poor Ray, or poor Paul: it was she who'd suffered the blows, really.

The whole town of Munich, the whole country in fact heard all about Paul's affair with Chris. Valentina herself brought it up whenever she had the chance, but only to defend Paul, she said, Robert said, against "ugly rumors." She'd go on about Paul's desperation during that period, Paul's confusion, Paul's grief. "I know you've heard these stories," Valentina said, Robert told me, drawing aside some acquaintance who hadn't heard anything at all. She would then spill all the stories and conclude, "It's all lies, it just isn't true."

Most people, you know, Robert told me on the roof of the Chelsea, had nothing particular against Paul—people liked Paul, they also couldn't care less about his moral or immoral behavior, that was her middle-class trip. You would go into the Eiche and see her with Rudolph's worst hangers-on, the ones who hadn't worked in the six years since Rudolph croaked, nodding sagely and endorsing all Valentina's emotional fantasies. But other people, said Robert, found it all jejune and cheaply manipulative, her "bravery," her abject devotion to these men she'd attached herself to. It all looked specious and histrionic, said Robert. All those stories she used to lay on with a trowel, about her humble beginnings, how she'd never tasted caviar until Rudolph fed her some "from a tiny silver spoon," the way she posed as this motherly presence, utterly guileless, utterly devoted. Let's face it, said Robert, it's enough to make you puke.

It was exactly that lead-solid bourgeois mentality of hers, said Robert, that Rudolph had despised and hated his whole life, *and yet he fell in love with it,* go figure that one out. Paul, too. Paul had his stupid side as well, said Robert, a weakness for big-tit women who acted like his mother. Paul and Rudolph wanted to be depraved, said Robert, but in the end, these depraved revolutionaries craved the bourgeois mother and the bourgeois lifestyle, they both needed a *femme de ménage.*

So, Robert said, she spent her days and evenings locked up with Paul's madness and then had her nocturnal life among the sodden old hangers-on. In those bars, Robert said, Valentina got the English nickname *Tragedy Ann.* Paul lived like an invalid by then, said Robert, sliding into an irreversible opera plot of his own invention. Valentina's affair with Mutti was going limp and intermittent. Some nights she turned up in the Kleist Casino, sulking at a corner table while Mutti ruminated behind the bar. Obviously they were not getting on, Robert said, what did she expect? Everybody knows that Mutti prefers fucking very slight, ethnic sixteen-year-old boys.

If Paul expected a phone call from Rita, Robert told me, or you, or me, or Weiland (he'd gotten quite friendly with Weiland, Paul did a big part in a film Weiland shot around that time, in Berlin—it was the one time he was away from Valentina for several weeks, according to Weiland, Robert said, Valentina phoned every night and kept Paul on the telephone for hours) . . . Well, he'd be waiting for a call, and then she would say, half-kidding, "Are you sure you want to talk to him?" or her, whoever. "She always wants something." "He's so self-impor-tant." "Oh, and you can listen to all his problems." The light touch. She left the hint that they could have more fun just the two of them. And she made it fun, she had to.

He loved to hear how Mutti's penis was bent and how Mutti couldn't always manage an erection, or all about her supposed nights of passion in Morocco with Rudolph. Or she got him going on politics and all his obscure theories, Valentina the acolyte, Robert said, she was his favorite type of listener, he told her all his stories about Theodora and Justinian, and Tiberius's "little fishes" in the Capri grotto, or the one he liked to tell about Count Ciano flying his plane over Merle Oberon's estate in the south of France right after the war, dropping thousands of roses down every day and finally crashing the plane on her front lawn.

Or they went bar-crawling, places like Philomar Bar, where Valentina picked up Turks and brought them up to the flat so Paul could watch her getting banged out on the balcony, right above the people eating dinner on the café terrace. Then they got into stealing things, shoplifting things at the supermarket, at book-stores, finally at people's houses. They dropped in on people Paul hadn't spoken to in months, turning up unannounced, chattering a mile a minute, whizzing through the apartment admiring things, making phone calls, pretending to want a drink and a nice cozy chat, and then they jumped up five minutes later, claiming some urgent appointment. They dropped in on Alex, for example, who was now living with his mother in a big apartment in Schwabing, and after they left, Alex noticed an expensive set of cufflinks missing from his bedroom.

As far as I know, Robert said, no one ever accused them directly of waltzing off with a piece of jewelry or an object d'art, it would've been too cruel—and besides, they were clever, they never stole anything the owner would notice missing right away. So there was always a slight doubt whether they'd actually taken it.

Throughout June and July, Robert said, Paul informed his friends that he'd accepted an acting job in Paris that began in early August. At the beginning of August, Paul told the cleaning woman he would be away for three weeks. Valentina had read somewhere, Robert said, that the best way to do it involved taking sleeping tablets in a full bathtub: you'd lose consciousness, then slide below the level of the water and drown. She would fly to Berlin for the weekend, return on Monday, let herself into the flat, discover Paul's body, and call the police. All the papers were signed, and Paul was ready . . .

". . . I picture it like this," Robert said: the tap gushing hot water into the mint green tub. Steam clouds rising, the square white floor tiles, an oval throw rug a damp shade of burgundy. Beethoven No. 6 on the tape deck, the phone machine in the living room clicks on, a message from somewhere. Paul's naked, he puts on his robe and walks to the table, pours a glass of Chianti, unscrews a plastic tube, shakes a dozen pink tablets into his palm, then tips his hand so the capsules slide onto the black-veined marble table. Who's calling? Now it would be a mistake to speak, a conversation might pull him back into being. He lights a cigarette. He walks through the hall. He fiddles with the taps in the bathroom. A nice lukewarm stream. He goes back into the living room. He shakes out a few more tablets. He looks at the carpet, the drapes. He stands up again and closes the terrace doors. He crosses into the living room, turns the tape over. He shuts off the kitchen light. He returns to the bathroom, turns the water off, feels the water, looks at his face in the cabinet mirror: "I guess we won't be seeing each other anymore."

He crosses the hall. He gathers the pills. He washes them down with Chianti, which burns. He switches off the living room light and turns up the volume on Beethoven No. 6. A morbid thing to be listening to. He returns to the bathroom, shrugs off the robe, tests the bathwater with his foot, then steps into the tub, lowers himself, stretches out his legs, lowers his back until it rests against the slope of the tub.

He hears air flowing in and out of his lungs. He closes his eyes. He remembers things. Bits of music. Voices. Swimming in a river full of sharp rocks, sunlight through branches, a smell of gardenias. The veins in his father's nose. Ray masturbating with salad oil in Corsica. Black squirrels on a green lawn. Rudolph eating a sandwich from the Stage Deli on Broadway. Beethoven, grandiose and pathetic. *Here is little Effi's head whose brains are made of gingerbread.* Rudolph. *Eh quoi? eh quoi? Est-ce ici que la vérité je prétends en vérité que d'ici.* Winking when he hung up the phone on some professor of cinema from Fairleigh Dickinson University. *Der Stein der Stein in der Luft, dem ich folgte.* Life of the mind, it's a great thing. *When they want something they never give up.* Some professor with a badly basted harelip. *Le huit mai, quel truc fantastique, ce naufrage du Titanic!* Line down the spur of his nose, like the line above Valentina's lip. *Tu vas t'asseoir sur ton gros cul noir, je mets les pompes en route, on va voir.* Creases, chalky cuticles. Bit them in college, also inside the cheek, until you get canker sores. *Eh quoi? eh quoi? Niemand knetet uns wiederaus Erde und Lehm, niemand bespricht unsern Staub. Niemand.* A wine may be entitled to the DOC Chianti Classico, even if its producer is not a member of the consorzio. Types of shit. Grainy, lumpy, pebbled, smooth, milk chocolate in color. *Pourquoi pas, je vous demande, pourquoi pas? Aujourd'hui elle interdit le suicide, hier elle interdisait non moins bruyamment les anesthésiques.* Fat coils. Adderlike. Speckles with grains of chewed-up peanuts. Runny. Streamy. Bad metallic taste of a seat belt. Steam. Windows that light up pink. *Wer in diesem Schattenviert schnaubt, ser unter ihm schimmert auf, schimmert auf, schimmert auf.* Cobblestones. Venice. The little humpbacked bridges. Milton. Bergamo. That funicular railway and the violin factory. The Jesuit school. *Wir brockelten auseinander und broselten wider in eins.* Then you won't, well, you can never, if they hadn't, if I hadn't, what do they mean anyway, if it's all, then you don't, where's it all go? Where's it go to? Drains out through rocks, earth, through caves, stalagmites, dripping crystals, gushes up in steampipes, what about geysers, do they, what do they do? Or lava, it cools and leaves porous charcoal in granite or on black beaches or heavy flaps of lead if it rains they have water then and then . . .

. . . Okay, said Robert, and now she's coming, not in a Chanel suit, she couldn't possibly be wearing a Chanel suit, even though it's the most appropriate thing, because if they made them in her size she'd look like a Prussian horse cantering through the airport. It was, Robert said, probably something a little more suburban in aubergine tweed, or midnight eau du Nil. The blouse, however, had a campy white ruffle like a crepe calla lilly. Flat lizardskin pumps she bought from Bennis-Edwards in New York. Besides her luggage, she had one of her vast leather purses on a shoulder strap. Dark nylon stockings rather than sheer, a touch.

She stopped in a transit lounge and ordered herself a brandy, a Rémy Martin, homage to Rudolph, quaffed one then another, then noticed her hands were still shaking and drank yet a third

Rémy Martin, paid with a hundred-mark note, collected her change, took a cab to Giselastrasse, touched up her makeup on the way, and tried reading in the cab, the diaries of Anaïs Nin, her current heroine.

She let herself into the building. She stood in the vestibule composing herself for the horror. Since there was a heat wave on, for all she knew he might've started decomposing already in the bathwater. Not a pleasant thought. She took the lift to the third floor, paused again outside the flat, studied the fiber doormat. She thought: What if he changed his mind? What if she opened the door and he was standing there? Then what? She could imagine him deciding the timing wasn't right, then wanting to try again. What on earth have I let myself in for, she thought, Robert said. She turns her key in the lock. She pushes the door open. She sees the empty hall, the pale gray wall-to-wall carpet, the low bookshelves along the hall, the Elizabeth Taylor silkscreen. It's stuffy in there. A definite crime scene ambiance.

She steps into the hall. She calls out. She looks in the kitchen: everything's the way she left it. Last week's mail is piled on the kitchen table. There's a saucepan in the sink. She might as well go ahead, she thinks, Robert said. She steps into the hallway to the bathroom. The bathroom door's open, he's left it open, she stops at the threshold, she sees it, a little bit of it. Creepy dead flesh— must be his leg. No smell yet. The robe's on the floor. She goes out to the living room phone, thinking to call the police. She decides to take a better look first, calm down, she thinks, Robert said, compose yourself, get ready for a shock. Jesus, well, he didn't go under after all. The face looks slightly caved in. Water just to the chest, the skin looks all bone white, except behind his shoulders, and down behind his leg it's green and black—Jesus Christ, he's breathing! She screams once and runs out of the flat, slamming the door behind her, leaving the suitcase in the hall.

She finds Mutti over at the Kleist Keller, his white linen sleeves rolled, swabbing ale mugs in a gray broth of dishwater. The old hag of a chef rolls out of the kitchen, thumbs clutching a platter of greasy pork for a table of three. It was a sweet dead dusty hour of the afternoon. The folkloric plates on the wainscoting caught the sun on their glaze.

What's up? Mutti said. You've got to come to Paul's, Valentina told him. Something terrible has happened. What, right now? Mutti bunches his apron and tosses it on the sodden drainboard, leaves a half-topped jug of pilsner foaming under the tap. In the street he follows her half a block in the wrong direction. They double back to his car. In the car she cries, forehead pressed to the window. Tell me what's happened, he says. He's messed everything up, she says. She spills the entire story. He couldn't face anything, she says, in the end he wasn't strong. First all that mess with Ray and the clinic and now this, I knew it!

Mutti follows her into the building, up the lift, into the flat. The thing in the bathtub made his heart stop, he told Robert, the skin in front had the color of a boiled egg, but the underside was all charred-looking, and where the colors met there were striations like obsidian sunk into the bloated flesh. Valentina was hysterical. Mutti remembered the pharmacy drawer and forced her to take a Valium.

We have to call the police, he said. We can't, she shrieked. Don't you see? He's in a coma, he's half-dead, they'll put him on a respirator and keep him alive as a vegetable, maybe for months, years even, this is the last thing he wanted, she told him, to wake up and find out that he *ruined everything*. Well, Mutti told her, if he wakes up he won't be a vegetable, will he. I hate this, she told him, this is exactly the kind of awful position he'd love to put me in. She stormed out of the hall. Mutti followed her. She clawed at the terrace doors, flung them open. You're not making sense, Mutti told her. You don't know him as I do, Valentina told him. It's just the kind of absurdity he adores. He's done this to get back at *me*, isn't it obvious? Mutti slapped her. Get hold of yourself, he shouted. We let the police take care of it, and just forget about it. Valentina looked at him as if he were crazy. Mutti, she told him, you don't understand. We've got to help him a little here. It's what Paul would want. All you have to do, push him under just a little. Just push his head under and finish it.

Mutti searched for something to say. That's murder, he said finally. You can't murder a dead person, Valentina told him. Think, Mutti, think, if this were somebody in your family, someone you loved, they have a fatal disease and want to be put out of their misery, and they come so close! What if it was you? You're in terrible pain, you can only think about your pain, you're reduced to the animal level, and when your pain's coming to an end, you're dragged back to suffer. Oh, horseshit, Mutti told her, he wasn't in any pain to begin with, besides, he added, you know what you can get for murder?

They went back and looked at Paul again. Mutti thought an autopsy might show whether Paul, in the state he was in, could have shifted position enough to go under and drown. He couldn't feature handling all that soggy skin, he told Robert, for all he knew, it might come sliding off the bone like boiled chicken. Anyway, he told Robert, I wasn't about to take that responsibility.

We could just leave him here, Valentina suggested, hopefully. But Mutti prevailed. A half-hour later Paul was on a gurney, being wheeled to an ambulance. Mutti gave a statement to the police and went back to work. Valentina accompanied the paramedics. Next was intensive care, adrenaline injections, doctors and nurses, technology. She had to produce the address of Paul's parents in the countryside.

Mutti told various people bits and pieces of this story, Robert told me, and those people told others. Meanwhile, he said, Valentina was busy hiring a private-duty nurse, an elderly woman who'd briefly looked after Ray when Ray first came back from Australia. Paul had to be turned and his joints had to be agitated carefully, to promote some circulation to the dead skin where he'd lain in the same position for three days. He was still unconscious, but the doctors felt he'd come out of it eventually.

The parents arrived, completely shaken up and confused. Valentina immediately took them under her wing. She posed, Robert said, as Paul's *fiancée*. Imagine, Robert said. They'd both been told any number of times that Paul was queer, in fact he was one of the better-known queers in Germany, yet both of them, the old mum in particular, never wanted to believe any such thing, and even though her favorite son was on a respirator and half of him looked like it had been deep-fried, she found herself relieved that he'd finally found himself a girlfriend. Maybe the old dad was a little more skeptical, Robert said, it's hard to say, but he's also ten years older than the old mum, hard of hearing also, a little cranky, a little doddering, plus, Robert said, he's had his own medical interludes, various internal organs going on the fritz, touch of diabetes, various surgeries, little kidney things, so the old dad had to rest, meaning, basically, that he nodded out every half hour or so. Whenever the father exerted himself, he got all winded and then he got sleepy. The mother is half-blind with cataracts, Robert said, she's not senile or anything, but confused, and naturally grateful that Valentina's taken charge of everything.

Valentina tells them that Paul's "accidentally" swallowed too many sleeping pills, tells them he's had insomnia for months, so he took tablets, and then he nipped a little wine, forgot he took the tablets, and took some more—then he passed out in his bath, maybe also hit his head, et cetera, et cetera. She also explains that the doctors don't want any of Paul's friends crowding around, especially at this early stage of recovery—so when the friends start showing up at the hospital, they find Valentina and these two decrepit lawn elves from the Black Forest parked on a vinyl sofa outside the ward, the father snoring away, the mother suspicious and wary, and Valentina tells them the doctors have absolutely forbidden all visitors. The persistent ones, Robert said, found the private-duty nurse blocking the door of Paul's room.

Robert said he got the nurse talking, a few months later, with a few hundred marks' gratuity, and this is how it was: after four days Paul came out of his coma, at first for a few minutes, opened his eyes, moved his head. They had all sorts of topical anesthesia on him. They couldn't give him anything internally at that point, and every inch of his body hurt, except where it was just dead. He passed out. The next day he remained conscious a bit longer. They brought the parents in. Valentina came in. He didn't say anything. He couldn't talk yet. The following day he spoke. To Valentina. The nurse heard him. Give me back the paper, he told her, I want that paper I signed, I want to tear it up. Valentina was all smiles: Don't be absurd, she told him, of course I tore it up immediately, Paul.

His episodes of consciousness weren't as progressive as the doctors expected. There was a question of brain damage. They couldn't really measure it until the dead nerves came back, which could take weeks, even months. Some parts of his skin were dead, other parts caused this blazing pain. He had to be moved frequently, to avoid sepsis. They had to experiment, get various parts to settle just so against the sheets. He had begun talking, though.

The parents stayed a few nights in Munich, in a hotel rather than in Paul's flat, but the father disliked being so long away from his beloved Black Forest, and they began driving in every couple days. Valentina stayed all day at the hospital, sitting with Paul, whispering in his ear, reading the newspaper aloud "to keep his brain alive," she claimed, while various people attempted to see him, each attempt thwarted by what Robert described as a virtual conspiracy of medical personnel. Meanwhile, the private-duty nurse heard things like: They say it will take months, maybe even a year. By then, you know, you could be as bad off as Ray was. Or: They think maybe you have that stuff in your rectum that Ray got. Another time the nurse heard: I'm exhausted, Paul, I can't take this anymore, I've got to go away from here, for some months, I can't stand it anymore. On another occasion, Robert said, the nurse said she heard Valentina tell him: You'd think some of your friends could be bothered to visit you. Not one has showed up, and I've called everyone. She had already instructed the switchboard not to put any calls through, as Robert later discovered. Paul had begun moving his arms a little, not enough perhaps to use the telephone, but he could talk, if the receiver was held against his ear.

The nurse told Robert that Valentina never stopped talking once she came into the room, always in a low, tragic voice. She sounded, the nurse said, as if she was lecturing him. He would nod miserable agreement, the nurse said, or whisper something that caused her to shake her head, he'd whisper something else and get the same reaction, and then, once every so often, the nurse said, Robert said, it seemed Paul hit on something that she actually agreed with, and she would say, Exactly, or Excellent, or, That's the idea. The nurse also noticed the way Valentina swept into the room each morning, planted her big pocketbook on the bed, practically between Paul's legs, as if she owned the place, the nurse told Robert, and she'd leave it there all day, she said, unless she needed a Kleenex or something, always the same routine, day after day, that dreadful bag on the bed, she'd even leave it there when she got her lunch in the cafeteria, the nurse said.

After ten days they took Paul off his IV and fed him orally, mashed-up goo of some type. He started to talk more when the parents visited, but he still had some trouble speaking. He tended to pronounce single words instead of phrases or complete sentences, the nurse reported, but you could ask him if he meant this or he meant that, and then he could nod or shake his head, and sometimes he would go on for a while, talking, but as days went by, Robert said, the nurse saw his depression coming back. It was heartbreaking, the mother told Robert later, the way Paul seemed displeased by his own recovery. Sometimes, the mother told Robert, they got there first thing in the morning and found Paul in a fairly sanguine mood. But then, she said, Robert told me, she and the father would go eat their lunch while Valentina fed him, and when they returned, Paul was sullen and uncommunicative. You just had to feel awful bad for him, the mother told Robert. Well, Robert said, one morning around six the regular hospital nurse came in and found him dead in his sleep, which was something no one expected. So they did an autopsy and discovered an overdose of Mandrax.

"She's so convincingly middle-class," Robert told me. "She told the head doctor she had it prescribed for her nerves, what with all the stress. But, since she hates taking drugs, she filled the prescription and never used it. So she didn't notice it missing from her pocketbook."

I poured the last drops of vodka into Robert's glass. He looked at his watch. The party below had seen a second wind. We heard a whinnying laugh over the bleat of a whetted clarinet. I stared at my folder of notes and closed it.

"I guess we can skip why and because," I said.

Robert Scheib stretched. "Oh," he said, "I think Valentina genuinely enjoys the aura of widowhood. Widowhood and litigation. There's a sense of high drama you get with both. I wonder—do you suppose they've got any vodka down there?"

*

Two mice fell into a bucket of milk. The first one cried for help and drowned. The other kept swimming around and around, and in the morning he woke on top of butter.